THE
TELL-TALE
HEART
ATTACK

OTHER BOOKS BY LINDA M. AU

Humor Essays:

Head in the Sand . . . and other unpopular positions
Fork in the Road . . . and other pointless discussions
Train of Thought: Travel Essays from a One-Track Mind
Travel Documents

Novels:

Secret Agent Manny
Gray Area

MORE RED INK MYSTERIES

The Scarlet Letter Opener (Red Ink Mystery #1)
Charlotte's Website (Red Ink Mystery #3)

another *red ink* mystery

THE TELL-TALE HEART ATTACK

Linda M. Au

vicious circle publishing

Copyright © 2019 by Linda M. Au
Vicious Circle Publishing

The Tell-Tale Heart Attack (Red Ink Mystery #2)

ISBN: 978-1-954973-02-2

Cover artwork by Mike Ferrin (mikeferrin.org)

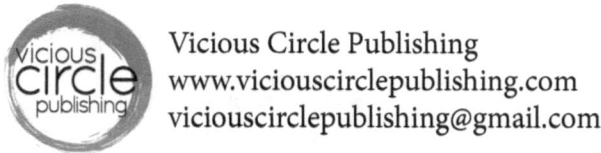

Vicious Circle Publishing
www.viciouscirclepublishing.com
viciouscirclepublishing@gmail.com

For the real-life Raging Avocados, a team brave enough to name themselves after a vegetable

CHAPTER 1

HAD TO GET THROUGH TO THE DOCTOR'S OFFICE right away. Time was slipping away, and I could almost feel a clock ticking in my chest. I reached into my purse and let my arm snake around inside it, trying to find that ever-elusive phone. Where? *Where?* I knew it was in here somewhere, in this huge black hole I called a purse. I really had to stop using tote bags as purses. It only encouraged me to carry around way too much crap.

I glanced at the clock on the wall. It wasn't just my imagination then. It really had been forty-five minutes already, with no end in sight. Only the doctor could help me now.

Ah, there it was, wedged under my bulging wallet (the old nylon one that was falling apart), my glasses case (those cheap readers I bought in a three-pack, knowing I'd lose two pair within the first week... and I had been right about that, by the way), and the granola bars I always carried with me in case of emergencies. This was beginning to feel like an emergency, though not a food-related one. I clamped my fingers down on the phone and plucked it out of the purse before it could slip out of my grasp and go running away once again. Damn thing had a mind of its own. Most technology does.

I swiped the screen and the home page came up. Two more swipes and I had made it into my list of contacts and then found the information for Dr. Camp. A light tap and I heard the comforting ring of Dr. Camp's office phone. I closed my eyes and sighed, trying to breathe slowly and deeply. Perhaps everything would be all right after all.

Two rings. Then three. Then, a fourth, which worried me. Usually someone picked up by the second ring. I knew for a fact that the office was open today, so when it rang a fifth time, I nearly gave up. Then, the call connected and someone answered.

"Hello, Dr. Camp's office. How may I direct your call?"

"Yes, hello. This is Maggie Velam. I'm a current patient of Dr. Camp's."

"What can I do for you, Maggie? Are you calling to make an appointment?"

"Not exactly."

"Then how may I help you today?"

"I already have an appointment."

"Ah, I see. When is your appointment?"

"Forty-five minutes ago. Somebody put me in Exam Room 5 and forgot about me. I'm sitting in here in this paper gown waiting for the doctor."

"Oh dear!"

I hung up, frustrated and still freezing my exposed butt off. *"Oh dear," my ass, lady.*

FUNNY HOW FAST YOU GET SERVICE in this country once you do something a little out of the ordinary. Dr. Camp was in Exam Room 5 within thirty seconds of me hanging up the phone. I tried not to wonder how long I would have sat in that room in that paper gown if I hadn't had a cell phone with me to call the front desk. If this was any indication of how the rest of my day was going to pan out, I might as well go back home and give up. The bed might be the only safe place left. All this fuss for a routine checkup.

Finally I was fully dressed and back in the car, sitting in the parking lot, rearranging the junk in my purse one more time in a vain attempt to put things I needed most in more accessible spots. But, in a giant black hole made of fabric, there really aren't *any* easily accessible spots. Besides, I wasn't solving my purse problems by sitting here; I was just weighing the pros and cons of heading home instead of going to my son's baseball game.

I took off the emergency brake and shifted the car into drive. Ultimately I'd regret it if I missed another of Seth's games. And I wasn't going to let a doctor with poor time management let me miss it. One of the upsides of being a freelance proofreader and typesetter was that my schedule was flexible. And now that Seth had moved back out on his own, I didn't get to see him as much as I did when he'd been crashing at my place in between jobs. Going to my son's adult baseball games was a great way to be an active part of his new life as a bona fide grown-up, even if it did feel a bit like the many times I'd sat in the stands at his Little League games fifteen years ago. The only difference was that now there was a lot less crying. Most of the time, anyway. At Seth's last game, where the Raging Avocados had lost miserably—falling behind right in the first inning and staying there for the entire seven innings—there had been a lot of weeping and gnashing of teeth. Big babies. It was only a game, right?

Okay, perhaps I had shed a tear or two myself. After all, no mother likes to see her twenty-six-year-old kid lose because of the ten-run rule. It's embarrassing. For both of us. In any case, I wanted to be there to cheer Seth and the rest of the team on to victory. Or to cheer them on to a perfect attendance record. They gave out trophies for that stuff now, didn't they? Or was that just elementary school?

I parked along the street just outside the ball field and again searched for my phone in the tote bag purse. This thing was like a clown car for accessories. The phone hadn't had time to sink to the very bottom so I found it more easily this time. I texted Seth to let him know I was here.

"*I'm here. Team ready?*"

The answer came quickly. "*Yup. Along 3rd base.*"

"*Will be right up.*"

"*Frank's already here.*"

Well, that answered *that* question. At least I hadn't had to ask outright. Seth volunteering the information was a lot less awkward. I had precious little experience juggling two adult children and a new boyfriend. The children I could handle, but throwing a brand new beau into the mix was completely uncharted territory for all of us. So far I had kept things low key, but there were things that didn't fall into place easily when adding a middle-aged male adult to a tight little family of three. We had our own quaint dysfunctions, and we were used to them. Bringing in Frank had only meant that those quirks were now easier to see and harder to explain.

I hadn't meant to fall for another member of Seth's baseball team, but sitting in the bleachers every week all spring and summer had meant I had plenty of time to watch and get to know the other players on the Raging Avocados, including one of the newest members, Frank. Let's just say there were at least two Avocados on this Earth that I really liked. All the others—the rest of the team plus the vegetables—I could still do without. I checked my hair and face in the rearview mirror, dropped my phone back into the monster tote, and got out of the car. Time to meet my adoring fans. Well, Seth and Frank, at least. I had fought hard to get out of that paper gown and back into real clothes so I could get here for the game. And not a moment too soon.

"DOWN BY THREE IN THE THIRD," Seth said, grousing a little more than usual, considering most of the team was used to losing a lot worse by this point in the game.

"Aw, Seth, don't give up so soon. There's still plenty of time to catch up." I smiled. The rest of the team grumbled aloud as they walked by me on their way to the dugout. Frank sauntered past, gliding a hand across my knee as I sat perched in the bleachers two rows up from the ground. He winked, then passed me a crumpled piece of paper he'd filched from his T-shirt pocket, and I felt my heart flutter ever so slightly. This having a boyfriend thing was kinda nice. I unfolded the note—a computer printout in Frank's ubiquitous Comic Sans font (his biggest personal flaw)—and read: "Hey, sexy! Dinner later?"

I beamed but tried not to do or say anything too mushy within Seth's hearing or sight. He was plenty old enough to know that kissing wasn't supposed to be icky, but if it involved his mom and some guy who wasn't his dad, then it was pretty icky.

The awkwardness stuck with me throughout all of these games now, because Seth's father, George Roberts—my ex-husband—was also on the team. I'd purposely missed a handful of Seth's games simply because I wasn't in the mood to endure seven innings of George and his wacky hijinks on the field. Seeing a new boyfriend on the same ball field was sometimes too much for my fragile psyche.

Frank opened the cooler at the end of the section of seats where the friends and family of the Raging Avocados were sitting, including me, and grabbed a bottle of Sport-Aide. He turned to the rest of the team, who were already in the dugout.

"Sport-Aide! Yeah! Seth brought my favorite again! Anybody else?" he asked, waving his bottle around. Most shook their heads and said no, but both Seth and Allen, their left fielder, nodded enthusiastically.

"Oh, hell! Grab me one! I hate 'em but I'm thirsty!" called Allen the accountant, a six-foot-six hulk of a man who reminded me of Babe Ruth, once I imagined Ruth letting himself go, gaining a hundred pounds, and then smoking and adopting John Belushi's diet of Little Chocolate Donuts. The unkempt beard and long stringy hair pulled back in a loose ponytail, along with the enormous team T-shirt with the sleeves haphazardly shoved up, completed the look. The look that said: "I am completely unaware that other people have to look at me like this."

Frank nodded, grabbed two more Sport-Aides out of the cooler, and dashed to the dugout to join his comrades. Seth and Allen took the second and third bottles.

"Don't blame me if this tastes bad. Blame Seth. He brought it."

"I swear, Frank, if I toss my cookies over this stuff, I ain't never doing your taxes again." He belched.

"You don't drink Sport-Aide!" said George, in a way that sounded almost personally offended.

Allen chuckled. "When there ain't any beer around, I'll drink anything. It's freakin' hot out here for October." He easily twisted the cap off his bottle, guzzling a long pull of the neon green liquid. He gasped as the first gulp went down.

"Good lord, that stuff is nasty!"

George snorted at him. "Well, when you're used to drinking beer the way you do, I bet even water tastes nasty."

"Nah, that's not it. Why I'm drinking something that's the color of toxic waste is beyond me. Who brought this stuff, anyway?"

"I did," Seth replied. "You know, not everybody wants to guzzle down beer while they're trying to get some healthy exercise." He smiled but it was clear his little joke wasn't appreciated. "There's bottled water in there, too, Allen."

Frank drank his Sport-Aide a little more slowly than Allen did, and Seth was too busy yammering, as usual, to get around to even opening his bottle. To my mind, Frank and Allen looked as if they were swigging water from the spent fuel pool of the nuclear power plant twenty miles down the river. Although I'd never seen it, I always imagined it was neon green and glowing. Around here, the nuclear power plant jokes were old but persistent. If only they were funny.

Based on the way the Avocados were playing, Allen and Frank wouldn't get to bat this inning, or the next. I was guessing we'd see only the minimum of three batters... as had apparently happened the last two innings. Being the home team this time wouldn't even help them. Only die-hard family members and friends attended Avocado games this late in the season, when all hope of a post-season was lost.

Frank continued to sip his Sport-Aide, but Allen had finished his entire bottle within a few minutes. He wiped the back of his bare arm across his mouth and let out a long, loud "Ahh!" as if the foul, glowing liquid was actually refreshing. I wasn't fooled. He was just savoring the guys'-night-out quality of these games, win or lose. Seth had mentioned to me that Allen played not for the sport (he hated baseball) or the physical activity (he hated exercise) or the fellowship (he hated everyone). He did it to get a full night out of the house, where he ran a private accounting business. Apparently his wife was a bit of a nag. Having watched Allen in action, though, I began to wonder if perhaps she and I might be fast friends if we ever met.

I admit I was musing in just this vein when I heard a wheezing choke come from just outside the dugout, followed by a loud, awful thud and nearly a dozen people gathering around a large pair of up-turned cleats (which was all I could see from my vantage point)—cleats that twitched a few times and then were still. The rest of the team members gasped and broke from their huddle, each looking around for assistance of any kind.

"Help!" Sandy yelled over her shoulder. The petite team catcher seemed to break free from the mass of large men around her as she quickly became the only person doing anything about whatever had just happened in their midst. She pushed past them all and headed straight for the rest of us sitting in the bleachers.

"Call 9-1-1!" she yelled, and all of us began reaching for our phones. Of course, I was the last person to *locate* my phone, and I was still scouring the inside of the tote bag from hell while a friend of Sandy's was already on the phone with someone at the other end of that emergency call. I really had to get a smaller purse. With com-partments.

By this time, the rest of the team had dispersed somewhat, each one heading for someone with a phone. I looked back to see that the owner of the prostrate cleats was none other than Allen. Seth was hovering over Allen, feeling for a pulse, patting him on the cheek—a rather unresponsive cheek, I noticed—and whispering things in tones far too quiet for me to make out all the way over here in the stands. I stood and jumped off the bleachers, heading over to be with Seth as he tried to provide comfort, if not much first aid, but Seth stood and shook his head at the rest of us. We were all looking back toward him and Allen now.

"He's dead," Seth said simply. "I think."

No one said anything, and the visiting team on the field quietly walked back to their own dugout, unable to decide on anything better to do. All I could think was that Allen should have *eaten* an avocado now and then, instead of just raging as one. Or, at least, some sort of vegetable, or fiber, or something. Make *some* sort of effort. The man probably wasn't even fifty yet.

But at least that annoying wifely nagging he hated would now stop. Sometimes you had to find a way to look on the bright side of things.

CHAPTER 2

WE WEREN'T ALLOWED TO LEAVE the ball field for several hours. The EMTs arrived on the scene quickly—we weren't all that far from anything in this urban setting for the game—but along with them came the local police, meaning lots of questions and interviews for each one of us on the scene. That, of course, included two full baseball teams and a set of bleachers with more than a dozen other people. And because Seth and I were the ones who stayed with Allen (well, with Allen's *body*, anyway) until help arrived, we seemed to get the brunt of the questions from all parties, police and emergency personnel. Seth held up well, considering he had just watched a friend of his die right in front of his eyes, although I knew we'd get back to my apartment and he would crash hard.

I, of course, couldn't blame him. Not quite a year ago, I myself had had a similar encounter with the authorities, having found the local newspaper editor dead behind his desk. You try to be a good, decent citizen, and then something like this happens and it feels almost like punishment when everyone is all over you with questions. It was an ugly feeling. I felt for Seth today because I'd been there myself.

Despite the time involved in getting ourselves extricated from the scene, there wasn't a whole lot to tell. The team had all been in the dugout, making sure the right player was headed up to bat at the bottom of that third inning, and the usual banter was flying back and forth among all of them. It was a lot of what made playing baseball as an adult so much fun. Seth's stories about his games—the rare ones I didn't attend—usually involved more details about what someone else said or did off the field than details about the game play itself. I shuddered to think just how long Seth and I might have been detained had there been a lot more to tell. Sure, Allen had been a bit ornery before the game started, but that was just his way. Some people were permanently cranky and negative, and Allen was certainly one of those people. The others on the team tolerated him because he could run so fast when he wanted to. For such a large behemoth of a man, Allen could move like the wind around those bases when the occasion called for it.

But sadly, it now seemed as if his particularly bad health habits had caught up with him. A person couldn't eat and drink the way Allen did and not suffer the consequences. He didn't typically drink Sport-Aide during the games—he was definitely more likely to reach for a cold beer out of that cooler—but Seth had opted to bring Sport-Aide and even iced tea. The weatherman had been calling for warm enough weather that it was probably wise to do without the beer in favor of something with electrolytes in it. But, typically, Allen's first choice was anything alcoholic. And don't get me started on his choice of snacks and food. I'd attended a few of the barbecues and picnics with this gang throughout the season, and it was clear that Allen must have had some sort of death wish, if you had to judge solely by the way he ate and drank.

And now, apparently, his wish had come true.

"So, ARE YOU OKAY?" I asked Seth once we were back at my place. I had offered to make his favorite meal—pepperoni casserole—if he wanted to crash at my apartment tonight rather than spend the night alone at his place. He'd nabbed the opportunity the second I offered it, which told me he was going to need to collect his thoughts and feelings about losing Allen so suddenly, right before his eyes.

"Sure, I'm fine," he responded, nodding unconvincingly and sinking a little further into the couch. Vlad, my little mutt companion, was already on the couch, nestled up under his arm so that Seth could scritch him behind the ears more easily. I had to appreciate Vlad's ability to selflessly put himself out there for the good of another living being. Well, either that or he knew Seth was an easy shill for bacon-flavored dog treats from the cupboard in my kitchen. I didn't call that little terrier "Vlad the Inhaler" for nothing.

"More pepperoni casserole?"

"Nah, I'm good."

That's when I knew things were bad. No seconds on pepperoni casserole was serious business.

"How can I help?"

"It's fine. What you're doing is fine. Just letting me hang out here is plenty."

Even though Seth had finally gotten his own apartment in the spring, he didn't seem particularly proud of it or excited to ever actually spend time there. I never knew whether it was the lumpy couch he'd picked up at the Goodwill, the underlying odor of whatever had apparently died in his bathroom during the previous tenant's stay, or his uncanny ability to take even the simplest microwave dinner and screw it up. Whatever it was, he still preferred time at my apartment. Especially meal time. But perhaps it was Vlad, after all. Seth wasn't allowed pets at his place, and Vlad had always been Seth's buddy most of all. He seemed to tolerate me as the person who brought home bags that contained his food, but preferred Seth's undivided attention to my half-hearted "I'm working here" pats on the head.

"You're welcome to stay as long as you like."

That was probably a dangerous offer to make, since Seth had

spent nearly half a year at my place the last time I said that. This seemed different, though. This was important.

"Probably just today, Mom. I'm sure I'll be fine tomorrow when I wake up."

"How's your dad taking it?"

I wasn't sure I wanted to ask that question—anything having to do with George Roberts set my teeth on edge—but Seth's perspective on his dad was obviously a lot different from mine. This wasn't about me, after all.

"Well, we talked after the police left."

"I know. It's why I headed back to the car. I figured you two would want to talk privately for a bit. Gave me time to get back here ahead of you to set up the office daybed for you. Is he okay about all this?"

"Dunno. Allen was closer to him than to me, so he's probably not doing all that hot. But you know Dad. He's not always on top of his own feelings anyway. I'm guessing this will sink in sometime in the next few days."

"Were they close then?"

"Dad was the reason Allen joined the team in the first place. He'd been telling Dad his doctor said he should be exercising more, and Dad thought this would be a good way to ease him in that direction."

That seemed amazingly thoughtful and proactive of ol' George, but I bit my tongue and didn't say that in front of Seth.

"I'm not sure how much good that exercise was doing him when he spent time in between innings grabbing another beer from the cooler."

"I know. It was going a lot slower than either of them wanted, but it was still a step up from sitting home watching TV while drinking the beer, you know?"

"Fair enough. Still, such a shame to see something preventable like this happen."

"Agreed."

"I'm glad you were there for him, Seth."

"Wasn't anything I could do, though. That sucked."

"I know. I hope it helped when your dad came over alongside you."

"Allen was already gone by then."

"Then I hope it helped you instead of Allen."

"It did."

That's when I had high-tailed it out of there to go sit in the bleachers awaiting the unending interviews by the police, and by anyone else with a uniform that didn't say "Raging Avocados" on it. As much as I wanted to help Seth at that moment, I also knew that it was his dad's job and not mine. Might as well let George do something right for the kid for a change.

"Have you talked to your dad since we got back here?"

"Nah, I said I'd call him again in the morning. See how he's doing."

"Okay then. Are you sure I can't talk you into more pepperoni casserole?"

He glanced at the empty bowl he'd been clutching tightly. "You know, I think maybe I would like a little more."

He got up from the couch and headed in my direction, Vlad at his heels. And, I knew everything would be just fine. Eventually.

CHAPTER 3

DAMN, GIRLFRIEND, I wonder if you're under some kind of curse or something. That's three dead bodies for your family in a single calendar year. Might wanna check your closets to see if you left any corpses in there!"

"No skeletons in my closet, Helga—literal or figurative. But you have no idea how many times I've wondered about the odds of this happening at all to both Seth *and* me, let alone in a single year."

Helga reached for another packet of sweetener at the other end of our table and tapped the end to get all the contents down at the bottom, before ripping it open and dumping it into her coffee cup. I'd lost count after her third packet.

"How's Sethy doing?"

"Fine so far, but don' t ever let him hear you call him Sethy."

She snorted a laugh into her cup. "Aw, half the fun of that boy is teasing the living daylights outta him. You know I live for that."

"Yes, dear heart, I know you do. But, he doesn't."

She winked at me. "He's a sweetheart. And so are you. This was a lovely surprise today."

"Eh, I needed to get out of the house anyway. Freelance work was staring me in the face all morning, so I knew lunch with you would get me out of the funk."

"And I definitely needed to get out from behind that desk today, so I appreciate the offer."

"That bad?"

"Yeah, kinda. The new editor guy still feels like... well, the new guy."

"It's been the better part of a year, Helga."

"I know, but you don't work with him on a daily basis like we do. He's just not fitting in.'"

"Sorry to hear it."

"Never thought I'd hear myself say this, but I almost miss Lee Gerber."

"Don't start, young lady."

"Ha! You know it's true! He was a creep, but he was definitely a hot topic of conversation!"

"I wonder if his having been murdered behind his desk had anything to do with that."

"I meant *before* that!" You know we couldn't stop yammering on about the guy."

"You like to yammer on about everyone, so that might not be the best yardstick." I grinned.

"My my, aren't we feeling ornery today?"

"It's not that. Just still feeling a little out of sorts about what happened to Allen. And the fact that it happened in Seth's presence. I know what this feels like and it's not fun."

"Well, at least this was natural causes and not murder. Doesn't have the same fear factor we had to deal with after Gerber Baby kicked the bucket."

"Yeah, about that natural causes thing..."

Helga frowned over her coffee cup and slowly lowered it to the table. She folded her hands together and tented them on the table carefully.

"Please tell me you're not doing that nitpicker proofreader thing with this one."

"Nah," I said, brushing her comment aside with a quick swipe of my hand, spoon waving back and forth between my fingers. "I learned my lesson about amateur sleuthing."

"And what lesson was that?"

"Leave it to the professionals."

We both laughed at that, and our impromptu lunch date continued without much ado, except for the snorts of laughter from Helga as she laughed at her own corny jokes. God, I loved this woman. Just what I needed after another run-in with the dead.

SETH WAS AS GOOD AS HIS WORD and left in the morning to go to work and then back to his own apartment. I'd somehow missed a phone call from Frank last night while Seth and I were gabbing and decompressing after our harrowing experience at the ball field. It hadn't dawned on me that *Frank* might want to talk about what had happened. He was, after all, also a member of the Raging Avocados and had known Allen, too—as a teammate, at least, if not a close friend. Plus, he would likely be concerned about how Seth and I were doing. And yet it hadn't occurred to me to call him, or to even be on the lookout for an incoming call from him. I'd tossed my cell phone on my desk in my office at the back of the apartment when I came in, having headed back there to put sheets on the daybed and get it ready for Seth to stay overnight.

So, there sat my cell phone on my desk, with the missed call notification, and I hesitated before picking it up. Why was I hesitating? Probably because I didn't want to rehash what Seth and I had already talked to death in the past twelve hours. I didn't get a charge out of the tawdry and horrific retelling of gossip-worthy events. Even knowing it would be with Frank this time didn't make it any more appealing. If anything, it felt worse.

I decided to let Frank's call go unreturned in favor of some hot coffee and a little freelance work I'd gotten behind on. So, when the phone rang before I'd even left the room with it, I hesitated. Then I realized it would look like I was purposely avoiding him. And even though I kind of was, I didn't want him to think that.

"Hello?"

"Maggie. It's me. Frank. You and Seth all right?"

"Yeah," I sighed. "We're fine. Uncomfortable night last night but we're doing all right, I suppose."

"Good to hear. I called last night but you didn't pick up."

Was he fishing?

"Yeah, I didn't see you'd called till this morning. I tossed my phone in my office when I got home last night and just never heard it ring. Sorry."

"No problem. I was hoping it was just that you were dealing with the fallout of... what happened."

"Allen's death, you mean."

"Uh-huh."

"We were. Seth stayed here last night. It was kinda rough on him, being right there, holding Allen's hand when... when he passed."

"Poor kid. I can only imagine."

"How well did you know Allen?" I asked.

"Not much beyond the baseball games. We had a few beers after a few games this year, but not a whole lot more than that. Seth probably knew him a little better than I did. This is my first year with the team, after all. Seth's been doing this for, what? Three years now?"

"At least three. I think he was going to the games four years ago but wasn't a part of a team yet. Allen's only been a part of the team since last year. George brought him on board, as a matter of fact."

"George? Why?"

"For Allen's health. Thought it might do him some good to get some exercise in between those beers."

"Wow. George. Huh."

So my instincts about George doing one good deed weren't that far off kilter after all. Of course, Frank's knowledge of George, beyond sharing the outfield with him this past summer, came mostly from me, and I had a sneaking suspicion I wasn't the most objective person to talk to about the life and times of George Roberts.

"Frank," I said quietly, after allowing him a moment of reflection on George Roberts and his minuscule altruistic side. "Is there any way we could cut this short? I didn't get any work done last night with Seth here, and now that he's gone back home, I'd like to dive in and see if I can wade through some of these projects."

"Oh, right. Sure. Was just checking in on you. Glad to hear you're all right. That you're *both* all right."

"Mm-hm."

"And if you hear anything more about Allen, please let me know, okay?"

"You mean, like, funeral arrangements?"

"Yeah, like that. The funeral arrangements. Let me know about those, for sure."

"I will."

Click.

I held on to the phone a moment longer after Frank hung up. But since I had enough work to keep me busy till next summer, I shook the thought loose and plunked the phone down on my desk again. Time to warm up the second cup of joe and get cracking.

"ARE YOU TRYING TO TELL ME it wasn't natural causes?" I asked Seth for what seemed like the tenth time.

"Pretty much, yeah. At least, that's what his wife is saying."

"Geez, I know people can be in a little bit of denial about stuff like this, but it doesn't seem likely that she'd think her husband was in good health. Would she?"

"She swears he was healthy as a horse."

"A fat, beer-swilling, couch potato horse, maybe."

"Mom!"

"What? You know it's true. The guy was grossly out of shape."

"He could run like the wind."

"That doesn't mean he wasn't out of shape. I'm out of shape, but at least I'd admit it. And, if the zombie apocalypse happens, you can sure bet I'd be able to run like the wind too, given the right circumstances."

"Point taken, but geez, Mom. Have a heart."

"Oh, Seth, I wouldn't say that to his *wife*. Just to you. We're just talking here, aren't we?"

He sighed and rolled his eyes. "I suppose so. But I just thought you'd want to know that this whole escapade might not be over just yet."

"Why does this not surprise me? And why does this feel oddly familiar?"

"I know. I thought the same thing. I'm not really up for going through all that all over again. Are you?"

"Of course not! I'd like the rest of my friends, family, and acquaintances to simply die of old age, thank you very much."

"You and me both." Seth fiddled with the baseball cap on his head, lifting it up, flapping it around once or twice, and then cupping it back onto his head.

"So, exactly what does Mrs. Allen-whatever think happened to her husband, if he didn't just keel over from bad lifestyle choices?"

"Her name is Alice Joneston. And she apparently thinks it was foul play."

Egad, how I hated that concept. Having been at the forefront of the murder of our local newspaper editor last year, all due to being in the wrong place at exactly the wrong time, I wasn't eager to hear that this town might be in for another horror show so soon.

"Like, murder? Really?"

Seth nodded. "Yup. Exactly like murder."

"Have you talked to her yourself? Why would she think something like this in the first place?"

"I did talk to her a little this morning. I stopped there to drop off Allen's cap and glove, which ended up in my car after the game the other night. She was going to go to the police later today to bring it up with them."

"Did Allen have enemies? You know, besides the entire bean sprout growers industry?"

Seth frowned at me. Sometimes my snark wasn't fully appreciated.

"She didn't really want to say, and I can't blame her. But you gotta know everybody has enemies... somewhere."

"Such a glum outlook for someone so young," I said, sighing.

"It's true. I'm not sure I agree with her that it's likely, but I gotta say it's not outside the realm of possibility."

"Honestly, if we're going down this road at all, I gotta say that the most likely suspect in my mind would be dear ol' Alice herself. Allen never really had anything very nice to say about her during the games."

Seth shook his head. "You're right. He didn't. But still, I always assumed that was just the way husbands and wives acted in public, especially a guy at a baseball game without his wife."

"Such a *really* glum outlook for someone so young!"

"Well, look at how you and Dad talk about each other."

"And look at how that turned out."

He said nothing. I didn't think that was the point he was hoping to make.

"At any rate, Mom, I encouraged her to go to the police, while it was all still fresh in everyone's minds. If there is foul play involved, I bet it'd be easier to sniff out early on."

"Agreed. And, if it's true, I hope they catch the bastard who did it as soon as possible. I don't need this a second time in one lifetime."

"Anyway," Seth added, an obvious segue coming, "I gotta get to work. I just wanted to stop by to tell you that, in case you got wind of it some other way before I saw you next."

"Much appreciated. I'll keep my mouth shut about it for now, though. No sense starting the rumor mill up early."

He nodded and turned for the door. "Thanks again, Mom, for letting me stay here the other night. I really wasn't in a good frame of mind to be home alone in the apartment."

"No problem. You know you're welcome here any time."

I grabbed him in a swift impromptu hug from behind as he headed out the door.

"Love you, Mom."

A kiss on the back of his neck, and he was gone. I didn't like seeing him entangled in this mess, and I secretly hoped that whatever tests were done on Allen turned up a cholesterol count of a thousand and a blood glucose level of twice that. Maybe some high blood pressure and a brain aneurysm for good measure. Whether or not Alice would get peace of mind out of it wasn't my concern. I just wanted Seth to be able to rest easy at night knowing he had a friend whose life was cut short by too many sleeves of Pringles and not by someone who'd had it out for him. Besides, there wasn't a mark on Allen's body. We all saw him chatting one minute and then keeling over on the ground the next. How exactly could any of that have been foul play?

CHAPTER 4

POISONED."

"What?" I said, even though I'd heard Seth just fine over what was sometimes a bad cell phone connection here in my apartment building.

"He was poisoned."

"You're kidding, right?"

"Nope, not a bit. Allen was poisoned."

"How? Who?" I still didn't quite know how to respond. It had been three days since I'd last spoken to Seth about Allen's death, and I subscribed to the no-news-is-good-news way of thinking about things like this. Hadn't heard a peep out of Seth in that time, so I assumed Alice's hunch that it had been foul play was nothing more than bad prophecy. Kinda like the end-of-the-world predictions we all had to endure once or twice a year these days.

"Well, we don't have all the details yet, but it was definitely poison. Well, an overdose of some drug that probably led to a heart attack."

"Oh my gosh," I said, again at a loss for words. "How did anyone poison him when he was right there at the game with his teammates and friends? You guys were at the bottom of three long innings when Allen dropped dead."

"Mom."

"Sorry. When Allen... *passed away*."

"Thanks. You've been hanging around Helga too long."

"Could be right." Helga had some of the most colorful ways of saying anything that I could imagine—and I could imagine quite a bit.

"The Sport-Aide. They think it might have been in the Sport-Aide."

"The Sport-Aide? Seriously? Allen doesn't... *didn't* drink Sport-Aide. He drank beer. A lot of beer."

"I didn't bring beer. I was trying to help out and discourage Allen from drinking so much of it, at least during the games, so I brought no beer and a lot of Sport-Aide last week." He sighed.

"Oh, I see, so—wait!"

"What?"

"*You*? You brought the drinks?"

Somehow I'd forgotten. Until now, it hadn't been relevant.

"Yeah. It was my turn. It was my cooler. It was... my Sport-Aide."

"Oh, Seth, no."

"Oh, yes," he answered.

"Now what happens?"

"Now apparently I have to go in for questioning. They're letting me wait till tomorrow morning, which makes me think they don't consider me a serious suspect or anything, but I have to be at the station by nine o'clock."

My heart skipped a beat. I could actually feel it, and it was a thoroughly unpleasant feeling.

"Do you want me to meet you there?" I asked.

"Would you?"

"Would I? Seriously, Seth, did you think you had to ask?"

"Well, I didn't want to impose—"

I could hear his voice crack at the end of that sentence, and I could hear the fear in his voice. He'd been trying to keep calm, but now that he'd let it out, I knew he was going to lose it, and soon.

"Impose? Oh, sweetheart, please. Do you want to come over here and stay tonight? We can go over together in the morning then. You wouldn't have to drive."

"Isn't Annie due home later today?"

"We can make room. I do have a sofa, you know. Quite comfy. Just ask Vlad."

He laughed softly—nervously, too, but at least his sense of humor wasn't completely gone, yet. "That'd be great."

"I have a few more projects to tackle here—maybe two more hours of work—and I can take a break for the rest of the day. The rest can get pushed back a little. I'll write to those clients and let them know... without actually telling them anything incriminating."

"That'd be great, too."

"Come over any time after about two o'clock, okay? I'll be here."

"Yeah, okay," he said, and I realized he'd been speaking more quietly with every phrase. I could barely hear him now.

"Everything will be fine, Seth. You know you're innocent. I know you're innocent. They'd have to be idiots to think you'd be so bold and stupid as to poison your own Sport-Aide and bring it out in public for everyone to see. Plus, no motive, right?"

"Uh-huh." Even quieter. Hardly audible at all.

"You didn't do it. Just focus on that, and I'm sure the police officers will see it, too."

"I didn't do it. Right."

"Seth?"

"Hm? Yeah?"

"You didn't do it... did you?"

"Mom!"

"Sorry. Just... covering all the bases. No pun intended."

"*Mom.*"

"Just... oh, Seth... come on over any time you want. We'll have dinner once Annie gets home from college."

"I hate to impose," he said softly. "Can I bring anything along?"

"Anything but the drinks."

Click.

Sometimes I couldn't tell when to just turn off the sick sense of humor. This was apparently one of those times.

"THEY SAID IT WAS SOMETHING called tri-trifluoperazine, or something like that."

"The poison?"

"Yeah, only it's not a poison. It's a drug. They use it to treat depression, schizophrenia, anxiety—stuff like that."

"Oh," I said. I really didn't have much to add to this discussion. I'd never heard of the drug, and blessedly, neither had Seth before today.

"It's why they seemed to gloss right over me as a suspect."

"Meaning what?"

"Pass the gravy," Annie butted in, half-listening to her brother's tale of potential woe.

"Annie!" I scolded, as Seth picked up the gravy boat and handed it to Annie.

"It's okay, Mom," Seth said. "It's over. I added what little information I had to their investigation and I was out of there. No harm done."

I was glad to see he could be so cavalier about what had happened, but a mother worries.

"Still, it had me worried all morning. Annie, you really should be a little more sympathetic toward your brother."

"He said he's fine, Mom. And compared to last night when I first got here, he's tons better. I can tell he's his normal old self again."

"Thanks," Seth replied.

"You know, as long as you don't take 'normal' too literally," she added, poking him in the side with her fork and smiling.

"You two!" If they were tossing jibes back and forth at each other, then all was right with the world again. They both smiled at me, wide grins full of fun. Even I had to admit that Seth seemed hugely relieved to have that interview behind him, along with any hints of suspicion that might have flown in his direction.

"Once they realized I'd never taken any sort of drug for depression or anything like anxiety, it was obvious they were going to start looking somewhere else."

"I assume you mean, looking at people who might have easier access to such a drug?"

"Yeah, precisely that. I'd never heard of it before they said it to me."

Annie coughed a laugh. "Then it's a good thing they weren't looking for someone with ready access to Mountain Dew or Fallout 4."

"Hey!"

I tossed a quick glance in Annie's direction, and she grinned wide. I laughed in spite of myself, and even Seth finally gave in and laughed, too.

"You guys ready for dessert?" I asked, standing with my own empty dinner plate and heading for the kitchen.

"Whatcha got?" Annie called behind me. Seth didn't ask, and I knew it didn't matter to him what I was offering; he'd be having some, for sure, whatever it was.

"Pumpkin spice pecan cobbler," I said loudly.

"Isn't it a bit early for pumpkin spice crap?" Annie called.

"It's October," I said in my own defense. "Do you not want some then?"

"No, I wasn't saying *that*," she countered. "Never that."

I laughed. "Okay then, three helpings of pumpkin spice cobbler crap coming right up."

Sure, it was good to have Annie home from college for a visit, but it was even better to not have Seth in the slammer for a murder I was sure he hadn't committed. Despite Allen having died at the hands of an as-yet-uncaught murderer, life was still pretty good in my neck of the woods.

CHAPTER 5

WHAT DID I TELL YOU, GIRLFRIEND, about ever getting involved in another murder?"

"I think you were against it," I said.

"Then, what the hell?"

"Helga," I said, sighing and handing the manila envelope I'd brought over the high counter between us. "I was just in the wrong place at the wrong time. So was Seth."

"That's kind of what you said last time, if I remember."

"And last time it was true, too."

"It's like one of your super powers, woman. Getting all enmeshed in crap that doesn't have anything to do with you. And then not being able to get yourself out of it again."

"Well, I have to disagree with you on that last part. Both Seth and I are going to be out of all this soon. The police don't seem to consider him any sort of suspect after all. Allen was poisoned with some sort of drug used for anxiety and depression. Nobody in our household has ever had to take drugs for anything like that."

"Eh, keep it up with these murder investigations and you might be singing a different tune there, young lady." She shook her head and waved the manila envelope back at me from her side of the counter.

"Yes, *Mom*," I said with just the right amount of snark. Helga could certainly handle a high amount of snark, especially from her friends. She giggled in response.

"So what's this thing then?" she asked, changing the subject and continuing to wave the envelope around.

"The rest of the project from Fiona. Took me a few extra days because of Seth staying with me after Allen died. We kind of had our hands full for a few days there."

"I can imagine."

"Oh, I'm quite sure you can!"

Helga had been right in the thick of things with me and Seth last year when editor Lee Gerber had been murdered. Helga had not only helped us get more heavily involved in that investigation, but also helped us get back out alive ourselves. I was sure she, of all people, would have no problem imagining what the past few days had been like around my apartment.

"Anyway," I continued, "Fiona knows what it is. She's been waiting for it since last week. The last section here also had the most errors, so the proofreading really slowed down there at the end."

"Gotcha. I'll make a note of it and make sure she gets it. She'll be back in tomorrow morning."

I sighed and leaned down a little closer to Helga, trying to position myself across the high counter between us so I wouldn't have to talk so loudly.

"What do you know about Allen, or his wife, Alice?" I whispered.

"Allen? Barely knew him, really. Saw him at a few of the games with you guys, of course. He did my taxes two years ago till I figured out how to do them myself. Why?"

"No reason. Just curious."

"Oh, hell no, missy! You ain't getting away with a 'no reason' answer there! You definitely have a reason for asking me, and you're damned well going to tell me what it is!"

"Well..."

"Well what?" Helga asked, coming up out of her desk chair and standing so she could lean in close to me.

"Well, it's just that..."

"It's just that *what*?" she asked, a little more loudly than she probably wanted to. "What?"

"It's just that Alice—Allen's wife—was sure it was murder right away. And I have no idea why or how she could know that, given the, uh, state of her husband's health that day. Or, that whole summer, really."

"So you think he was generally unhealthy?"

"Helga, you saw him at those games! He was always winded, always sweating like a pig, always drinking beer. Let's just say he was probably mighty comfortable with comfort foods."

"Do you think maybe Alice was just in denial about all that? That she didn't want to deal with the thought that her husband was a fat slob who wasn't on intimate terms with anything leafy and green?"

"Yeah, that's what I thought at first, but Seth took her quite seriously when she first spouted off to him that Allen must have been murdered. He didn't seem to think she was being naive or foolhardy or anything like that. She seemed... I don't know... determined. Sure of herself."

"Well, Maggie, I didn't really know Alice, just Allen, and even him only through other people. She could just have been completely convinced that someone had it out for her husband. Some people are just naturally paranoid, as you probably know."

I snorted. "Yeah, I think I used to be married to one, as a matter of fact."

Helga tittered in response. "Yes, I definitely think you were. Speaking of ol' George, how is he handling all of this? He was the closest thing to a friend that Allen had on that crazy ball team."

"I don't quite know. Not firsthand, anyway. Seth talked to George the other night and said he was sounding a little off, compared to usual, but otherwise seemed fine. I'm actually headed out after this to drop off a few neckties George never took back after the divorce. Said he needs them for a job interview, and naturally, he couldn't find them and called me to help track them down."

"How the hell did they end up in your apartment? You moved out of the house, not him!"

"It was stupid. They ended up getting packed in a box of my own stuff because they'd been in a small box similar to the one where I kept my hair accessories. The boxes got mixed up."

"Hair accessories? You mean, from back when you still had hair?"

"Hey! I still have hair! The haircut's not *that* short!" I protested.

"Uh-huh. Okay, Kojak. Whatever you say. Want a lollipop?"

"You can knock off the ancient television references any time now, Helga. You're making me feel old."

"Why? Just because both of your kids would say, 'Kojak who?'"

"Yeah, that. And knock off the haircut jokes. Any friend whose first response to my new haircut is, 'Hey, it'll grow back,' is no friend of mine."

She laughed out loud. "Touché! But seriously, it will."

"It will what?"

"Grow back. The hair. It'll grow back."

"Smart ass."

I WAS MORE THAN A LITTLE FRUSTRATED with the weird vibes I was getting from Seth the next time I saw him, almost a week later. We were at another Raging Avocados game, me in the bleachers with the other friends and family members, wearing my matching green T-shirt and acting perhaps a little more fangirl-ish than either my son or my boyfriend would have liked. Frank had learned to tune it out fairly early on, but Seth had a much longer history of me having embarrassed him in public, so his knee-jerk reactions came a lot quicker than Frank's. Granted, it seemed the other folks in the bleachers were there out of a sense of familial obligation, but I was there because two people I liked were playing on the same team. I wasn't yet ready to say "loved" in regard to Frank, but I did feel an odd swell of pride when he played well, when he hit a long fly ball that the outfielder couldn't catch, when he himself ran down a long fly ball hit by the other team. At those times it was tough to rein in the cheering, the giddy applause. If Frank was embarrassed by it, he never let on. Seth, though, would roll his eyes any time I even showed up in a green T-shirt, let alone when I responded to anything he did on the field.

Well, he was just going to have to get over it. This week, in particular, it was even more important—the first game they'd played since losing Allen. I noticed immediately that no one had brought a cooler of drinks for everyone to share. Certainly not Seth. Nobody would have touched the stuff, even if he'd brought an expensive brand of beer. Didn't matter that the police had officially exonerated him. People were just weird about stuff like this. And I didn't blame them. If that Sport-Aide had been brought by someone else other than Seth, I know I wouldn't have wanted Seth to go anywhere near it. Even if it wasn't an issue of thinking that person was a murderer, it was at least a matter of personal security. Someone had gotten to those bottles of Sport-Aide and tampered with them. The police were still investigating whether the bottles had been fiddled with on site at the game, or whether this was a case more akin to the infamous Tylenol tampering case of 1982. Allen didn't really have any enemies, unless you included his nagging wife, the one he complained about so often during the games. But that had seemed like little more than the stereotypical marriage of a drinking, insensitive husband and a nagging, complaining wife. I wouldn't have looked at Allen and thought, "He needs to be dead." Then again, I didn't have to live with the man. He could have been absolutely unbearable, for all I knew. Alice might be guilty only of justifiable homicide.

At any rate, I sat at this first game post-Allen and tried to act as I normally did. Seth was probably torn between being his usual embarrassed self and being relieved that his mom was able to continue acting the same, minus any awkwardness or moody silences that could have been brought on by the events of the last game.

The Avocados had taken a week off, so this was a makeup game. Not that they were in the running for any sort of playoff berth. This was a fairly casual adult league—pay one flat fee per season and get assigned to a team if you were new. If you'd played here before, you could choose your own team. Or, a newbie could be chosen by an established team as long as they all agreed on the new player coming in. This was apparently what had happened with Allen last year. George had recommended him for the team, asking them a favor to let Allen in, citing his need for the exercise and camaraderie and touting him as a damned fast runner, which he was. He was also loud, brash, and rather blunt when he'd had a few beers. He especially seemed to like beers brought and paid for by other people.

"Go, Seth!" I yelled as Seth walked out from the dugout swinging a blue aluminum bat. He was wearing a batter's helmet that didn't seem to fit quite right, but in such an informal league, you took the equipment you had and worked with it. Seth wasn't going to be the one to spring for new equipment when there was still a perfectly good, cockeyed helmet he could use.

He looked my way and gave me the stink eye. Time for ol' Mom to just shut up, I guess. I'd save my yelling and screaming for when he actually hit the ball. Which, sad to say, wasn't a whole lot more frequently than when he was ten and in Little League. Which, also sad to say, is why I yelled with glee so easily when he hit the ball soundly nowadays. He didn't hit the ball at all this time, but at least I was used to it by now. He and Frank were at opposite ends of the batting order, so I could turn my attention back to my tablet, which I'd brought along in case of a lull in the action. And with an extremely amateur ball game like this one, lulls in the action were the lion's share of the action. I looked away from the playing field as Seth skulked back to the dugout, and I caught a glimpse of Alice standing just outside the fence far off left field, next to the lone tree that stood near the cinder block restrooms. She was purposely standing under the tree, so the leaves would hide her from the ball park's overhead night lights Even in shadow, though, I could tell it was her.

She didn't routinely come to any of the games, but I'd seen her not only at the funeral last week, but also during the picnic for the entire team and their families at the beginning of the season. She hadn't looked all that excited about the upcoming season, but she'd brought a marvelous macaroni salad and had managed to loosen up a little and even enjoy herself by the time the sun went down that evening. I hadn't, though, seen her at an actual game all season. I'd wondered about that—all the other team players seemed to have at least one or two family members or friends in the bleachers during games—but assumed she just had better things to do than watch her husband drink beer and cuss and belch. She likely got enough of that at home the other days of the week. It wouldn't have surprised me if the poor woman wanted a day off once a week. I pictured her sitting home on game nights, reading trashy romance novels, eating Godiva chocolates, and listening to Michael Bublé songs. After I'd spent a few of those game nights with her charming husband, I certainly wouldn't have begrudged her the alone time. And I was getting Allen in diluted doses because there were several dozen other people around. She had him all to herself on the other nights of the week. Yes, she certainly deserved a little "me" time once a week.

As I watched her standing alone in the shadows, still unnoticed by everyone else, I realized that she now had *all* nights of the week as her alone time, whether she liked it or not. I wondered if indeed she liked it. And if she felt guilty about liking her freedom. I couldn't explain why she was standing back there under that tree, present at her first Raging Avocados game of the season, and, tragically, the first one in which her husband wasn't present. Was it curiosity? Sadness? Guilt? Something else entirely? I couldn't see her face well enough to tell what she might be thinking or feeling, but I was certainly curious. If I stood and headed off in her direction, would she welcome the contact, or would she dash away like a deer along the side of the road? I looked back at the dugout to see if any of the players had noticed her standing there, but of course they were all busy chatting or batting. I seemed to be the only person to notice that Alice was there at all.

I stood slowly, trying to look as if I was eyeing my tablet and not noticing her. I climbed down off the second row of bleachers, tablet still clutched in my hands, and tried to look casual as I sauntered— no, meandered—in her general direction. Maybe she would simply assume I was heading for the restrooms.

But no, it seemed as if she didn't want to be seen. As soon as it was clear I was heading out along the third base line toward the outfield, toward the break in the fence near where she was standing, she pivoted and hurried off. She was initially hidden by the cinder block restroom building, and by the time I reached the break in the fence myself and rounded the corner out of the field, she was gone. All our cars were parked right along that street just past the restrooms, but I didn't see any headlights come on. Either she had gotten to the ball field some other way, or she was sitting in her dark car waiting to see what I was going to do before starting up the car and turning on the headlights, thereby giving away her location.

I didn't really want to press her into a conversation—my curiosity wasn't that strong to put her in an awkward and probably grief-inducing position—and so I headed into the ladies' restroom instead of standing outside looking up and down the street for her. I went through the motions of having to go, then came out of the stall and began to wash my hands in the sink. When I turned off the water, I heard the unmistakable sound of quiet sobbing coming from somewhere nearby. She wasn't in her car after all. She'd come into the ladies' restroom and was in the other stall, trying to time her sobs to be hidden by the sounds of a flushing toilet and a sink with running water.

"Alice?" I asked, standing still at the sink and trying to sound as helpful and encouraging as I could in the echo chamber of this restroom. At least we were alone. There were only the two stalls and nowhere else for anyone to hide.

"Alice, it's me. I'm Maggie... Seth's mom."

She didn't say anything from inside the stall, and the quiet sobbing had completely stopped.

"I'm also George Roberts's ex-wife."

Still nothing.

"George told me he was the one who encouraged Allen to join the team last year."

Still nothing. So maybe I should just go and leave her alone? I hadn't a clue what the right course of action was here. Did she feel like a caged animal at the zoo right now? After all, she couldn't come out of the stall without encountering me, something she obviously hadn't wanted in the first place.

"Alice, listen. I don't mean to make you feel uncomfortable. Really I don't. I just thought maybe... maybe you came to the game for a reason. To... see... how things were. Or to maybe talk to somebody on the team or something. No?"

I thought I heard a sniffle from the stall, but the bad cinder block echoes were making it tough to figure out what I was hearing out here by the sink. A cheer went up from outside, back at the field, and I fleetingly wondered which team was doing the cheering. Were the Raging Avocados still up to bat? Had someone scored a run? That would be just about my luck, too. The team finally does something cheer-worthy and I'm in the ladies' room with a grieving widow and miss all the fun.

"Alice, I know you're in here. I saw you out by the fence when I was sitting in the bleachers. I know it's you. And I don't mean to make you uncomfortable—"

Sniffle. Sniffle. Sob.

"No, really, I don't. I want to just let you know that, if you want to talk, I'm a good listener."

I'm not *really* a good listener—no more so than anybody else on the planet, anyway—but everybody says that when they're trying to get someone to open up. And right now I really wanted Alice to open up to me. I wasn't even sure why. The last thing I needed was to get entangled in a situation like this again, a situation involving murder and intrigue. Because the one thing I knew after last year's experience was that murder and intrigue weren't all that intriguing. They were, however, painful, difficult, painful, awkward, and painful. Did I mention they were painful? Because they were.

And here I was, in an ugly cinder block bathroom talking to a virtual stranger, asking her to open up about her husband's murder. Voluntarily. For no apparent reason other than some sort of morbid curiosity. And it wasn't just a morbid curiosity. It was a wholly misplaced curiosity. I needed to get involved in another murder like I needed a hole in the head. And the last time I checked, I hadn't really needed another hole in the head.

"Hello?" a small voice asked from somewhere inside that second stall. "Are you still there?"

"Yes!" I said quickly, and far too loudly. "I'm here. I'm Maggie. What can I do to help you?"

She sighed, which I heard clearly because of the insane echo in here. "Just... just let me come out and wash my hands and maybe splash cold water on my face. I probably look like a mess."

I smiled. "Oh, I'm sure you're fine. It's just us girls in here. Definitely, come on out and wash up."

The door latch sounded like a bullet shot out of a gun as she yanked it back, but then she was outside the stall and standing at the second sink up against the far wall. I watched her carefully but said nothing. And I tried to watch her without seeming like I was staring at her. But, of course, I kinda was staring at her. At the rate I was going, I was going to be a really bad friend.

As she soaped up her hands and then rinsed them under the faucet, I stood quietly. She dried her hands under the automatic hand dryer and then turned to face me. Her eyes were clear and she seemed a lot stronger and more self-assured than I would have anticipated, given her recent hiding in the stall. Maybe she did need to just gather her thoughts and feelings a little before dealing with me. I had, after all, accosted her in a ladies' restroom. Not exactly great behavior to pull on someone you didn't know, especially if they're already in a fragile emotional state. And I suspected widowhood due to your husband's murder qualified as a fragile emotional state. At least, it would have meant that for me. Even with George.

CHAPTeR 6

ALICE AND I DIDN'T EXACTLY BECOME FRIENDS—we didn't have enough in common for that—but we quickly developed a sort of mutual respect for one another. We started getting together once or twice a week for coffee, and in the beginning she just needed to vent. The emotional release was important in her grieving process. And even now I hesitate to call it a proper "grieving process," because hers came with a boatload of guilt attached to it. Guilt at not having been there when Allen died, when everyone else seemed to have spouses, significant others, and family members in attendance. Allen had always been there alone, without anyone tagging along to watch him play. She also felt supremely guilty that she hadn't been all that happy in her marriage to begin with, so being suddenly free of Allen was a sort of blessing in disguise. She hadn't really told anyone else about this part, for obvious reasons. The fact that Allen also had a nice insurance policy meant she would probably be able to keep the house and work only part time to maintain her current standard of living.

I could see why this would make her feel guilty. She'd gotten her secret wish, something she had wanted for many years, and all of it at the expense of Allen's life. She hadn't specifically wanted that part—just the freedom from having to live with him—but she now realized she had even more freedom than a simple divorce would have given her. And, of course, a lot more money, too. I cautioned her not to go around blurting out this part to anyone who would listen. It did, after all, make her look rather guilty. A *real* guilt, not the false guilt she harbored for being a survivor. I was sure she hadn't had anything to do with Allen's murder, and so our budding relationship continued. In fact, since I inadvertently became her only confidant about these things, her view of our friendship was likely more personal and precious than my own. I still saw myself as doing her a favor, giving her a hand up and out of her grief, even if some of it was wrapped up with feelings of guilt and shame. I hadn't wanted any trouble by becoming her friend. As I'd been telling myself for the past few weeks, the last thing I needed was involvement in another murder.

"How many times have they questioned you now?" I asked Alice during our most recent coffee gathering.

"Three times so far. This time was the longest. And, to be honest, the most frightening."

"Frightening? Why?" I asked in between sips of my dark roast. I was going to need a lot more caffeine to get through the rest of this already too long day. And it wasn't even lunchtime yet.

"Something changed. The way they treated me. It felt... different somehow."

"Different? Not in a good way, I take it."

"No, not at all. They were looking at me funny this time." No matter how Alice meant that, it certainly wasn't good. "Funny, how?"

"Like they suddenly didn't believe a word I was saying. Or even a word I'd ever said to them before. By the time they let me go, I felt sick and wanted to throw up.

"But you didn't, I hope."

"No, the feeling passed once I got outside in the fresh air. But, I tell you, Maggie, it was awful. Just awful."

"But they didn't actually accuse you of anything, right? Or tell you not to leave town? That sort of thing?"

"No, nothing like that. But it wouldn't surprise me if they said that next time." She turned her attention to her own coffee mug, slurping it loudly enough that I could hear it across the table. She seemed nervous, and I really couldn't blame her. The spouse got the most scrutiny in a situation like this, and if you added on her own extreme dissatisfaction with her marriage, you had an obvious, likely suspect. The cops were just doing their job the way most of us would have done it. No other suspects were jumping out at them, anyway. Poor Alice was front and center, caught in the crosshairs, if you will.

"Do you really think they're going to call you in *again*?" I asked. "At some point they're going to have to stop asking you those same questions over and over and move on to someone else, aren't they?"

"Not if they think I did it," she said bluntly. She looked up from her mug and directly into my eyes, a sort of pleading in her gaze that made me both sympathetic and uncomfortable. She wanted me to find some way to help her, but there wasn't anything a lowly proofreader could do for a possible murder suspect.

"Well, good grief, they're taking their good old time about it then. Allen's been dead for weeks. If they think you had anything to do with it, they should simply arrest you. If they don't think you did it, then this is a horrible way to treat a grieving widow."

"Even if she's not exactly grieving?"

I balked. "Well, you get my point, Alice. They should either put up or shut up about it. This isn't fair to anybody to just drag things out like this."

"Well, until they decide one way or another, I'm going to be a little bit paranoid, looking over my shoulder. I swear any time I see a police car now, I freeze up and panic."

"I can imagine," I said, shaking my head slowly. Assuming she was indeed innocent—and I was assuming that very thing—this had to be the worst thing to add to this period of mourning for her. Guilt. Shame. Sadness. Some element of grief. And now paranoia and fear.

I thought I'd had it bad last year when Lee Gerber had been murdered, but at least I had never really been a suspect beyond that very first day. And that was only because I had been the one to find Gerber dead, slumped over his desk. Just bad luck, and bad timing. Alice, on the other hand, hadn't been anywhere near Allen when he'd keeled over. In fact, the likelihood that she could have found a way to spike that Sport-Aide in Seth's cooler while she was home eating bon-bons and watching rom-coms on the television seemed incredibly far-fetched. Surely the police saw that, too, and would soon turn their attention elsewhere to find Allen's killer. Right?

"Well," Alice said, standing up from the table we'd been occupying for the past hour and a half. "I gotta get home. I want to start looking through some want ads online."

"For what?" I asked, swigging down the rest of my coffee and looking longingly into the bottom of the now-empty cup.

"A job."

"I thought you were going to be all right for a long time with the insurance money."

"Well, sure, once I actually *see* it. But with the investigation ongoing, the insurance company said they have to wait and see what happens with the authorities. I might never get it."

"Well, that majorly *sucks*," I blurted out, loud enough that the people at the next table heard me and frowned at us. I lowered my voice by half. "How long do you think you'll have to wait then?"

She shrugged, putting the empty mug back on the table in front of her. "As long as the entire investigation takes. Apparently they need a wrap-up, a decision of some sort. As long as everything is up in the air, so is the insurance money."

"I'm sorry, Alice. Really I am." Yeah, more useless platitudes from Maggie. I sighed.

"It's okay. Some days I don't know what to do with myself anyway. I think a part-time job doing something simple would be really good for me, you know?"

"Well, then, I wish you well. Check some of the job sites out there in addition to the local papers. I'm not sure what sort of job you're looking for or qualified for, but if you want something part time, I bet you'll find plenty of opportunities out there."

I didn't really know anything about her job history, but many entry-level jobs didn't require a heavy set of skills. Alice might already possess lots of employable skills. And she was probably right that getting out of the house for a few hours a day would do her some good and help her not to obsess about both Allen's death and the never-ending investigation that had been weighing her down for the past few weeks.

"Thanks, Maggie. You've been a friend right when I needed one."

"I try. Sorry I can't get you out of this mess. But if there's anything I can do to help you in your job search, let me know. Will you?"

"Definitely. I'll text you when I have some leads or when I think I can meet again like this. I really look forward to these times out together."

"I do too," I answered, and I found that, despite some of the awkward moments, I meant it. It felt good to be needed by someone other than my kids. And Frank didn't count. Not yet. That whole budding relationship had its own quirks, but helpfulness and need hadn't really entered into it yet. It was still a light romance born of fun and convenience for us both. Once one of us began to feel too desperate, all bets would be off. Neither of us needed a significant other right now. Just a good friend, and possibly a default date for Friday nights. Knowing Alice truly needed me right now felt good. I only hoped I could help her in ways that meant something in her life.

CHAPTER 7

ANNIE AND SETH BOTH SEEMED TO BE STARING at me across my small kitchen table. I'd made their favorite foods for dinner. I'd even baked their favorite dessert again, the pumpkin pecan cobbler. So, why were they both eyeing me suspiciously? Maybe I was just imagining it. Ever since Allen's death I'd been a little punchy about how people were looking at each other in my familiar circles of family and friends. Perhaps they were just looking at me funny, as usual. It was so hard to tell with grown kids, anyway.

But when I got up to start the coffee maker, I distinctly noticed that they were both watching my every move. What was up with that?

"What?" I asked, turning to face them directly, the sauce pot in one hand and the trivet in the other.

Seth, face still blank and mostly unreadable, replied first. "What do you mean, 'What'?"

Yeah, this was going to be a great conversation. I could see that already.

"I mean, what are you two staring at? You look like you think I'm a spy or something." I put the saucepan back onto the stove burner and put the trivet on the countertop.

Annie snorted and put down her fork. "A spy? Mom, seriously."

"Seriously, yes," I countered. "Both of you have been giving me the stink eye all through dinner. Tell me right now, what's up?"

Annie shot a knowing glance over to Seth, who nodded almost imperceptibly. Almost. I caught it.

"Okay, one of you two had better just come out with it. I can see there's something going on here that I'm not privy to. And it's about time I *was* privy to it. Cough it up, one of you."

I stood in the kitchen and folded my now-empty arms across my chest in that defiant "mom" way that all kids know and fear, even the grown-up kids. Seth sighed.

"Mom," Annie started, "we don't want you to take this the wrong way, but..."

"But what?" I chimed in, cutting her off a bit too fast but not really caring because they were the ones being rude by staring at their mother without a good explanation. Right?

"But we're a little bit worried about..."

She hesitated a little too much, not a good thing to do when talking to the likes of me when I'm pissed off or upset. I tend to blather on and on and cut people off.

"About what, exactly? Spit it out, girl."

"Mom," Seth interjected, "be nice. We're just worried about you, that's all."

"Worried about me? Why? I'm fine. Seth, you're the one we should be worried about! You're the one who had to watch someone you know die right in front of you. You're the one who had to answer questions from the police. You're the one who carried a cooler with Sport-Aide in it that somebody got their hands on and—"

"MOM." Seth stood from his place at the table but didn't move or come toward me. He just stood there, jaw set, waiting for me to shut up and let one of them talk for a change. It took me a moment but I picked up on the cue and shut up. I waved a hand in their direction, giving them permission to finally break in and speak their piece. Whatever they had to say to me, I should at least let them say it before I bit their heads off.

"What?" I asked, a lot more quietly than the first time.

"Mom," Annie said, also quietly. "It's Frank we're worried about."

"Frank? Why? He's fine."

"No, we don't mean we're worried *for* him. We're worried *about* him, *for* you."

I frowned, not following her line of reasoning. Why couldn't the daughter of a professional proofreader speak good English and communicate well? Sometimes I felt as if she spoke the way she texted people. But that was neither here nor there right now. There was a salient point buried in her fractured King's English. I had to find a way to dig it out.

"Still not following you, baby girl. What would Frank have to do with worrying about me?"

"Let's face it, Mom," Seth said, now moving from around the table and coming into the kitchen with me. Annie rose to follow him. I tried not to feel ganged up on by my own offspring. "We hardly know Frank. It's like he appeared out of nowhere."

"He appeared out of West Mifflin," I corrected. "Not quite the same thing."

Annie snorted. "Mom, you know what we mean. He's not really from right around here, like mostly everyone else on the team. We just don't know him."

"Nobody knew Allen when he first showed up, either," I said. "How is that any different?"

"It's completely different!" Annie said, spinning on her heels in a little fit of frustration at my obvious lack of understanding. "Allen is the one who's *dead*, not Frank!"

I rubbed my eyes, hoping to ward off the headache I could feel starting just behind them. "Let me get this straight. You're saying you can't trust Frank because Allen is dead and Frank isn't?"

"Yes!" Annie cried out, flailing her arms and acting as if finally we had landed on logical ground. I, on the other hand, felt that potential headache rapidly turning into a real one, right smack between my eyes.

"Still not making any sense whatsoever, kids. Sorry."

"Mom," Seth said, coming up to me and startling me by putting a hand on my arm. My eyes had been closed and I hadn't expected anyone to touch me, so I jumped a little, thereby startling both Annie and Seth in return.

"Geez!"

"Sorry, Mom," he said. "Anyway, listen. Allen is dead."

"Yes, I know."

"And somebody killed him."

"Yes, I know that, too."

"And we don' t know yet who it was who killed him."

"You're batting a thousand, kiddo. Let's try for the home run now, shall we?"

"And it could very well have been Frank."

"Strikeout! Sorry. You had me until this last point. What kind of logic did you use?"

"Let's sit down, okay?" He kept his hand on my arm and led me—and therefore Annie, too—back to the table, where we took our original places and sat together. "And let's take this slowly."

"Oh, good grief!" I said, giving up on the headache avoidance and throwing my hands up in the air. "You don't have to treat me like a child or like a hospital patient. Just be clear about what you're saying. And be even clearer about what you're accusing poor Frank of, because that part is still *really* unclear."

I looked at them both, hoping this was some sort of ridiculous prank. But Annie, of all people, was the least likely person I knew to be part of a prank. Especially one as tasteless as this.

"What if Frank is the one who poisoned Allen?"

There. Seth had just blurted it out. And it landed on the table in the middle of us like a big pile of dog shit. *Plop.* There it was. And none of us wanted to touch it or even look at it now that it was out there.

"Oh, you cannot be serious."

"Yes, we can."

"What are you two thinking? Don't they teach anything in these schools anymore?"

"Mom, we were homeschooled."

"You know what I mean! And Annie, you're in college. You should really know better, for sure." I leaned over and held my head in my hands, sighing.

"Think about it. Except for Allen, Frank is the newest member of the team," said Seth, leaning across the table as close as he could. I saw his hand snake out toward me, and I swatted at it to keep him from touching my arm again.

"So, the new guy is automatically a murderer? Simply because he's the new guy?"

"No, but we know everybody else a lot better than we know Frank."

"And," Annie said, sounding as if she was going to launch into a tone of chastisement, "you're not dating any of the other guys on the team."

"Or the other girls," added Seth, in what I assumed was a pathetic attempt at humor to lighten the mood.

"Yeah. Wait, what?" Annie said, turning to Seth and frowning.

"Never mind. The point still stands. You spend a lot of time with Frank these days, and what if he's... dangerous?"

I rolled my eyes and then caught myself, realizing I would look a little too much like my twenty-year-old daughter if I kept it up. "I thank you both for your concern about Frank, but I can assure you he's harmless."

"How can you know? How long have you known him?" Seth looked way too serious for the slacker he usually was. This was starting to creep me out.

"Longer than either of you."

I knew that was a lame comeback as soon as I said it. Now they were the ones rolling their eyes.

"Wrong answer."

"Seth, I really am touched by your concern. And yours, too, Annie. But I think I can handle myself just fine."

"So suddenly you're this awesome judge of character?" Seth said. He had folded his arms across his chest, and I felt as if he was trying to sound like my dad instead of like my son. Except that my dad wouldn't have looked this stern.

"Okay, I deserve that. If only because I married your father."

"Mom."

"Sorry. Not sorry." I smiled, hoping to ease the tension, but I realized that I was the only truly tense person in the room.

"Will you stop kidding around for one second?" Annie asked.

"I'll stop kidding around when you two stop accusing my boy-friend of murder."

"We're not really accusing him…"

"Oh, really? Then what else would you call it? Because from where I'm sitting, it sounds a lot like an accusation. You're trying to make it sound like it's just general concern, but you two have both gotten really specific about it at this point."

I hated going on the defensive and then switching to the of-fensive like this but I couldn't risk them starting to treat Frank any differently because they were secretly harboring suspicions about him having murdered Allen.

"It's not completely out of the realm of possibility, though, is it? Can't we just be a little protective of *you*, for once?" Annie said, switching to a gentler, more pleading tone. She was smooth, I had to grant her that.

"Well, of course it's possible. Just like it's possible that Seth killed Allen. Nobody really has an airtight alibi here, do they? That Sport-Aide was spiked with that drug at some point before the game even started. So, since we're not sure when it was spiked or by whom, then nobody is safe from suspicion."

"Not even Frank," said Seth.

"Okay, yes, then not even Frank. But that doesn't mean we have to have an intervention to let me know how worried you both are. I'm sure I get your point now. And, I'll be careful when I'm with Frank. Not that I'm completely sure I know what that even means, but…"

"It means, Mom, that you really shouldn't be completely alone with him for a while. At least until the police wrap up their investi-gation and arrest someone."

"Arrest someone *else*, you mean."

Seth sighed. "Yes, sure, whatever you say. Arrest someone else. Someone who's not Frank."

I nodded. "Thank you. Now, is this inquisition over for tonight?"

They both nodded at me and smiled.

"Good. Now, who wants dessert?"

"Me!" they said in unison, and I was glad we'd finally found something all three of us could agree on.

CHAPTER 8

FRANK WAS DRIVING A LITTLE TOO FAST for my liking, but that was nothing new. I was pretty sure this was a "guy" thing, this driving too fast on winding back roads. The only comfort I had was that he already knew these roads like the back of his hand.

"Frank," I said as calmly and coolly as I could. "Do you mind slowing it down just a wee bit? You know I get a little queasy on these back roads if you take the turns too fast."

"Well," he said, smiling from his side of the front seat. "Let's just say I know you *say* you get queasy. I'm still not convinced it's not just mind over matter."

Boy, how I hated this argument. We'd been dating only about three months, and unless my math was off, we'd already had this particular argument—whether dear ol' Maggie was prone to motion sickness or whether it was psychosomatic—nearly half a dozen times already. Sure, they weren't usually full-blown arguments—more like semi-playful banter about the concept of motion sickness—but they were annoying nonetheless because, to me, they always sounded a bit condescending. Frank's view on such things was obvious from the very first time I mentioned it, on this very road during one of our early dates. I was all right if I myself was driving here, but if I was a passenger in a car going anywhere over the *low* speed limit around these parts, my head always started to feel yucky and I started to feel nauseated. Nothing seemed to help—not staring out the front windshield, not looking out the side window, not closing my eyes. And Frank's first reaction was the one he still had any time he took us along these roads and I mentioned how I felt: he was completely unconvinced that there was anything medically wrong with me. He saw it as a ploy to get him to just drive more slowly. Of course, that wasn't a bad idea in general, but adding on my own personal discomfort somehow made it seem to him like I was trying to manipulate him into doing what I wanted. Apparently he hadn't figured out yet that, if I wanted him to drive more slowly, I would have said something like, "Frank, slow the hell down." I wasn't the mealy-mouthed young thing I'd been in my first marriage to George.

There were only a few things that annoyed me about Frank, but this was one of the big ones. I had a particular sticking point with men who spoke in a condescending manner—called "mansplaining" in some circles—and although Frank didn't indulge in it much, this was one area where he remained unconvinced and unable to budge. He'd tried on each of these occasions to talk me out of it. To simply explain to me (in small words with few syllables, which will always win a woman's heart, let me tell you) why what I was feeling was just silly. Calling me silly while I was trying not to puke my guts up in his car wasn't one of his more endearing qualities. It was a good thing he had plenty of others.

We'd met through Seth's baseball team, the Raging Avocados. I hadn't attended any of the games the first year Seth played—he hadn't really mentioned that he'd joined a local league, partly because he wasn't all that good back then—and at the start of his third season Frank had shown up, joining the team sometime in late spring and helping them limp into next-to-last place by playing first base in a pinch, when he wasn't needed in the outfield. Hard to believe, but without Frank showing up they'd be dead last. "Dead last" was probably not the best choice of terms now, after what happened to Allen. This season, when Seth invited me to a game, I was tickled pink to sit in the bleachers with other family and friends. Seth had struck out three times that game, so it wasn't his best performance, but I found myself watching the smooth game play of the first baseman that day, the one with the salt-and-pepper gray in his hair but a spring in his step.

After the game, a bunch of the players and some of their friends walked to a local bar a few blocks away to celebrate their near-tying score. (For the Avocados, this was a major step forward.) Seth had invited me, mostly out of a sense of obligation since I had driven an hour to see the game, but within the first half hour, Frank was the one buying me appetizers and beer.

Sure, it wasn't the most romantic "how did you meet?" story, but it was the only one we had. And, what I had seen in Frank in those early days was still true. He was, at heart, a gentleman, and he enjoyed fussing over me when I let him. Of course, I didn't often let him, which led to its own sort of squabble. I didn't fancy myself a feminist by any stretch of the imagination, but I also knew that I appreciated being appreciated. I think everybody does. So, I allowed a little bit of fussing, so long as it didn't make me feel as if I was a weakling. It had been way too long since anyone had fussed over me, except my parents. And, of course, that kind of fussing didn't really count. They were almost required by law to fuss over their only child, weren't they?

At any rate, there we were in Frank's car, on our way back to my apartment after a lovely evening of dinner and a few brews—more hopeless romantic evenings out, of course—when I began fighting off that queasy feeling. Frank slowed the car to a rate of speed that usually got rid of the motion sickness, but this time it didn't. This time, even when we were off the winding back roads and driving on the straightaway four-lane roads leading into my small town, the stomach churning continued. I took a few deep, calming breaths and closed my eyes, trying to will it away. (After all, it was all in my head, right?) When that also didn't work, I gave up and gave in.

"Frank, can you find a good spot to pull over? Like, soon?" I leaned over, clutching my hands across my torso.

Frank glanced over but essentially kept his eyes on the road. I mentally thanked him for that. "Are you all right?" The concern in his voice was evident.

"Not really, I think, no."

"Are you going to, you know, throw up?"

"I... I think maybe I might, yes." I doubled over completely and closed my eyes, hoping to ward off the inevitable.

"In my c-c-car?"

Another "guy" thing to say, so of course he'd said it.

"Yes, in your *c-c-car*! Pull over!"

Within seconds he found a spot where the shoulder was wide enough to pull over. He smoothly rolled to a stop and threw the car into park, turning to see if I needed help.

"Do you need help?"

"No!" I snapped. "I'm pretty sure I remember how to throw up."

With my eyes still closed, I fumbled for the door handle, found it on the third try, and quickly pushed the car door open. I stuck my head out and promptly puked everything I'd just had for dinner, including the two expensive microbrews, onto the grassy ground just to the right of the car. Behind me, Frank said nothing and didn't even move. That was probably wise on his part. *Stand back, Frank, nothing to see here...*

Once I was sure I was done, I stayed doubled over but reached near my feet to find my purse. I fiddled around inside the bottomless pit of doom and finally found the packet of tissues I always carried with me. I sat upright and wiped my mouth off, tossing the tissue into Frank's small trash bag attached to his stick shift. In my eagle eye peripheral vision, I saw Frank make a face at that, but hey, what else did people throw in trash bags except, well, trash? I avoided making eye contact with him until I could rummage around in my purse some more and find the pack of gum I knew was in there somewhere. Freshen up the breath a little bit. Beer smelled nasty enough on the breath when all you did was drink it and keep it down. Letting it make an encore reappearance doubled the nastiness. A little spearmint gum would keep me from being supremely offensive.

"Are you all right?" Frank asked again.

"Better, but not really all right."

"Do you need a doctor?"

I frowned. "Why would I need a doctor? It's just motion sickness, and besides, you keep telling me it doesn't exist anyway."

"Well, you know... because of... what happened."

My mind wasn't clear enough to get his drift yet. This conversation was taking forever. "What happened? What do you mean?"

"With... Allen. With the poison."

Oh, good grief. The thought hadn't even occurred to me. I had assumed that this was brought on by Frank's insistence on taking the back roads to my place and inducing a worse-than-usual case of motion sickness. The thought that it might have been something else, something far worse and far more sinister, now began to worry me.

"Oh my gosh," I said, clutching my waist again, but this time out of fear rather than discomfort or pain. "I hadn't even thought about that. But, it wouldn't happen again. Would it?"

I looked at him now. He was frowning.

"How would I know?"

"Well, you mentioned it, that's how."

"I just made the connection because my first thought was food poisoning. Then, once I'd thought *that*, the word 'poisoning' just led me into the other thought!"

"A doctor then," I agreed, and Frank turned back to the wheel, put the car into drive, and pulled away, heading toward the medical center. My stomach still felt like it was doing flip-flops, but this time I wisely refrained from voicing my troubles and blaming them on Frank.

At the time it seemed like a wise decision not to blame Frank. By the next day, I wasn't quite so sure.

I WOKE UP FEELING NAUSEATED, only to realize it *was* all in my head this time. All of the previous night, though, it hadn't been a figment of my imagination at all. Frank had gotten me to the medical center in the nick of time, to coin a phrase, and the emergency room doctor had made the decision to pump my stomach. What else they did while I was knocked out is anybody's guess, and I was pretty sure I didn't want or need to know what else had happened. I was okay with lost pockets of time in this situation. Sometimes that NBC slogan of "The More You Know" was a load of horse shit, to be honest.

This time the nausea quickly passed, replaced with the uncomfortable remembrance that I hadn't eaten since the restaurant last night, and of course all of THAT food was long gone, left along the side of the road. So, the last nourishment I'd had that had actually stayed in my system was lunch yesterday. One glance at my phone on the bedside table told me it was still the middle of the night. In fact, it was nearly four in the morning, and I'd already awakened twice since Frank had finally left the hospital a few hours earlier when they officially checked me in and gave me a bed in a semi-private room.

I lay here now, hoping Frank had called Seth as I had asked him to do. And that he had had the good sense to not let on that this might be anything other than simple food poisoning or motion sickness. After all, right now we really didn't know for sure what had caused the severe vomiting and mild dehydration I'd been suffering from when Frank brought me into the hospital. It had all the earmarks of simple food poisoning and it was only our recent brush with Allen's death and that *deliberate* poisoning that made either of us think otherwise. I vaguely remembered Frank saying something about me having been poisoned on purpose to the emergency room workers last night, but whether or not they took him seriously was anybody's guess. I hadn't exactly been in the right frame of mind to add a whole lot to the conversation while I was concentrating on not puking on everybody's shoes. A feat, I might add, with which I was mostly successful. Mostly. That reminded me that I had to apologize to that one unfortunate nurse when I saw her next. I hoped those sneakers she was wearing were machine washable. Or at least inexpensive.

All sorts of to-do lists passed through my mind as I lay there in the quiet stillness of the hospital room. Although I was in a semi-private room, there wasn't anyone in the other bed so I had some blessed privacy, making those to-do lists a lot easier to run through in my head. Two freelance projects were due tomorrow—wait, *today*, actually—but I wasn't going to get back to my desk, I assumed. Even if they let me out of here sometime later today, I had a feeling my day wouldn't be spent proofreading a theological tome from the 1800s. That fun and excitement would have to wait until another day. I'd have to make sure everyone whose projects were now on hold got word. Maybe I could email a few of them on my phone while I was still here.

My mind drifted further, and before I knew it, I was drifting back into dreamland. Turns out, dreams in such a state are particularly odd and vivid, because I went from being in this antiseptic hospital bed to standing alongside dear ol' Allen. Dead Allen and I were standing in some sort of line, waiting for something. I tapped him on the shoulder in order to ask him what we were all waiting for, and he turned slowly to look at me. I gasped when I caught sight of his face, already decaying and half falling off his skull. His eyes were limply hanging out of the sockets because the muscles that would normally hold them in had deteriorated and were also falling off the front of his face.

"What?" he said, through lips that dangled down like bits of twine, flapping outward as he spoke. "What do you want?"

He didn't seem to understand my horrified gaze, so I tried not to look at him the way I felt. That was a losing battle, let me tell you. But it seemed best to maintain a normal conversation so that he didn't notice his own gory state and freak out.

"Nothing, really, I'm just wondering why we're all standing in line here. What are we waiting for, exactly?"

"The Grim Reaper, obviously," he said, clucking his tongue at me, which loosened a few of his upper teeth, which toppled out of his mouth and onto the ground between us. "Shit," he said as he watched them bounce. "Not again."

My stomach lurched and I threw a hand over my mouth, trying to keep myself from vomiting on his shoes. Too late. I woke myself up with a wave of nausea and sat up just in time to pull my head over to the side of the hospital bed, where I promptly spit bile onto the shiny tile floor next to the bed. I grabbed the call button on my lap and pressed it hard. Twice, just to be sure.

Half over or not, it was going to be a long night.

CHAPTER 9

MOM," SETH SAID, GRABBING MY HAND AGAIN and looking around furtively to make sure no one was listening in. Annie was the only other person in the room, and the door was closed, but Seth was already paranoid and freaked out, so he wasn't in the mood to trust anyone, even the hospital staff. Maybe especially the hospital staff.

"What?" I said, putting my other hand on top of his and patting it in the most reassuring way possible.

"I knew it. I knew something like this could happen."

"You did not." I rolled my eyes at him exaggeratedly, on purpose, so that he might understand my level of frustration.

"I did. *We* did," he amended, pointing to Annie with his free hand. She began nodding like a puppet under his control.

"You did not."

"Yes, we did!" she said, adding absolutely nothing to Seth's argument, except maybe emotional momentum. If I had thought they were a united front before, they were double that now. I was going to have to placate them a bit in order to win the battle, if not the war.

"So tell me, please, you two. What exactly did you *know* would happen?"

"We knew Frank was trouble," Seth said without so much as blinking.

"Frank was the one who brought me here last night!"

"After he *poisoned* you!"

I shook my head. "And if he meant to kill me—for some reason unknown to both man and beast—why would he then drive me straight to the medical center the minute I got sick? It was *his* idea to come here in the first place. I just thought it was motion sickness, which it usually is."

"Mom, I've never seen you throw up over your motion sickness," said Annie, crossing her arms defiantly, tapping her foot as she stood on the opposite side of my bed from Seth. It would have been cute and charming had it not been annoying and misplaced.

"Ah, but I've seen *you* throw up over *yours*," I countered, and she simply frowned at me. Annie had a long toddler history of puking her guts out on the way to church every week, so we'd learned early to drape her in a receiving blanket—a sort of motion sickness drop cloth—in her car seat because somewhere around Exit 32 on the parkway, she'd invariably throw up. She'd inherited my motion sickness and then some, poor thing. We kept crackers and baby food in the diaper bag for a long time, so she could at least start to make up for whatever she couldn't eat before we loaded her into the car for the weekly trip.

"This is different," she said, citing no actual evidence for this but obviously believing it wholeheartedly.

"How?"

Seth exhaled loudly. "Mom, it's obviously different. When Annie was a baby, nobody was being poisoned and dying at the same time!"

"Ah, but Allen didn't throw up, did he? He just kind of keeled over."

"About an hour after he drank that Sport-Aide."

"You mean the Sport-Aide *you* brought to the game?"

"Mom."

"What?"

"You got sick about an hour after eating that food, according to the doctor."

"Is that your only evidence of foul play? That same hour? You're going to have to do better than that. Pretty flimsy."

"We don't think so."

"I do. We were eating at a restaurant. It's not like Frank was cooking dinner for me at his house or anything."

"Mom."

"And it's not like he served dinner with a nice chianti and some fava beans, either."

"*Mom.*"

"What?"

I blinked at them both, looking as doe-eyed as I could. I knew I was playing devil's advocate here, and I was trying to appreciate their protectiveness of me. But when it was this misplaced, it only caused strife between us. But, I also knew that my trying to make light of it could backfire on me. They were starting to feel belittled. I could see it on both their faces. Time to ease back a little bit and give them a way to save face. Even if I thought they were being ridiculous, they didn't see it that way.

"Seth," I said, hoping to change the subject. "Could you hand me that glass of water on the table next to you?" I pointed directly at it.

He lifted the glass, peered into it, and then shook his head. "Do you know who poured this?"

"The nurse," I said.

"Which one? Have you seen her before?" Seth was cocking one eye at me, half open, and I felt as if all that was missing from this interrogation were the lie detector and Detective Columbo with his cigar.

"Seth, she's been in and out of here all night. I've already had a few swigs from that very glass of that very water. And look, I'm not throwing up or dying or anything. Now, can you please hand it to me?" I asked, holding out my hand in supplication.

He met Annie's gaze across the bed, and she nodded wordlessly. He handed me the glass, and I freely drank of the probably untainted but possibly dangerous water. These kids. They needed to lighten up a little bit.

"See? Just water."

Suddenly I dropped the empty glass onto my lap, where it nearly rolled off onto the floor. I grabbed my throat with both hands and gasped, making an extremely loud gargly noise and letting my tongue loll out of my mouth to one side.

"MOM!" Seth yelled, and Annie very nearly screamed, before I dropped my hands into my lap, pulled my tongue back into my mouth where it belonged, and smiled at them.

"See? Just water. As I said."

I picked up the glass from my lap and held it out to Seth. "Would you mind putting this back on the table there? Thanks so much."

"*Mom.*"

"What?"

"That's not funny."

"No? Because I thought it was a riot."

"You would." Annie was frowning at me as if she were about to ground me for my bad behavior.

"Mom, seriously, just tell us you're going to steer clear of Frank, at least for a little while."

I shook my head. "No. Why should I? There's no evidence that anything happened that doesn't have a logical, reasonable explanation."

As I said this, the door to my room opened and a doctor walked in.

"Mrs. Velam?" he asked, walking to the end of the bed and grabbing the clipboard with my chart on it before sidling up to the same side of the bed where Seth currently stood.

"Miss," I corrected.

"Oh, sorry, my bad," he said and smiled. "I'm Dr. Carter."

"Yes, I remember. From last night. How am I doing?"

"Well, good... and not so good." He looked at the chart a little more but then closed everything up and held the clipboard at his side.

Seth and Annie both crossed their arms across their chests, and I simply frowned. "Go on."

"It looks like you're definitely out of the woods, and I'm going to give the green light for you to have a proper meal when I leave here in a few minutes."

I smiled. "That's good news. My stomach's been yelling at me ever since I woke up this morning."

"I can imagine," he said, smiling in return. "However..."

Oh, here was the bad part. I could feel it even now. Seth and Annie both looked like they were wound up so tight they would fly off in opposite directions, and soon, as the doctor spoke again.

"It wasn't from motion sickness."

"So," I said, maintaining some small sliver of hope that this could still end uneventfully with a quiet hospital discharge and a short, boring recuperation at home. "So, it was food poisoning then. From the restaurant?"

"Food poisoning, yes. Two other people came in after we admitted you. Same restaurant."

"Two?" I squeaked, trying not to look at either Seth or Annie.

"We thought it might be deliberate, like the poisoning at the ball game a few weeks ago," Seth chimed in. I bit my tongue.

"Oh, so you've heard about that case?" asked Dr. Carter, turning to Seth.

"Yes, we've heard about it. My mom and I were the ones who were right there with Allen when he died."

"That was you?"

"Yes, it was. I thought maybe Mom's new boyfriend, Frank, had something to do with this—and with Allen's death."

"Seth," I cautioned. "Let's not start hurtling accusations we can't prove."

"She won't listen to reason on this," Seth continued, "but we told her that Frank was trouble."

Dr. Carter was frowning now, apparently unsure who to take

seriously but not wanting to discount any possible option. He was going to get caught in the crossfire in a minute.

"And just who is Frank, and why is he trouble?"

I sighed, jumping in before Seth could get his own tainted response out. "He's my boyfriend. The man who brought me in here last night. We were out having dinner and I got sick in his car on the way home. Coming here to the E.R. was his idea, not mine. My kids here are just trying to be protective of their mom." I hesitated a moment, holding my hand up in front of Seth as he drew in a breath to speak. "Frank is the first man I've dated since the divorce from their father. I think they're just being overly cautious and seeing problems where there aren't any."

I smiled at Dr. Carter, hoping that my calm, reasonable response would win him over.

"Probably so," he said, "but your friend Allen *was* deliberately drugged. By someone who meant for him to die." He lowered the clipboard and banged it against his thigh—*tap, tap tap*—and I began to feel more than a little bit perturbed at being ganged up on by these three people who were supposed to be helping me, not making me more upset.

"Listen, doctor, can we talk about this later? Right now I'd like to just find out what I need to do in order to get out of here and get back home."

He nodded. "Of course. Let's get you home where you can recuperate best."

"So it can be soon then?"

"I can sign the release papers as soon as you eat some lunch and hold it down for at least three hours."

I sighed. "I feel fine."

"I know. And you seem fine, too. But it's house rules. We need to be sure you'll be all right once you get home. I'll have the nurse get you something simple and bland for now—maybe just a turkey sandwich, some crackers, things like that. Once you show those are going to stay put, you're out of here. Deal?"

I nodded. "Fair enough. Deal."

"Oh, and can one of these fine young people stay with you for the next few days? To keep an eye on you and make sure you don't overdo it?"

Seth and Annie both nodded, but it was Annie who chimed in first. "I'm off on fall break right now so I'm staying at Mom's place anyway. Easy enough since I'll be there through the weekend. Not heading back till Tuesday morning."

"Good," said Dr. Carter. "Perfect. And Miss Velam, will you behave and let your daughter know if you feel the least bit sick after you're back home?"

I nodded. "Of course." It seemed a small price to pay in order to get to go home today. I was sure I was in for quite a few anti-Frank lectures once we were all back at my apartment, but I felt reasonably sure I could endure them and even tune them out. A mother doesn't get to be a mother for several decades without learning how to tune out the kiddos every once in a while. This seemed like just the right time to do it. A lot of creative smiling and head nodding and we'd get along just fine for the next few days. Now, if only I could get her to keep my office clean while she slept on the daybed this weekend. Ah, but I was probably asking too much. I had to be realistic, after all.

IN THEORY, IT WAS MARVELOUS to be back in my own bed again after a horrendous night's sleep in that hospital bed. Sure, I slept like a log once I was back home, with Annie there to make sure I was properly fed. That is, as long as you call eating Stouffer's microwaved dinners being properly fed. And, I did. Anything was better than spending another night in a narrow, uncomfortable hospital bed. Except, that is, for waking up to the sound of yelling and arguing from somewhere near my living room. It wasn't the television. It was two actual human voices. Two *male* voices, which is what really threw me off. I swung my legs out of bed and planted my feet soundly on the carpeted floor. My bathrobe was carefully laid out for me at the foot of my bed, and I stood—a little shakily—and put it on, cinching the belt snugly. The arguing and yelling continued, and, in fact, got a little louder, as I slid my feet into my slippers and headed out the bedroom door and down the short hallway toward the living room.

I wasn't thrilled to find both Seth and Frank standing there in front of me, my front door wide open. Frank was in the archway of the door, and Seth was trying to shove him back out into the hallway of my apartment building.

"*Get out!*" he yelled as he pushed on Frank's chest one more time.

Frank opened his mouth to reply, but he caught sight of me standing in the hallway just outside the living room.

"Maggie!" he called. Seth turned to find me staring at both of them. Annie was nowhere in sight. I assumed she'd gone out on some sort of errand and had asked Seth to hold down the fort here while she was out.

"Frank! Seth! What the heck is going on out here?"

I sounded a bit too scolding and motherly toward these two grown men, one of whom wasn't even one of my offspring, but the situation seemed to warrant it.

"Mom!" Seth shouted back at me, turning to face me fully and lowering his hands to his sides. "You're awake."

He stated this with a great amount of surprise, which I would have found amusing in other circumstances.

"Yes, of course I'm awake. And I have a feeling people on the other side of town who were sleeping are also awake now. What's going on between you two?" I turned my gaze to Frank in the doorway, but I got no real answer from his blank look. Whether or not he had shown up here on the offensive, it looked as if he had not anticipated such a hostile reaction from Seth.

"N-nothing," Frank said, sounding way too much like a toddler in trouble, trying to hide something from Mom.

I rolled my eyes at them both, while walking slowly toward the couch. I wasn't well enough for this much standing just yet, and the couch looked like a better place to be while I continued this conversation.

"You okay, Mom?" Seth asked as he saw me heading toward the couch. "Here, let me help you." He stepped toward me and stretched a hand out in my direction. I batted it away.

"Never mind. I'm fine," I said, snipping at him more out of a sense of annoyance at my own lack of stamina than at anything I had just seen going on here. "Just tell me you two weren't heading toward fisticuffs just now." I made it to the couch and sank down into it, immediately hoisting my feet up onto the coffee table and sighing.

"Fisticuffs?"

"Yes, Seth, I was trying to make light of whatever I was witnessing here when I came down the hallway. Now, at least one of you two boys has some 'splaining to do." I looked up at them both, only to see them turn toward each other. As if they had practiced it, and as if they were part of a bad sitcom, they shrugged in unison.

"Seriously? Surely one of you can come up with a reasonable account of what was happening here just now." I grabbed a throw pillow from the couch and laid it across my midsection, gripping it tightly in an effort to keep from becoming too upset. There had to be a way to make this a little more humorous than it felt at the moment. Because it didn't feel the least bit funny, and I wasn't even sure whose side I was on.

"Maggie," said Frank, instinctively trying to step into the living room from the hallway. Seth launched into an immediate knee-jerk reaction and stepped in front of Frank, blocking his path into the apartment.

"Stay right there and say your piece, mister." He was completely serious. Frank, on the other hand, looked completely perplexed and a bit forlorn standing outside in the hallway.

"Seth," I said, in my best mother-knows-best voice, "let him in. We're in America. Remember? Innocent until proven guilty?"

Seth turned to me but stayed at his spot blocking Frank's way. "This isn't a court of law, Mom. This is your home. And I'm not entirely sure this man is welcome here right now. Is he?"

"Maggie, what the hell is going on here?" called Frank from somewhere behind Seth. He tried to move himself either left or right in order to see around Seth, but Seth was sensing Frank's intentions even while facing me and was bobbing and weaving in response, keeping me from seeing Frank's face in order to gauge my own reaction to what the poor man was trying to say back there.

"I think I know, Frank, but if Seth would only *let you in the door*, maybe we could have a civilized discussion about all this."

"All *what*?"

"See, Seth, this is why you need to step aside and let Frank into my apartment. *My* apartment, remember? Now, let him in. He doesn't even have a clue why you're suddenly treating him this way."

Seth frowned at me, clamped his jaw firmly, and crossed his arms across his chest defiantly. I rolled my eyes.

"Seth, you've crossed the line from being the helpful son to being the annoying hindrance. Could you *please* just step aside and let Frank in? Then maybe we can talk this through together." I clenched my own jaw and crossed my own arms across my own chest, across the throw pillow. Seth sighed, looked at me again, and finally stepped aside to let Frank cross the threshold of the apartment.

Men.

"So, what happens now?" Seth said. Suddenly he was upset with me for being calm and not freaking out on Frank. Well, I wasn't going to succumb to scare tactics, not when relationships were at stake. Seth seemed perfectly willing to burn bridges, but since this one was *my* bridge, I wasn't going to let him burn it for me.

"Well, we ask the right questions, and we do *not* make assumptions, my boy." I turned my gaze to Frank, who was now technically inside my apartment but who still looked as if he might dash back out into the hallway—and down the stairs and away from me and my family drama—at any moment. I had to hand it to Seth: he looked fairly intimidating for a young, ectomorphic guy who had "gamer geek" written all over him.

"Maggie, can you please tell me what's going on here? Why the Spanish Inquisition as soon as I get into the building?" He glared at Seth, who turned away immediately and looked at me instead. Apparently Frank could give as good as he got. I was impressed, and I smiled without thinking of how Seth might react.

"Mom! Whose side are you on?"

"Seth, there aren't 'sides' here. My best guess is that there is a huge misunderstanding, and I'm hoping we can clear things up fast so I can get back to bed and get enough sleep."

Seth's look changed from anger to a sheepish sort of guilt. "Sorry, Mom. I really didn't mean to wake you up or get you involved in all this."

"When you shout and scream in my small apartment, Seth, there's no way I'm not going to hear it."

"I realize that now, but—"

"No, no buts, Seth. I'm awake, and I'm going to mediate this skirmish from here on out. Frank," I continued, making eye contact with Frank and trying to look apologetic and sympathetic at the same time. "Honey, Frank... I don't know what Seth has already said to you, but—"

"Nothing, really. Well, nothing that makes sense. As soon as he opened the door, he freaked out and started yelling at me about staying away from you from now on. And how he was 'onto' me. What is *that* about?"

"You'll have to excuse Seth for his incredible rudeness—" At this point I gave Seth the mom-glare that I knew he loved so much. "Apparently I haven't taught him the basics of human interaction."

"Mom."

"Seth. No. Let me speak. And, more importantly, let Frank speak."

Frank scoffed. "Speak? I don't have any idea what I'd speak about. I still don't have a freaking clue what's going on here. Mind telling me what all the fuss is about?"

"Have a seat here next to me, Frank," I said, patting the couch cushion.

"No!" Seth positioned himself between Frank and the couch, and poor Frank balked even as he started to move his first step forward.

"Seth, knock it off. We're just talking here." I motioned for Frank to come on over, and I used my other hand to shoo Seth off to one side. "Frank, have a seat. Seth doesn't bite." Seth gave me a huge frowny face. "Do you, Seth?" The frown deepened. "Do you?"

"I'm going on record that I am not in favor of this conversation."

"Thanks, Seth. Duly noted," I said as Frank stepped around Seth and around the coffee table, finding a spot next to me on my couch. He reached out as if he was going to touch me, possibly hug me, but one loud cough from Seth behind him made him withdraw his hand as if he had touched a hot stove burner.

"Seth!"

"What?"

"Sit!"

"Woof," Seth said snidely as he plopped down in the armchair across from the couch. "I'm not a dog, Mom. Sit. Stay." He rolled his eyes and suddenly looked more like the fifteen-year-old I remembered all too well instead of the twenty-six-year-old sitting across from me right now. Who knew young men could do the drama queen thing almost as well as their female counterparts?

"Knock it off, Seth. Not in my home, okay? Now, first question is for you. Where the heck is Annie? She was here when I went into the bedroom to sleep."

"She said she had some errands to run. And I think she was going to stop at the grocery store for some stuff."

"Grocery store? Why? The fridge is pretty well stocked."

"Not with stuff she wanted, apparently. She said something about Oreos. And Diet Dr. Pepper."

"Wait, what? Oreos and *Diet* Dr. Pepper?"

"Don't look at me, Mom. I'm just telling you what she said."

I shook my head. There was no accounting for taste sometimes. I was still trying to figure out how the Diet Dr. Pepper canceled out the calories and sugar in the Oreos, but I suppose a gal had to measure out her daily sugar allotment in ways that made sense to her. I was the one who ate pasta and then backpedaled on all those carbs by having nothing but bacon and eggs for breakfast every morning. Same difference, right?

"Did she say when she thought she would be back?"

"Nope. Could be any time now, though. She's been gone over an hour."

"Okay then. Now, Frank," I said, scooching to the right just a tad so I could better face Frank next to me on the couch. "I apologize for Seth's rude behavior, but please cut him a little slack. He's had quite a scare about his mom, and he's feeling a little bit vulnerable and a little bit protective of me." By this point, Seth was not only rolling his eyes at me but was also turning beet red with embarrassment. But, one more glare from me as I spoke, and he knew not to make a fuss at this point.

"Maggie, babe. Seriously. I know exactly how he feels. Remember, I was the one who was with you when you... got sick." Now he did reach out and take my hand, and I let him. Awkward or not, I was going to have to navigate between these two men in my apartment, and I was going to have to be Switzerland in this cold war in front of me. Well, bad analogy, I suppose, but the truth was in there somewhere.

"I know. And that's why Seth's rudeness is particularly offensive. Right, Seth?" One more time with the mom-glare and Seth finally seemed to soften. A little. Not a lot, but perhaps enough.

"I don't get it, though," said Frank, and it seemed as if he was purposely not making eye contact with Seth now. "Why is he so damned pissed at me?"

"You could look at me and just ask *me*," said Seth from across the small room.

"No," I said, interrupting them both before this escalated into another standoff. "Don't ask him. Ask me."

"Okay then. What's up? Why no love from Seth?"

"Do you want the short answer or the long one?" I asked, pursing my lips, not sure coming right out with it was the best way to go.

"Just the clearest answer for now, thank you."

"Well, the short version is that Seth thinks you may have been the one who poisoned Allen."

"What?" Now Frank turned toward Seth, who sat deathly still in the armchair. He was avoiding direct eye contact by looking at something fascinating on the ceiling. Of course there was nothing on the ceiling, but his focused gaze tried to convince us otherwise. I suspected Frank was just as unconvinced as I was that there was anything at all up there worthy of attention. Not even a ladybug or stink bug. Just plain blank white ceiling as far as the eye could see.

"Seth, don't you have anything to say for yourself?" I asked quietly. He continued to stare above him and said nothing.

I sighed, weary of the relational garbage already. I wondered if this was Seth's overreaction to my having a boyfriend or if he truly believed that Frank was a possible murder suspect. Perhaps this murder investigation was simply the easiest way to make Mom's life miserable with her new boyfriend. If there hadn't been a conveniently timed murder to pin on someone, might Seth have come up with some other semi-heinous crime to patch onto Frank's back instead? Accuse him of robbing a bank or drowning puppies, perhaps? I might never know. All I had to work with right now was what was in front of me: a son staring at the ceiling in a self-imposed catatonic state and a boyfriend sitting next to me, stunned into silence by the aforementioned son's accusations. Well, his *silent* accusations, anyway. He hadn't actually said anything yet. I was the one who'd voiced it for him.

"Seth, please speak," I said and crossed my arms across my chest again.

"What do you want me to say, Mom?" he said finally. "You already said it all for me. Yes, Frank, I think it's entirely possible that you could have been the one who poisoned Allen. We don't know you all that well, do we?"

Now he stopped staring at the blank ceiling and turned a frowning, disapproving gaze on Frank himself. Frank, to his credit, didn't flip out or lose his cool. He met Seth's gaze and held it for what seemed to me, as the woman caught in the middle, a complete eternity. It was probably no more than five or six seconds.

"Look here, young man. I think I really like your mother, and I don't think—"

"You really like my mother?"

"Yes, that's what I said. Why?"

"Gee, Frank, old pal, don't overdo it with the emotions, okay? You might make one of us swoon."

"Seth!" I yelled, standing up and starting to cross the room around the front of the coffee table. Frank held out an arm in front of me to prevent me from doing so.

"It's okay, Maggie. Let him say it. It's probably better that we get all of this out in the open where we can better examine it and deal with it. Time to nip all these bad feelings in the bud, I think."

"Nip them in the bud?" said Seth, seeing this as an affront because he could and because he felt it was his duty, I suppose. "Bad feelings? So that's what you think this is all about? Just some bad feelings? And not, say, an actual murder of an actual human being?"

Frank shook his head. "I think you're using Allen's unfortunate death as a way to get me out of your mother's life."

"While she still *has* a life, yes, that's precisely what I'm doing. Because I think you're dangerous."

"Boys!" I said and moved to stand directly between them. "This is insane. And it stops now. Seth, you're going to apologize right now. And Frank, you're going to let him." I looked from one to the other and back again, hoping to see one of them break ranks and soften so we could move on past this ridiculous situation. Then, sensing that it was going to have to be Seth first, since he was the one who'd come with his teeth bared, ready for a fight, I turned to face only Seth. He took a few extra seconds to work up the nerve to look directly at me, but when he did, I met his gaze and held it. He finally softened and looked away.

"Fine, Mom, I'll shut up about this, but I really would like to see Frank come up with some sort of alibi to exonerate himself." He was back to avoiding eye contact.

"Alibi?" Frank said, and I spun around to face him directly now. I hoped my look, stern as I could make it, communicated that I wasn't going to stand for any more anger or self-righteous indignation. Frank, too, softened under my icy stare. "Maggie, I'm just not sure what he means by alibi."

"What?" called Seth from behind me. "Don't you know what an alibi is?"

"Of course I know what an alibi is. But since nobody has any idea how, when, or why that Sport-Aide was spiked, exactly when might I need this alibi to cover? What time period are we looking at here? Because the way I saw it that day, Allen drank that Sport-Aide—the stuff *you* brought to the game, I might remind you—and then, within an hour, he collapsed and was dead. Beyond that, *before* that, we really don't have any sort of timeline to start with. Do we?"

Seth glared at Frank, having leaned to one side in the armchair so that he could see around me. So much for standing between them in order to restore order. They would find a way to glare and stare at each other no matter what I did.

I turned to Seth, sidestepping a little so that it was clear I was giving up the hopeless cause of keeping them from looking at each other. "Seth, he has a point. How can any of us have any sort of logical alibi when we don't know when the crime was committed? That is, the crime of spiking the Sport-Aide."

Seth blinked at me. I could almost see the wheels turning inside his adorable young man head. He desperately wanted to find an answer that could still incriminate Frank, or at least cast a lot of doubt on his motives toward me. I was going to have to have a little heart-to-heart talk with Seth once Frank left. If this was simply a son's knee-jerk reaction to Mom having a boyfriend for the first time since the divorce, then he was going to have to suck it up and deal with it. I wasn't in a position to run off and marry Frank any time soon—my first marriage would have taught me nothing if I made that sort of mistake twice—so I just couldn't fathom why this was putting Seth out of joint so much.

Because, frankly, I was having a hard time with any other explanation of why Seth was adamant about Frank's potential as a suspect. The logic didn't hold up. There was no reason Frank would want someone as innocuous as Allen dead in the first place. Perhaps if the two of them had been seen fighting not long before the murder, then maybe it would be logical to think there was some sort of motive there, even if it would have been more like a crime of passion than a fully premeditated murder. Still, no one had seen or heard anything like that between Allen and anybody. Even their neighbors said that Allen and Alice hadn't been fighting much in the days before Allen's death. So, if the police weren't in a big hurry to arrest *Alice*, the person with arguably the most inclination to murder Allen, then why was Seth so gung ho to string Frank up for the murder? Yes, I was definitely going to have that talk with Seth.

In the meantime, I had to defuse the testosterone-laden man-bomb about to go off in the middle of my living room.

"Okay, Seth and Frank, I think it's time to call off the dogs on this one. At least for now. Frank, let's just pretend Seth never said anything about any of this. And Seth, unless you come up with something better than the fact that you don't know Frank all that well and that you just don't like me dating someone, then I'm going to have to ask you to let it go."

Seth opened his mouth and was obviously going to pipe up with yet another gripe about Frank, but I held up my hand in a "stop!" gesture and shook my head.

"I mean it, Seth. No more. Now, I'm exhausted and really would like to get some more sleep. The arguing out here woke me up, and I fully intend to head back to my bedroom and get some more rest. After I get a drink of water."

I turned toward the kitchen, half expecting one of them to chime in with some snide remark about the other one. I was amazed to hear nothing but silence behind me as I padded toward the kitchen for my glass of water. "Can I get either of you fine fellows anything to drink while I'm out here?"

"Mom, you should let me get you that glass of water," Seth said, getting up out of the armchair and heading in my direction. "You're right that you need more rest."

"Seth, it's just a glass of water. I already have the cup out and that's the hard part. Honestly, I think I can manage a glass of water. It was refereeing the fight in there that wore me out, not this."

He was now in the kitchen with me, looking suitably sheepish. "You're right. I'm sorry. Bad timing. It's just that when I opened the door and there he was, I just—"

"Seth, not now. Not again. I know you didn't plan this. But, still, it happened. Next time learn how to restrain yourself. A little self-control goes a long way, mister."

I turned to find him standing there with a big pout on his face. He could really spread it on thick when he wanted to. I reached out to hug him, and he fell into my arms gladly.

"Sorry, Mom. I love you, that's all."

I kissed him lightly on his temple, which I could reach only by standing on tiptoe. "You're a good kid, Seth. I appreciate the protectiveness. Just don't let it get the better of you, okay?"

He nodded, looking a little more emotional than he probably wanted to in front of his mother. I smiled at him and grabbed my water glass off the kitchen counter where I'd put it down in order to hug him.

"That's fair," he said and smiled in return. We walked arm in arm back into the living room, only to find it empty.

"Frank?" I said, glancing around the room but seeing no sign of him. I walked over to the living room window, which overlooked the main street, and I saw Frank's car pulling away from the curb. "Huh."

"What?" asked Seth. "Is he out there?"

"Yeah, I just saw his car leave."

"Huh."

The front door opened just then, and Annie came in carrying two grocery bags. "Was that Frank I saw leaving as I was coming in?" she asked.

"Yes, honey," I answered, turning toward her and smiling broadly. "He was just here to see how I'm doing." Actually, I had no idea why he was here. He'd never had the opportunity to say why he had come because Seth had jumped all over him the second the door was open. It was a good guess, though. Why else would he have come around? I looked at Seth warily, as if to say that we'd just go with that story and leave it at that. I didn't want to get into this discussion all over again, not with both my overprotective kids here, and no Frank here to defend himself.

"And how *are* you doing?" she asked, brushing past me on her way to the kitchen to put away what I assumed were her Oreos and Diet Dr. Pepper, food of the gods.

"Better," I fibbed. "But I'm just up to get a glass of water and head right back to bed. Frank was just out here when I came out, so I've been up for a little while now. Time to get some more sleep, I think."

"Oh, okay," she called from the kitchen. "Glad he's gone. How are you feeling? Not feeling sick or queasy anymore?"

"Nope. Feeling pretty good in that department." I ignored her swipe at Frank. Due to the little skirmish between the two men in my life, I was feeling a little unsettled in the tummy department right now. But that was probably because of the relational strife of the past half hour and not left over from last night.

"Any more word from the doctor while I was out?"

"No, sweetie, not today. They said they wouldn't know more till sometime on Friday. I don't really expect them to tell me much more than we already know, though. And either way, it apparently won't change how to handle my recuperation from this point on anyway. So, a phone call from the doctor is almost a moot point."

She came out from the kitchen and into the living room with us, where I had settled back onto the couch and Seth had again taken up residence in the armchair across the room. Annie curled up on the sofa next to me, with a small plate with a few Oreos on it and a twenty-ounce plastic bottle of Diet Dr. Pepper. I held my tongue.

"Do you want to visit a little bit while I'm up, or should we save that for later?" I asked her as she munched on the Oreos.

Seth gave me a pointed look that seemed to beg me to not stay up talking to Annie. I had a feeling that he was dying to get some time alone with her, out of range of my hearing, in order to give her the lowdown on Frank's visit. Which meant I was going to have some serious anti-Frank propaganda to undo once I woke up again later. Still, the thought of staying up any longer in order to defuse yet another relational bomb made me tired all by itself. I must have looked sufficiently weary because Annie clearly didn't want to keep me up. Besides, if I went to bed, the TV was all hers.

"No, Mom, go get some rest. We'll have plenty of time to gab. I'm here till Tuesday."

I smiled and stood, taking my water glass with me as I headed back to my bedroom. "Good night then," I said from halfway down the hall. "Don't forget to lock up and turn off all the lights before you go to bed."

"I won't!"

"Oh, and Seth?"

"Yeah, Mom?"

"If you hang around for the night, there are sheets in the linen closet outside my office back here. You can curl up on the couch."

"Got it, Mom. Thanks. Not sure if I'll stay over or not."

"No problem either way. If I get up in the morning and I see you snoring on the couch, I'll have a good idea that you stayed the night."

He chuckled. "Good thinking. Good night."

"G'night. Love you both!" I called, rounding the corner into my bedroom and closing the door behind me.

The rest of the night was a blissful blur of sound sleep and no dreams at all. And no nightmares. Perhaps I had worked through the potential nightmares ahead of time with Seth and Frank there in the living room. For whatever reason, I got the sleep I needed. A rare thing even when there wasn't a murder investigation going on under my nose. An even better thing when someone had been deliberately drugged and then died as a result. My children were both under my roof, and I was safe and sound. What more could I have asked for?

CHAPTER 10

THIS WAS THE THIRD TIME IN A WEEK that I'd used getting caught up on work as an excuse not to go out to dinner with Frank. Needless to say, both Seth and Annie had no problem with my repeated fibbing to Frank. I, on the other hand, was starting to feel a little guilty about it. I kept telling myself I was completely convinced that Frank wouldn't hurt a fly, or a fellow baseball player. And, besides, I really was behind on some of my freelance work. If I were being brutally honest, I'd admit that I'm always a little behind on my freelance work. It comes with the territory. New projects are always coming in, and other projects are always being finished. Completely clearing off my work desk would mean no more income—not a good situation for a freelancer.

I suspected Frank knew this, deep down, but he was surprisingly gracious with me about it, even when I bowed out of his offer of dinner at my favorite restaurant and a movie afterwards. The very same thing that had given me pause about spending time with Frank right now—that skirmish between Seth and Frank—was also probably the reason Frank seemed so understanding about my abdication of our budding relationship. He must have guessed that my children would now be in my ear constantly about him, voicing their fears and concerns about the possibility that Frank had had something to do with Allen's murder, stupid and impossible as it seemed when viewed from a more objective distance.

But, sadly, I didn't have the luxury of viewing this from afar. I was up close and personal with this situation, with my children right there cheering me on every time I said another no to Frank. I had to keep reminding myself that they meant well. And they did. Only on rare occasions did this feel like a contest they were holding with Frank—one the two of them intended to win at all costs. The best I could do now was to enjoy the relative peace and quiet that my time apart from Frank afforded me. Peace and quiet with my kids, at least until Annie was back at college and Seth decided I could handle life on my own again. I loved the boy dearly, but it wasn't a great stretch to see that he had used the alignment of Annie's arrival home and the whole Allen–Frank thing to weasel his way back into my apartment for a while. My apartment, which included access to my cooking, my refrigerator, and my washer and dryer. I decided to take it all as a vote of confidence and to enjoy the company while I had it. It was only another two days, after all. What could go wrong in two days?

A FEW DAYS LATER, ALICE SAT ACROSS FROM ME, her hands on the table, fidgeting uncontrollably with her handkerchief. She'd called me that morning to see if I could meet her for lunch, and although my own feelings about eating in public were currently more than a little tainted, I agreed. She had eaten a lovely flatbread sandwich, but I had chickened out and eaten a small sandwich at home and was now sitting across from her sipping just a hot tea with lemon. I dunked the tea bag one more time and wrung it out with my spoon, confident that I had a little more control over this drink— the cup of hot water and the untouched tea bag they'd given me— than I would have had with almost anything else on their menu. I privately wondered just how long it would take me to gain back my confidence in public eateries.

At least the tea itself tasted good.

"So, Alice, please don't tell me the police are still hassling you. Are they?"

"Yes and no," she said, casting her eyes down at her own drink, a Diet Coke, and tapping on the outside of the cup with both hands.

"I've hired an attorney." She said this without looking up at me, and I noticed her fingers were rapping on that cup in double time now.

"An attorney? Why?" I realized immediately that it was a stupid thing to say. There were some pretty damned obvious reasons why someone in Alice's position would need to hire an attorney, even if she were innocent. *Especially* if she were innocent. Alice looked up from her cup and simply blinked.

"Okay, sorry. That was a dumb question," I admitted, and she smiled wanly. "Did the police suggest it, or are you just being prudent?"

"A little of both," she said. "They still haven't officially accused me of anything, but I just always feel like there are eyes watching me, following me wherever I go. I finally realized that a consultation with a lawyer wasn't such a bad idea. Turns out I probably should have consulted one when all this started. But of course, back when this first started, I was suddenly m-made a w-widow... and I was kind of busy with things like a f-funeral and the p-paperwork that came with it."

Her stammering was tough to witness, but she somehow collected herself nobly and didn't give in to the fear and grief that always seemed bubbling just under the surface. I found myself occasionally wishing I had known Alice a little bit before this had all happened. Minus the grief and panic, I had a hunch she was a fine woman to get to know, even if her husband hadn't shared that thought in his final days and had been neglecting her terribly.

"So, what did the lawyer say?" I asked, cutting through the topical tributary we almost fell into and getting us back on track. I was sure this was the reason she had asked me to meet her for lunch in the first place. She needed someone to vent to about the fact that she now had to hire a lawyer to keep herself out of prison. The thought was more than a little sobering to me, and I wasn't even the person in question.

"He thinks my best defense right now, based on the situation itself on that day, is that I didn't have any sort of ready access to the Sport-Aide before the game. I'd been home, and Allen hadn't been the one to bring the drinks that day. I shudder to think how different things would be for me if it had been Allen's turn to stock the team cooler, and if those beverages had come from our house."

She shuddered then, and she wrapped her hands around the soda cup solidly this time, no longer tapping the sides. I felt a little shaky myself. She was right. If Allen had been in charge of team drinks the day he had died, Alice would probably be behind bars right now.

"Well, that's good, right?" I said, trying to smile and look as encouraging as I could. "Seems like an airtight alibi. Yes?"

"Mostly. But since the cops don't really have anything else to go on—it seems everybody but me adored Allen in one way or another—then I still have the most red flags against me right now."

"Oh, I wouldn't say *everybody* adored Allen."

"What do you mean? He seemed to get along great with all the others on the team."

"Sure, but that's mostly because he often *did* bring the drinks. Beer, mostly. And apparently a lot of it. Not always the best brand, but still more expensive than"—I touched the side of Alice's cup across the table from me—"Diet Coke."

She smiled. "That sounds like Allen. He assumed you could bargain your way into—or out of—anything with a case of beer."

"He was largely right, Alice."

She smiled.

"But that doesn't mean everybody loved him," I continued. My impression, from having seen him at the games I attended since he joined the team last year, is that they appreciated his strange skill set as well as the beer. But Seth often mentioned that Allen could be embarrassing when he was on the field in the second half of a game, after he'd had a few of those cheap beers. So, there's that, too."

"Well, that kind of makes me feel a little bit better, though I think I feel guilty about it."

"Don't. Right now you're in self-preservation mode, not grief mode. You can't let one encroach on the other, or you'll end up in the cops' crosshairs, Alice."

She nodded. "You're right. I may already be in their cross hairs, but I certainly don't have to make their job any easier, do I?"

"No, you don't," I added, sipping my tea and thinking back on some of the times Allen had embarrassed not only himself but the whole team with his shenanigans after too much alcohol. "And, here's a little something you might find interesting." I wasn't sure why I was suddenly feeling compelled to share the goings-on in my own life recently, but my intuition was telling me that Alice was a safe harbor for such information. After all, she had been sharing with me her own struggles with the police and suspicion, right? Might as well trust her as much as she'd been trusting me these past few weeks. "I've suspended my dates with my boyfriend, Frank."

"He's the first baseman of the team, right?"

"Sometimes, yup."

"Why? What's wrong?"

"Well, after I got home from the hospital, Frank came to my apartment the next evening, and he had a confrontation with Seth right there in my apartment. I was trying to catch up on sleep after that bad night at the hospital, and the shouting woke me out of a sound sleep. Turns out Seth had decided that the best suspect for Allen's murder wasn't you after all."

"Frank?"

I nodded. "Yup. And there he was, essentially accusing Frank of murder, and even attempted murder—of *me*—right in front of me."

"But you two ate at a restaurant, you said."

I nodded again. "We did. One I chose that very day, not one Frank had chosen. It was just food poisoning. So how could he have poisoned the food in advance if he didn't even know where we were going?"

"What was Seth thinking then?" She seemed morbidly fascinated by this, and I was glad to divert her attention away from thinking about her husband's death. Well, at least partially. Just about any topic even remotely concerned with what had happened was only one or two steps away from being right back to talking about Allen's murder. Still, even those one or two steps could make a difference.

"I say he wasn't *thinking* very much at all. But he got his sister behind him, too, and I'm stuck in my apartment with my two paranoid kids, who both think my new boyfriend is a cold-blooded murderer."

Alice shook her head. "Awful. Poor Frank."

"He's been pretty good about me saying no to dates since getting home from the hospital. I keep blaming it on work, but I think he knows. He knows Seth is my son, my firstborn, and that even if I completely disagree with Seth about Frank's involvement—or lack of it—I still might find it easier to lay low and avoid contact with him for a while. And, it *has* reduced the stress around the house a lot."

"Still, that's gotta be tough. Glad Frank is being a good sport about it. That's the kind of thing Allen would never have stood for. He was a pretty stubborn bastard in a lot of ways." Tears welled up in her eyes as she said this, and I blinked back a few of my own. "Still, I'm glad that Frank is a lot more reasonable." She managed a smile, and I reached across the table and patted the back of her hand. She was a soft, kind woman, and I wondered how someone like Allen could have been so clueless as to have stopped appreciating just what he had in Alice. Still, water under the bridge. Alice would eventually be fine. As long as she didn't end up in prison for a crime I was reasonably sure she had not committed.

"Well, let's see how long he'll wait before he decides that competing with my offspring isn't part of a healthy, honest relationship." I smirked and looked down at the last dregs of my tea, which had almost completely lost its heat.

"Seems we're all just a bunch of misunderstood souls," Alice said, in a moment of crystal-clear poignancy that almost made me cry right there in public. She was right. Between me and her, we were balancing on a tight rope of half truths and misrepresentations. Add in Frank, and it was starting to get a little ridiculous.

"So," I said, hoping to steer the conversation back to where it had started: why Alice had called me this morning in the first place. "What happens if the police call you back in for a third time?"

"Well, for starters, this time I don't go by myself. My lawyer comes with me. That alone helps me sleep at night. But I'm not sure it makes my situation any better. After all, nobody else really has a motive but me. Sure, none of us had access to that cooler of Sport-Aide except Seth, but nobody but me seems to have had a good reason to want Allen dead in the first place. And the spouse murder thing is so ridiculously... oh, what's the word I want here?" She glanced up at the ceiling, searching for the right word.

"Cliché?" I offered. "Common?"

She smirked. "Bingo. So common that I'm betting cops don't look anywhere else if they can see a spouse who's a little disgruntled or dissatisfied in the marriage. Add on something like an insurance policy, no matter how small, and you might as well throw a noose around the person's neck and call it a day."

"An insurance policy? Really? Because I'd say even in this day of raging feminism, most husbands probably have insurance policies that name their wives as beneficiaries. Don't they?"

"You would think so. And Allen's wasn't even all that huge. The house will be paid off automatically, but the policy would only have given me a cushion for the next five years or so to find myself a proper job of my own. And, of course, if I end up in prison over this, I won't see any of that policy, even if I've been falsely accused and know it. If the law doesn't agree with me, I'm screwed."

I shook my head. I was glad she had the attorney, but I wondered just how much he was going to be able to do for her unless someone else looked like a better target. How much were the police counting on putting someone away for this murder? It was a fairly small town. And we were a relatively safe community. Lee Gerber's murder last year had been a real shock to the system for us all, but we'd eventually had the comfort of knowing that his murderer had not been from around here. What if Allen's murderer was someone local, born and raised here, which seemed not only possible but likely? Would the cops be interested in wrapping this up quickly, and as quietly as possible?

"I think I'm out of tea," I said abruptly, for no real reason other than to talk about something other than life insurance, guilt, and murder.

"Well, I have to be going anyway. I'm on my way to see that lawyer again. We need to piece together a better timeline. A more thorough one. The more I can account for my time that day, the less likely the police will be to keep calling me in to account for myself. Time for them to start looking somewhere else for the killer. I'm tired of always being the target here."

She stood, putting the cup down on the table and grabbing her purse from off the back of her chair. I stood as well and quickly came around the table in order to give her a quick hug. She sighed as we hugged, and I thought I heard a small hitch in her breathing. I had a feeling she was going to barely make it back to her car before giving in to a crying jag in the parking lot. Couldn't say that I blamed her. I'd had more than one of those of my own lately, and I wasn't even the grieving widow. Sometimes the brokenness of this world felt overwhelming. We separated and she gave me a smile as she left. I waved and grabbed my own purse. I was lucky to count her among my friends.

Except that friends don't go around casting blame for murder on their friends' sons just to save their own skin.

CHAPTER 11

WHAT?" I YELLED INTO THE PHONE WHEN SETH CALLED. "Please tell me you're kidding." My heart was racing already. "Not kidding. Not happy, either." I heard him clicking his tongue over the phone, a nervous habit from childhood. That wasn't a good sign.

"And they're saying it has something to do with your cooler?"

"Yeah, I have to bring it down to the station."

"I thought you already did that."

"I know. I did. But apparently they want to look it over again. So I gotta go back down as soon as possible." He sighed loudly.

"I'm sorry, Seth. Do you want me to go with you, as a sign of solidarity? Or just moral support?"

"No, not really. I think I can manage this one all right."

We ended the conversation on a definite down note, and I had a bad feeling in my gut. I wasn't a big believer in a mother's instincts or women's intuition, but it just felt like something had shifted in my universe. Sometimes a person should listen to those little voices in the back of her head, because sometimes they're right. Who knew that the next time I would talk to my son, he'd be behind bars?

Well, *I knew*. That's who.

"TELL ME AGAIN. What do you mean, we have to go bail out Seth?" Annie had taken an overnight bus back home from college as soon as I'd called. I waited for her to arrive before heading to the police station to see Seth. She was beside herself with worry, and I wasn't sure if touching her, to comfort her, was a great idea or a terrible idea. She wasn't one who appreciated unsolicited pats on the back or attempts to rein in her emotions, but I didn't see that happening anyway. She was beyond help by this point. She hadn't ever seen her brother in jail, of course, so I was in completely new Mom territory. And I wasn't pleased about our new little adventure as a family. But, I grabbed my keys, tried not to hug Annie as we flew out the front door, and held my breath and prayed.

HE WAS ONLY IN A HOLDING CELL at the police station, and not in an actual prison, but the difference to me as his mother was a matter of semantics. My little boy was in jail. And, in the ultimate irony, for a crime he didn't commit. It was almost cliché.

"So, the cooler? They found something suspicious this time, or what?"

He shook his head. "No, I don't think it's the cooler. I think this was all planned out separately from the cooler, but now they're hoping to find something in or on the cooler to back up their theory."

"What theory would that be, exactly?" I didn't bother to try to hide my disdain for how the police were handling this situation. And Annie was holding back her tears for now, but I could see that the sobs would come, and soon. I weighed the pros and cons of staying here with Seth as long as they would allow me and getting the heck out of here with Annie before she emotionally imploded.

"The theory that Seth Roberts killed Allen. That's the theory." I sighed, but he kept on. "Apparently *somebody* came down here yesterday afternoon all hepped up on this crazy idea that suddenly they remember Allen and me fighting the day before he died. Which is totally bogus. I barely even knew the guy."

"I know. As far as I ever saw, you only had contact with Allen during games. Or, you know, right before or right after."

"You've been meeting with Alice lately, Mom, haven't you?"

"Yeah, but..." I hesitated, feeling as if I wouldn't like where this was going.

"Did she say anything to you? Anything that might have sounded as if she was going to do this to me?"

"You think *Alice* said that to the police? Seth, honestly. We just met the other day for lunch. The only thing she seemed concerned about was that the police were still looking at her as a possible suspect. In fact, after we got done, she said she was heading for a meeting with her lawyer."

"She has a lawyer?"

"Now she does. But I haven't talked to her since she met with him. Maybe—"

"Maybe what?"

"Maybe the lawyer put ideas into her head. You know, about you. *If* she was the one who talked. But she's kind of my friend."

"Why would she do something like this? She doesn't even know me! Does she want closure that badly?" His voice broke on this last phrase, and I wanted nothing so much as to reach through those bars, *past* those bars, and grab him and hug the stuffing out of him. I sniffled a little bit, and that was the last straw for Annie, who burst out into a long, wailing sob behind me. I turned and grabbed the one child I could hug, and she melted into my arms.

As I hugged her, I tried to keep talking to Seth. He and I needed to get to the bottom of this turn of events, or, at least, as close to the bottom as we could get. "I'm not so sure this is about closure, really. If Alice did this—and that's a big *if*—I like to think it's more about Alice keeping herself out of jail."

"You mean, she's trying to make me the..." His voice trailed off.

I frowned, not wanting to follow my thought through to its logical conclusion, but unable to avoid it, the more I thought about it. "Yeah, I think so. A scapegoat."

"Then she probably did it herself, right?" He looked like a caged, cornered animal, and not just because he was sitting in an actual human cage. If this had been a television commercial, Sarah McLachlan would have been singing in the background.

"Not necessarily, though that does seem a lot more likely now than it did before you called me. But she could just be desperate to clear her own name precisely because she *didn't* do it. She was completely beside herself when we met for lunch. She'd just hired the lawyer because the cops were starting to breathe down her neck and she wanted a way to combat what she felt was harassment. I don't know what to think. Who else might have talked to the police?"

"Mom, seriously, how do you know she wasn't just meeting with you that day so she could make sure you'd think she was innocent, too? Seems like a big stretch on her part, but it also seems like it kind of worked, didn't it?"

"How so?" I squeaked, feeling a little sheepish.

"Because here you are, talking to your firstborn son who's behind bars, and you're practically *defending* her." His voice broke again.

"No, no, Seth. No, I'm not. I'm just trying to reconcile what I saw in her with what I know about you. I really don't think Alice did it, the same way I don't think you did it. Isn't it possible that neither of you killed Allen?"

I hated putting it out there—I really just wanted the police to nab someone soon, someone not Seth—but I had to admit that I just never got a "guilty" vibe from Alice. But now I wasn't sure how much I could trust my own vibes about people, though. I wasn't any better a judge of character than anybody else, when it came right down to it. I just had a hunch. My nitpicking nature didn't necessarily extend beyond the written page, but I still had that hunch.

Seth was frowning, considering. "Sure, anything's possible. But let's face it. *Somebody* poisoned Allen. He didn't just poison himself, now, did he?"

"Mom?" came a small voice from behind me. Annie had slipped out of my grasp and was sitting a few feet from me, curled into a tiny ball of a girl, her knees drawn up and her arms holding them in tight, a little ball of flesh.

I turned to her. "What, babe?"

"Can we go home now?" She was trying not to cry, poor thing.

"Sure, hon. If you need to."

She looked past me, at Seth. "Sorry, Seth. I just don't feel good. I need to get out of here." She stood and waited for me to do the same.

"So do I, Annie," he said. "So do I."

I TALKED ANNIE INTO STOPPING at the Brighton *Bugle* newspaper office on our way home. I wanted to talk to Helga about Seth. I thought maybe she could give me some insight and remind me about the things we had gone through together during the investigation into Lee Gerber's murder last year. She and Seth had been a big help during that whole fiasco. Then again, he hadn't been behind bars at the time. Still, I had a feeling that Helga would be able to lend fresh insight into this latest development. At the very least, she would be able to cheer me up.

"So, whatcha thinking? Maybe we break this Alice chick's kneecaps or something?" Helga gave me a crooked smile from across the high counter behind which she sat at the main entrance to the Brighton *Bugle*'s offices and newsroom.

"I don't think we need to go that far. But I think Seth could use some sort of encouragement. He's not sure how long they're going to keep him in that place. I don't think they can hold him indefinitely. But he's there at least through today. No word on whether he'll be there overnight. Probably," I added, suddenly overwhelmed with fear and sadness. And, I had to admit, a lot of anger at my new ex-friend, Alice.

"Maybe I'll stop by there on my way home from work and see if I can cheer him up."

"If anyone can cheer him up, Helga, it's you." I managed a light smile and felt a little better. I had a feeling Helga would be just the balm Seth needed to endure a night in a jail cell. Maybe Annie and I could plan a little welcome-home celebration for Seth when he got back. Tomorrow. Had to be no later than tomorrow.

"I'll make it my life's mission then. Say, does the police station have anything like visiting hours? I don't want to get there too late, just to find out that they won't let me in to see him."

I shrugged. "I don't know, but I can probably find out for you."

"Nah, I can do that. Maybe more of a show of solidarity if I call separately from his mommy, you know? Anything to make it plain to these idiots that they have the wrong guy."

"Good thinking. And let me know what you find out. Not just about the hours they allow visitors, but also just keep your ears open for anything about the case. I'm curious to know just what they're thinking. If anything."

"Right. One question, though."

"Sure. What?"

"If Seth is the wrong guy—and he *is*—then who do we think is the *right* guy?" She wrinkled her nose at me, seriously looking for an answer.

"I have no idea."

CHAPTER 12

THE APARTMENT SEEMED UNUSUALLY QUIET. Granted, Seth didn't live with me anymore and Annie was usually at school, so the apartment was typically this quiet, or quieter. But it just seemed like a more brooding, somber silence when I opened the door.

Except for Vlad, who came dashing toward us. He wriggled his whole small doggy body at us, and Annie obliged by scooping him up in her arms.

"I'll take him out for a walk, Mom," she said. "We've been gone for hours and hours now."

"Thanks. I'll start dinner."

I decided against the pepperoni casserole I had been planning on making—Seth's favorite—in favor of a frozen lasagna. Easy, mindless, and no messy cleanup.

I was minding my own business while the lasagna heated up in the oven when there was a knock at the front door. At first I thought it was Annie and Vlad and that she had simply locked herself out and hadn't taken the key with her when she left with Vlad for his walk. But as I strode toward the front door, I passed the window and saw Annie and Vlad below, going down the sidewalk in front of my apartment building.

Just as I ran through the mental list of who could be at the door, it hit me and I was right. I opened the door to find Frank standing there, with a look on his face I couldn't quite describe. A little bit sheepish, a little bit confused, and concerned. Since Annie wasn't back yet and Seth obviously wasn't here at all, I seized the opportunity and waved him in quietly. As he came into the room and I moved to close the door, we brushed shoulders. A wave of emotional electricity surged through me, and I think he felt the same way because he instinctively turned to me then and we hugged fiercely. Not a hug of passion but, rather, compassion.

"Maggie," he whispered into my ear, still clinging to me tightly. "Are you guys all right?"

So, he'd heard. Sometimes being part of a fairly small town was a good thing. I wasn't so sure about now, though. In one sense, I was glad to not have to call Frank to tell him Seth had been arrested. But, on the other hand, I wasn't thrilled to realize that our family was part of the current local gossip. There was no good balance between these two things, so I concentrated on the fact that Frank had heard what had happened and had come over to see how we were holding up.

And no matter what else I was trying *not* to think right now, it felt good to have someone to hold onto. Someone who wasn't depending on me to be the strong one. And even though I considered myself a reasonably strong woman, I knew I was mighty close to the end of my strength. Even a little bit of outside support would go a long way toward buoying my spirits for the fight ahead.

"We're all right," I said back huskily into his warm neck. "Mostly. Seth is—"

"I know. I heard," he said, cutting me off. I suspected he did this so that I wouldn't have to actually say it. I was grateful for this small mercy.

"I'm hoping we can get him out of there sometime tomorrow, at the latest."

I pulled back from our hug, if only so we could hold a normal conversation face to face, instead of breathing everything into each other's ears and necks. I stayed in his embrace a bit longer, though, lingering while I still could. Annie would be back upstairs in the apartment in the next few minutes, and I was pretty sure she—

"Mom!"

Too late.

"What is *he* doing here?"

I looked past Frank after quickly breaking free of his grasp, and I saw Annie standing in the doorway, with Vlad under her arm, his leash hanging down onto the floor. Vlad was wiggling like an idiot, itching to get down so he could come greet Frank and sniff his shoes to see what exciting vicarious adventures he could smell.

At least Vlad didn't have a problem with Frank. Then again, Vlad didn't have a problem with *anybody*, really. Not the best watch dog with an attitude like his.

"I'm not sure yet, sweetie, but I'm guessing he came here to see how we're doing and to offer some support." I gave her the frowny mom-face, but it didn't look like she was going to pay much attention to it.

"That's right," Frank offered bravely. He didn't seem deterred by Annie's negativity, which I appreciated. His tone and demeanor seemed to find the right balance between reasonably defending himself and yet not being defensive. I admired his persistence and skill, though I suspected Annie wasn't ready to share my admiration.

"Nobody asked you," Annie said, addressing Frank directly, and bending down to put Vlad on the floor. Vlad dashed over to Frank and hurled himself—and his leash—around Frank's legs while undulating like a tiny snake dog.

"Annie!"

"Mom, don't even start to defend this man. Just tell me you didn't call and *ask* him to come over here. Did you?"

"No, I didn't, but that's not the point. This is *my* home and I said before I won't tolerate rude behavior to one of my guests. So, knock it off, missy. Right now."

She opened her mouth as if she was about to spew more hatred but then closed it when she saw my steely gaze. Nice to know I could still command a little respect, or at least appropriate behavior, from one of my kids.

"Thank you," I added. "Now, if you can go see if that lasagna is ready in the kitchen, that'd be great."

She took the subtle hint—*please leave us alone for a few minutes*—and skulked out to the kitchen with Vlad at her heels. He knew that, as fascinating as the new smells on Frank's shoes and pants were, the kitchen held a lot more promise if he was hoping to grab a snack or even a full meal. The food dish was in the kitchen, after all.

I waited till they'd both disappeared into the kitchen completely and motioned to Frank to sit on the couch with me. We sat and just looked at each other for a moment. I wasn't sure where to begin.

"First off, thanks. I know it wasn't easy for you to come back over here after the reception you got last time, so let me just make sure you know that I appreciate it immensely."

"Maggie, please. It wasn't difficult. Of course I was going to come see how you're doing. It wouldn't be right to do this over the phone."

"Well, I appreciate it. And Annie will, too. Someday. And Seth will eventually find a way to understand that you're here to help his mom in her distress."

He smiled a crooked smile. "Somehow I don't see Seth being all that thrilled that I'm here. But thanks for saying so."

"You're a lot more generous and forgiving than you know."

"Forgiving? For what?"

"For being kind to me, to *us*, despite the fact that my kids currently think you're the antichrist."

"I can't blame them, really. They're only concerned for their mom, and that says a lot to me about how devoted they are to you. Not all grown kids would be as fierce in their loyalty as yours are. So, here I am because I find I'm feeling a little bit loyal to you, too."

This guy always knew the right things to say. I started to tear up thinking he saw some good in how rotten my kids had been treating him. Perhaps once the real killer was arrested, and Seth was out of jail and back home, the kids would be able to forgive Frank—for something he hadn't done, I had to remind myself—and make amends. I wouldn't let them off the hook for their rude treatment of Frank. And I had to admit that I felt relieved that Frank wasn't giving up on our relationship just because my kids had been treating him like dirt. It wasn't a situation I would be able to live with long term, but since their mistreatment was due to a misunderstanding, I had every hope that the truth coming out would lend itself to healed relationships all around.

"Frank, thanks. I'm trying to keep myself from falling apart over this, but I'm not sure how well I'm succeeding. I'm glad I have Annie here to keep me anchored. The fact that I have to be strong for her means I'm not losing it here all alone."

"I'm glad, too. I'd hate to think of you here all alone worrying about Seth. I take it you've been to see him."

"Yeah, we just got back a little bit ago. He's doing as well as can be expected, but I think he's still in shock. It might hit him tonight now that we're gone and he has time to sit there and do nothing but think things through."

"So, what happened? Why the hell would they think Seth had anything to do with this?"

I caught a glimpse of Annie peeking around the kitchen doorway, half listening in to our conversation. The look on her face, as she quickly withdrew again, was clear: *Don't tell this man anything. He's only here to sniff out information he will use against us.*

I motioned her away and turned back to Frank.

"I'm not sure, but apparently Alice came into the station yesterday and mentioned Seth by name, saying he'd had a big fight with Allen the day before he died."

"But, he didn't. Did he?"

I shook my head. "No, of course not. What would they have fought about? They didn't even really know each other."

Frank nodded. "That's what I thought. Seth need any sort of character witness or anything?"

"I don't think this is the time for that. I think they're holding him right now because of what Alice said, but if they can't charge him officially soon, they'll have to let him go. If this goes any further than that, then maybe that's when we'll need more support."

I shuddered to think about this going any further, but I had to admit that we weren't out of the woods yet. Just because I found this whole situation ridiculous didn't mean everyone agreed with me.

"Do you need a lawyer for Seth?"

I hadn't thought about this yet, but it had been in the back of my mind since mentioning to Seth that Alice now had a lawyer. Bringing in the big guns of a law firm felt completely surreal. But maybe it was something I was going to have to consider. And, soon.

"Not yet. I'm still kind of hoping this all goes away on its own."

"Is that realistic?" Frank was frowning, and now he reached out to take my hand, stroking it calmly and gently on top of his own.

I sighed and almost started sobbing. Such a small gesture, at precisely the right moment, and I was no longer in control of my reactions and emotions.

"I have no idea what's realistic anymore. Let's face it. I don't think it's realistic that I'm sitting here while my son sits in a jail cell. So, 'realistic' isn't really part of my vocabulary right now."

"Dinner's done!" Annie suddenly called from the kitchen. I looked at Frank, who nodded in an overly understanding manner. God bless him.

"That's my cue to head out of here for now." He let go of my hand and stood. I stood too and smiled as warmly as I could.

"You don't have to leave. Stay for dinner."

Now we both heard Annie start to clank utensils around loudly in the kitchen. She'd obviously heard my invitation and was voicing her disapproval through cutlery. Frank shook his head.

"No, that's okay. I appreciate the invitation, but this has to be you and Annie tonight."

"But I think I need you here tonight."

"And I think Annie needs just *you* here tonight. Comfort her. You won't regret it. And, if you want to talk, there's always the phone, the computer." He smiled and took my hand in his again.

"Okay. Yeah, you might be right. Annie would really appreciate time with Mom tonight, I think."

"And you will, too. Honest. I'm not wrong on this."

I impetuously hugged him, grabbing him quick and pulling him close. I didn't want to ever let go, but I gathered the courage to let go and see him to the door.

"Thanks for checking in on us, Frank. I think maybe I'll sleep tonight after all."

He kissed me lightly on the cheek, ever aware of Annie and Vlad hovering somewhere nearby, and opened the apartment door. "Remember, call me if you need anything. Or even if you don't need anything but just want to vent. I'm a good listener."

I already knew this about Frank, and it warmed my heart to remember it now. "Thanks. I'll keep you posted on Seth and what I find out in the morning."

"Then I'm hoping to hear that he's back here where he belongs first thing tomorrow."

And with that, Frank was gone. I closed the front door, listening to his echoing footfalls on the stairs, and then watched out the front window as he looked both ways and crossed the street to where his car was parked. I hated to see him go, but he was right. Tonight had to be a time to focus on Annie, who was not only perturbed that Frank had shown up but who had been close to losing it at the police station earlier when we were visiting Seth. She would need some normal family time tonight. And that meant me.

And maybe a chick flick. Or two. Tomorrow was going to be a difficult day. I didn't need my acute attention to detail to know that. And, as usual, I was right.

CHAPTER 13

AFTER WHAT SEEMED LIKE THE LONGEST NIGHT of my life, and what was probably even longer for poor Seth, Annie and I packed up a few things and headed back to the police station. We rode in silence, no topic seeming safe enough to start before one of us would break into tears. Talking about the weather would seem almost cruel. Seth was in a windowless cell and couldn't see the weather outside. Talking about the rapidly approaching holidays seemed worse. The very thought that they might not be our usual, happy holidays would be crushing. So, we wisely said nothing and listened to whatever crap was playing on the radio. I wasn't really listening anyway. I was sure Annie wasn't listening, either.

We parked in the same spot we'd used the day before, giving me the sensation that we had never left and that Seth hadn't just spent a cold, dark night behind bars. Once we were both out of the car and heading toward the front steps, Annie veered over to me and grabbed my hand. She was almost crushing it, and I could feel her pulse pounding beneath the surface. I didn't dare tell her that I was as glad for the human contact as she was, that I needed it just as desperately. She had taken my hand so that she could be anchored to someone she assumed was stronger than she currently felt. Oh, how wrong she was. But I didn't let on that I was about to crumble. Somehow I managed to hold her hand firmly and walk straight-backed and tall into the police station. I suppose that was my super power for the day: to maintain an air of strength when I felt like curling up in a corner and sobbing.

The officer behind the front desk recognized us from yesterday. He waved us over with an all-too-cheerful "Hello! How are you to-day?"

I held my tongue and did not say, "How do you *think* we are?" Instead, I said simply, "Fine. May we see Seth Roberts? My son?"

The officer nodded. "Sure. His father is back there with him now."

I balked at this. For some reason, it hadn't occurred to me that George might show up. Didn't really seem like his style. Then again, how often had we been in a context like this, with one of our children in jail? Precisely never. I mentally gave George credit for being here for Seth, and Annie and I headed back to the holding cells once the officer signed us in and waved us back there.

We rounded the corner and immediately saw George sitting on a chair in front of the holding cell. He was hunched over, his elbows on his knees and his head cradled in his hands. I thought perhaps he was crying, or had been, or was about to. He heard us coming and looked up, startled.

"Maggie! Annie!" he exclaimed. "What are you doing here?"

"What do you mean, what am I doing here? Seth is my *son*. What are *you* doing here?"

Annie tugged on my sleeve, and when I turned to her I saw that she was frowning at me. I had crossed some sort of invisible line into inappropriate behavior, at least as far as Annie could see. Of course, she didn't have quite the same history with George that I did, so instead of making this about me and George, I relented and tried to relax.

I let out the breath I had been holding and extended a hand to George. He came to me and shook my hand, then just pulled me in to him for a big bear hug instead. At any other time, my kids would probably have found this display either uproariously funny or incredibly awkward. But, due to the current circumstances, they both seemed to find it somewhat horrifying. Annie looked as if she had seen a ghost, and Seth, from inside the holding cell, looked both confused and angry. I pushed back from the hug, and George got the hint and let go, backing away so much and so fast that it became its own awkward moment instead.

"Mom. Dad." We both turned to face Seth on the other side of those massive bars. He simply blinked at us. I didn't know what to say, so I just smiled weakly at him. George joined me in smiling, and we both sat on the long bench outside the holding cell. Annie stood next to the bench, her arms crossed, her foot tapping nervously on the tile floor. I secretly wished she had worn her Chuck Taylors instead of those clickety-clacking heels of hers. The echoing sound was unnerving, like a loudly ticking clock when you're in a hurry.

"Seth," I said, breaking the staccatoed silence instead of waiting for George to pipe up. "How are you? How did you do last night?"

"He just told me all that, Maggie," said George, sounding a bit more perturbed than he had a right to sound.

"So? I wasn't here to hear it, was I? So, I'm asking him now, so I can know, too." And I sounded a bit more clipped and terse than *I* needed to sound.

"No, you weren't here, were you? You could have been here an hour ago, like I was, but apparently you were still at home, probably drinking your third cup of coffee."

So now he was picking on my coffee-drinking habits? The nerve.

"For your information, George Roberts—"

"Mom! Dad!" Annie spoke up from behind us. "Knock it off. The last thing either Seth or I want to hear right now is the two of you squabbling." She rolled her eyes at us both, and I couldn't blame her. We were acting like children. And to think we had mostly worked out our divorce issues years ago. It seems a shared life event like this one didn't bring out the best in either one of us.

I couldn't speak for George, but I could see from the look on his face that he was as embarrassed as I was. Well, that was something, then.

"I'm sorry, sweetie," I said. "You're right, Seth," I continued, turning back to face him. "I apologize for my behavior. I'm just majorly stressed out about all this, and I overreacted."

Seth sighed loudly and sat down on the small cot that served as his only real furniture in the holding cell. "Imagine how I feel then." *Point taken, son.* George, eyes closed in some sort of odd reverie, hissed air through his teeth. I didn't know what to make of that. Was he mad at me? Upset about Seth? Irked that Annie had shamed us both? Hard to tell.

There had been a time when I could easily read George Roberts and all of his actions, facial expressions, and nervous tics. Now? Not so much. And although it would have been a good skill to have retained, for a time such as this, I was glad that so much of that part of my life was over. But a good guess meant he was feeling a lot like I was feeling.

"Seth," he said, so quietly I barely heard him, "I'm sure your mother and I will find a way to make sure you get out of here as soon as possible."

It was the right thing to say—to show solidarity of purpose for Seth's sake—but it was very difficult to hear "your mother and I" come out of George's mouth again after all these years. But Seth deserved to hear that his estranged parents could and would still work together for his sake. I smiled as sincerely as I could and nodded. It wasn't much, but I hoped he could see that I was willing to do anything necessary to get him out of here and free again. Even to work with his father to get it done.

As the awkward and semi-sincere nodding and smiling continued, the officer who had been out front came back to us and stood firm, putting his hands on his hips and sighing. "Well," he said, waiting until he had the attention of all four of us. We all turned in his direction, and only then did he speak again. "It looks as if your boy can go home now."

I do believe all four of our mouths dropped open in unison, like something out of a bad sitcom.

"What?" I blurted out, standing and grasping George's shoulder so tightly he'd probably have a bruise in the morning. "What do you mean?"

"Yeah," added Annie. "What do you mean he can go home now?"

"I mean, ladies, that there isn't enough evidence to hold young Seth here any longer. We'll be letting him go as soon as the paperwork comes through. That will probably be within the hour, in case you want to wait."

"You bet your ass we want to wait!" shouted Annie, her face now beaming. She ran into my arms and squealed like a small child—a small child with a big mouth—and I wasn't sure I had ever felt quite so happy as I did at that moment. Seth shot up off the cot and ran to the bars, where George met him with a handshake. I wished we could have hugged Seth right then, but our celebrating would just have to wait another hour. Annie continued to hold onto me tight with one arm, but she also opened up her other arm to include George in her hug. And, although I know she was just excited about the news and meant well, the last thing I wanted to do to celebrate my son's imminent release was to have a big group hug with George Roberts. One look at his face told me he felt exactly the same way I did. I tried to simply be glad that we had found at least one thing we could agree on.

It wasn't much to build on, but at least our son wasn't going to be in a jail cell much longer. Sometimes you had to focus on the little things, especially when they were really, really big things.

CHAPTER 14

SETH WAS SLEEPING IN MY OFFICE ON THE DAYBED, and I could hear the snoring from the living room, even with the office door closed. It was the most awesome sound in the universe. I was tickled that he didn't want to go back to his apartment alone, and that he didn't want to go back to his dad's house, either. I didn't fool myself into thinking it had anything to do with my company, or even the company of Vlad or his sister. I knew it was the cooking. And, I was getting out the ingredients for that pepperoni casserole, finally. It made my heart glad.

George sulked a little bit when Seth said he was going to head back to my place with me. Big baby. Seth had the wisdom to look a little sheepish about it, and he said, at least, "Well, Dad, all my stuff is still at Mom's house from when I was staying there last week. I should probably go get it."

Technically, this was true. He'd left his cell phone charger and a pair of socks at my place. Still, it was hardly enough to warrant his decision. He had several spare chargers, and probably a few more pairs of socks. I noticed that a bachelor's answer to running out of clean socks was not necessarily to do the laundry. It was just as often an indication that it was time to buy more socks instead. So, he wouldn't miss the pair he'd left at my house. But I wasn't about to tell ol' George that. He looked forlorn enough standing there outside the police station between our two cars.

"Okay then," he managed to say in a fairly steady voice. "I'll see you at practice tomorrow."

"Is there practice tomorrow?" Seth had asked.

"Yeah, for the last game this weekend. We might be able to finish the season in positive territory after all." He smiled in as winsome a way as George Roberts could manage, and Seth returned the smile sincerely.

"Actually, that sounds great. I think I could use the fresh air and a little bit of fun, too." Seth reached out his hand for yet another man handshake, and George took his hand and then pulled him into another one of those George hugs. I was just glad it wasn't with me again. Seth didn't seem to mind it quite as much as I had.

"Goodbye, son," George said, looking away from Seth and yanking his keys out of his pocket. "I'm glad things worked out for you. I'll see you tomorrow at practice. Four o'clock."

We'd piled into my car then, and Annie played with the radio the whole way back, chattering with Seth and giggling like a schoolgirl. Seth laughed at everything she said. These were the same two kids who usually were at each other's throats because they could never agree on anything. And here they were getting along like they'd been lifelong friends. I really wasn't sure I could feel a whole lot happier than I did during that car ride.

Except that, back at my place, it was pretty damned awesome to hear Seth snoring away in my office. Safe. Sleeping. And right under the same roof with us. This was going to be the best pepperoni casserole I'd ever made. And, the best company to share it with.

ANNIE AND I TAGGED ALONG WITH SETH to his baseball practice the next day. I think neither one of us wanted to let him out of our sight after the past harrowing day or so without him. So, there the two of us sat in the bleachers with other family and friends, only this time our whole family was the hot topic of conversation. Everyone was thrilled to see that Seth was no longer being held. Despite the fact that the Sport-Aide had come from Seth's cooler, it seemed as if nobody had ever suspected that Seth had harmed Allen. I appreciated the good will and positive vibes from everyone else on the team. Seth himself seemed none the worse for wear after his overnight stay in Hotel Holding Cell, and he cheerfully took his spot as shortstop and fielded like a pro. I enjoyed watching him play a game anytime, but watching him out on that field this afternoon was a balm to my mother's soul. The practice went well, and aside from Annie not being able to admit that she was actually bored after the first hour, it was a wonderful way to spend the first full day of Seth's freedom. George seemed unusually quiet out on the field, but I chalked that up to him still processing everything that had happened over the past few days.

The only difficult part of the afternoon was when Frank showed up halfway through the practice, shuffling out onto the field and trying not to attract too much attention. He glanced my way and gave me a quick wave in acknowledgment. I waved back and gave him a shy smile, but I immediately noticed that Seth was watching us. His cheery countenance immediately turned to a frown of frustration, and I was sad to see the good will disappear so fast. So, Seth was still angry with Frank and likely still thought he was somehow involved in Allen's death. That was discouraging. The bubble of happiness I'd been in since the day before was burst in a moment, and I felt my loyalties instantly divided between the two of them.

I saw George off in the distance in the outfield, and he was grinning like an idiot.

Then again, how else would an idiot grin, right? I fumed over his immature reaction to the animosity between his son and my boyfriend. Why did he have nothing better to do than wallow in a little bit of tension between his son and his ex-wife's beau? The man was just as petty and self centered as I remembered him from the last ugly days of our marriage.

Frank quietly took his spot in the outfield, put on his glove, and focused his eyes on the infield. Seth got himself under control as well and hammered his right hand into the glove in his left hand, bending his knees and adopting a good fielder's stance to get ready for the next pitch. The inning continued and I exhaled loudly, happy to see that both my son and my boyfriend were just going to learn to coexist out here on the baseball field, if not anywhere else. I'd have to work on that part later.

I turned to Annie, only to find her hovering over her phone, busily texting someone or posting something on Facebook or Instagram or Tumblr or wherever else girls her age were posting stuff these days. I liked to think I was up on all the latest online hoopla, but I had a feeling I had lagged behind in recent years. She was smiling at whatever she was reading, and she looked like the Annie I remembered a few years ago, before she had gone out into the world to college. It was a short glimpse, though, because suddenly we both heard a nasty shout from across the ball field, and her face hardened into a frown as she looked up before I did. I looked back onto the field, only to see Seth flinging his baseball glove to the ground and taking off straight for Frank in the outfield. This wasn't a play as part of practice. No, Seth was yelling like a banshee, saying things I didn't enjoy hearing my firstborn babe yelling about someone else I cared for.

"It was *you*! Admit it, scumbag! You and Alice! You both got together to get me in trouble, didn't you?" He was halfway to Frank by this point, and I drew in a breath and held it. Frank stood his ground, not moving toward Seth but not backing away, either. I was about to see the unstoppable force hitting the immovable object, and I had the feeling it wasn't going to be pretty.

And, it wasn't. Seth had lost all sense of propriety by the time he reached Frank, but Frank had been keeping his cool and simply awaited Seth's arrival. So, when Seth got close enough to leap into the air to come down hard on poor Frank, poor Frank was ready for him and simply held up his arms to ward off the downward trajectory of Seth. I thought I heard an audible crunch when they smashed into each other, and perhaps I did because they were both hurtin' fierce the next day. The skirmish lasted only a moment or two—neither of them were really fighters by nature, and Seth hadn't a clue how to handle himself in any sort of actual fistfight. Frank, of course, wasn't going to pummel his girlfriend's baby in front of her very eyes, so he merely got Seth into a chokehold and held him there for a moment before smacking him on top of his head. Seth swung his arms around wildly, fiercely, and he managed to whack Frank several times in the torso. I saw Frank wince each time, and I stood at my seat in the bleachers, having grabbed Annie's hand and gripped it in my own. I wasn't sure if I was holding her back from dashing onto the field to stop the fighting or if I was holding myself back. Either way, we stayed quiet and motionless there in the stands for what seemed like forever.

It lasted only a few moments. After Seth got in a few whacks, Frank had apparently had enough and tightened his chokehold on Seth.

"Stop!" Seth cried, and Frank immediately and abruptly let go, letting Seth drop like a rock onto the ground at his feet. Seth grabbed at his throat and coughed a few times. I took a single step forward onto the bleacher seat in front of me, but Frank caught my motion in his peripheral vision and held a hand up to stop me. He looked at me and shook his head. *No*, he was saying to me silently. *Don't be such a mommy. Don't come out here and embarrass your son. Stay there and let us wrap this up like two men.*

I stood still. His instincts were good ones. If this rivalry was ever going to end, I had to let them do things their way. Then perhaps whatever truce they enacted here would hold. Assuming it happened at all, of course. And, I wasn't sure it was even possible.

CHAPTER 15

HE WASN'T REALLY HURTING ME, MOM."

I wasn't sure how much to believe. I wanted to believe him and simply be over this entire episode—to not think that Frank had meant violence to my son—but I also knew that Seth was embarrassed by what had happened, and how easily an old fogey like Frank had bested him out there in front of the whole team. I hadn't had an opportunity to talk to Frank yet. We'd come straight home after Seth and Frank broke it off, and I wasn't ready yet to call Frank to talk to him about his side of the story. I briefly wondered why he hadn't called me, but then thought perhaps he was giving us some room as a family, on purpose.

The family thing, of course, had to remain loosely defined right now. George had continued to be some sort of odd add-on after Seth was released from the jail cell. We didn't know quite what to do with him, and right now he sat in my home office with Annie, discussing plans to get her back up to her college dorm tomorrow. It wasn't the first time he'd been to my apartment, but he typically remained near the front door. I was trying to remember if he had ever been back in my office. I didn't think so. At least they weren't sitting in my bedroom. That would have been even more awkward. Either way, I would be glad when some of this surreal situation was over and I got my life back.

I patted Seth on the shoulder from behind the couch where I was standing. He was stretched out on the couch, using the armrest as a pillow and wiggling his toes. "I know, Seth. Still, I'd like to see him apologize to you, but only after you more properly apologize to him. The way you came flying across that field at him! Scared me to death to watch it!"

"I'm sorry, Mom. I didn't mean to freak you out."

"But, you know, you did. Just exactly who was I supposed to root for in that little tussle?" I smiled down at him, and he shrugged, grinning.

"Me, of course. Your own flesh and blood!"

"Don't make me choose like that again, mister. Especially if you're the one who starts it. You're asking for me to defect."

He smiled. "When is Annie going back?"

"Probably tomorrow after breakfast. Your dad is in my office with her now trying to figure out when he can swing by to pick her up."

"So you're not taking her back then?"

"No, your dad offered, and frankly, I'm far enough behind on my freelance work that I could use the time to catch up. It's a four-hour round trip, as you well know."

"Oh yeah, I remember. Maybe I'll go with them." He sat up and swung his legs over onto the floor, stretching his arms over his head and yawning.

"Really? That's a lot of time in the car."

"I know."

"With your dad."

"I know."

"Alone. Just the two of you on the way back."

He chuckled. "Mom, I know. Remember, I don't feel quite the same way about Dad that you do. You know that, right?"

"It slips my mind on occasion. Projecting... transference... yada yada yada. Just ignore me when I do this, okay?"

He laughed again. "Fair enough. Anyway, I haven't decided for sure. I might not decide till morning."

"So you're staying the night then?" I asked.

"If you don't mind."

"Why would I mind? After the week we've all had, I'd just as soon have you right here under the same roof with me for a little while." I leaned over the couch and he picked up on my cue and leaned back so I could hug him—probably a little too fiercely for his tastes. But he knew a mom sometimes needs to be sappy and mushy. I was glad he indulged me at times like this.

Times like this. What did I even mean by that? It's not like we had ever gone through anything even remotely like this. Even last year's bout with Lee Gerber's murder hadn't involved us quite this much. Sure, I'd found the body, and sure, we'd tried to figure out who had done it—and who had then also murdered Brenda Johnson in addition to Lee—but even when the murderer had cornered me and Helga in the *Bugle* office, it hadn't felt like we were quite as personally involved as I'd felt when I had to visit my own son in a jail cell.

I SAUNTERED BACK TO THE OFFICE and peeked in the doorway. Annie was sitting sprawled on the daybed and George was sitting on my desk chair, scooting around the hardwood floor on its wheels as Annie chatted animatedly.

"Excuse me, gang. Do we have any ideas for dinner?"

"Mom, let's order a pizza! Have it delivered!"

George immediately looked away from Annie and over at me. I instinctively frowned—Annie had meant to include her dad in this great idea of hers, but I wasn't all that keen on it myself. I couldn't read George's face as he blinked at me. Did he want to be invited to share dinner with us? Did he feel this was as awkward as I knew it was going to be? How could I graciously get us out of this one without offending someone—either George (which wasn't a big deal to me, really) or the kids (because I'd purposely not picked up the ball and had refused to invite George to eat dinner with us)?

"Umm..."

"Mom? Please? It's just a pizza."

She rolled her eyes in that way that reminded me that she wasn't all that far past her teenage years yet, and I smiled weakly. "All right. Pizza it is." And I found the strength to turn to George, who still sat in the desk chair blinking at me in that unreadable way of his, and to smile again.

"Thanks, Maggie," he said quietly, and he lowered his gaze to the floor, scritching the chair left and then right in a tight half circle in front of my desk.

"No problem," I said, trying to sound as if I meant it, and looked again at Annie. "Pepperoni okay then?"

"You know it."

"Right. Sure."

Who knew a simple pizza could be a strange sort of bonding experience for two people who had officially said they no longer had anything in common? Well, I certainly didn't, that's for sure.

GEORGE BARELY SWALLOWED THE LAST BITE of his third slice before he was standing and wiping his chin with the napkin. "I gotta ske-daddle, you guys."

"Oh, already?" Seth said, reaching for the second-to-last slice in the second pizza box and not making eye contact with George.

"Seth, if your dad says he has to go, then he has to go." I didn't want to sound too eager to get rid of George, but I was *plenty* eager to get rid of George. Subtle little things had been reminding me for the past hour and a half that I had long ago left any thoughts of George Roberts in the dust, and for many good reasons. The divorce had originally been his idea, but it hadn't taken me long to warm up to it. And I felt I'd blossomed ever since. So, to have George back at my table, along with our two children, felt like some sort of time capsule had exploded all over my apartment. Of course, explosions aren't typically good things. Especially in one's apartment.

George, though he was so often a clueless lump of testosterone wrapped in man flesh, picked up on my hint, and he dropped the napkin on the table and clapped his hands together. "Yeah, kiddos, I do have to get outta here. I want to stop and fill up the car with gas on my way home so I'm ready to take you back to college in the morning, Annie. And I gotta let the dogs out."

Ah, George's two dogs. That was another whole story that I really was quite glad to not be part of. Once the divorce was finalized, George had replaced me with not just one, but two mangy mutts from the shelter. Noble though animal adoption is, one still should measure one's ability to keep up with said animals. George's two dogs, if you could call them that, were a mess. He'd gotten them as puppies—a rare thing to find in any shelter—but he hadn't spent any real time with them, training them. The few times I'd had to go over to George's house for anything, I tried to not even get out of my car. Once you're out of your car, you're a moving target for those mutts. It's like they can sense that you don't want them to come rambling up out of nowhere and have them jump up with their usually muddy paws. And then there was that one time the bigger one had missed me completely when he jumped up and had landed against the side of my car, slowly sliding down the side with his untrimmed nails, creating lovely scratch marks all the way down the driver's side door.

So, when George said he had to go home to let the dogs out, I was sure he meant it. God only knew what those two mongrels had gotten into while George had been away all day long. And, as if George's housekeeping skills weren't bad enough without two destructive dogs in his possession, the last thing he needed was to find out they had gotten bored of being left alone for so long and had decided to scratch up furniture, chew up chairs, and redecorate in the ways only unruly, untrained dogs can do when left to their own devices.

Seth nodded. "Okay, Dad. What time are you thinking of coming by tomorrow to pick up Annie?"

"Why?"

"I'm thinking of tagging along if it's all right with you."

George smiled. "Of course it's all right." He stopped abruptly. "Well, it's okay with me as long as it's okay with your mom."

I clucked my tongue. "George, he's a grown man. He doesn't need my permission."

"Not permission. Just hoping he'd be courteous by making allowances for your feelings. This past week has probably been a bit of a strain for you."

I tried not to overthink why he had just said that, or whether he meant it in a condescending way. George didn't really "do" condescension very well, mostly because I think you have to exhibit at least a little bit of actual superiority over someone in order to pull it off. George was a fairly clueless guy to begin with. To add on an enhanced sense of self that would allow him to feel superior to anyone, including me, was asking a bit much of poor George.

"It's okay. It's been a tough week for all of us. A little grace, a little slack, and we'll all get past it. If Seth wants to tag along with you tomorrow, that's perfectly fine. I have a ton of work I should be catching up on anyway."

And so, it was settled. The three of them left in the morning when George showed up around ten o'clock. And, armed with my third cup of coffee, I found that I could almost hear my work desk calling to me from my office.

CHAPTER 16

HELGA TOOK THE MANILA FOLDER FROM ME across the high countertop that separated us. Her perch there at the front of the *Bugle* offices always seemed like it had been designed for looks rather than function. I hated having to stand on tiptoe in order to hand anything to her down on the other side. But at least she got her exercise throughout the workday. That countertop, all by itself, turned her otherwise sedentary job into an exercise routine. A complete workout just by letting people in the front door who needed to hand her things.

As if on cue then, she had stood and *reeeeeached* across the countertop, smiling and winking at me. "How ya been, chickie?"

"I've had better weeks, Helga."

She snorted. "I can imagine. No, wait, I *can't* imagine. Not at all."

"I'm just glad it's over and that Seth is out of that God-awful place. I know it was only the one night, and that he was in there alone and all, but... well..."

Helga *tsk-tsk*ed at me. "Girl, you don't have to explain it to me. Nobody wants to see their kid behind bars, even if they're guilty as all get-out. Add on Seth being completely innocent, and it's just a horrible, horrible thing. Isn't it?" She now had my manila folder in one hand, fanning herself with it, and her other hand on her hip. She was shaking her head and still *tsk-tsk*ing at me.

"Ah, Helga, what would I do without you? Whenever I seem to need a little perspective, there you are, the rock of Gibraltar."

"You know," she chimed in, still fanning herself with my folder full of hard work, "what does that even mean? Is there a *real* rock of Gibraltar out there?"

"Perspective, yes. And apparently a little randomness thrown in for good measure. What made you ask that?" I said, chuckling.

"Dunno. Sometimes a phrase I hear all the time suddenly sounds weird. And then I start asking myself where it came from. And sometimes I actually answer myself." She laughed at her non-joke.

"That's what Google is for, Helga. Besides, I'm sure there is a Gibraltar somewhere. I think it's around Europe. And that whatever rock it's made out of is really, really sturdy."

"Apparently."

"So, you've got the proofreading," I said, changing to the subject we should have been discussing in the first place. "Anything else waiting for me here?"

"Nope. The rest of the projects coming in are digital, according to Fiona. Frankly, I'm surprised you still get anything in hard copy, young lady," she said, flapping that manila folder back and forth a little too harshly. I could almost picture the pages flying out of the folder if her hand slipped.

"Not much, I gotta admit. But you know, that one guy who's reprinting all the old theological tomes still really likes to work in hard copy. And that's okay. Once in a while I kind of like working with hard copy myself. I get to use my red pens and my slanted editor's desk again, like old times."

"Damn, girlfriend, you need to get some real hobbies. Nobody should get as excited as you do about pens and paper."

"It's a sickness, I tell ya."

She laughed. "Oh, honey, I know! I've seen the symptoms in you for a long, long time."

She resumed the fanning, and I pointed at the folder, raising one eyebrow in question.

"Oh, the fanning? Too hot in here."

I raised the eyebrow again.

"Menopause, toots. Menopause."

CHAPTER 17

S O, MAGGIE, I WAS THINKING..."

Hearing that phrase from Helga always made me nervous. Once Helga got thinking about something, just about anything could happen. And it often did. Most of the time it was lighthearted fun, but there had been times Helga and I got in over our heads. I was already wondering if this was going to be one of those times.

I slid the sugar bowl across my kitchen table, and she clutched at it as if it were a life preserver on the Titanic.

"And, just exactly what were you thinking, Helga? Because you know what happens when the both of us get involved in something, right? You remember, right?"

"Aw, now, Maggie, don't go spoiling my fun. You know I'm only trying to help."

I smiled. "I know, Helga. I just don't want a repeat of what happened when we were 'just thinking' about Lee Gerber's murder."

She frowned. We'd almost gotten ourselves killed last year getting in over our heads trying to figure out what happened to editor Lee Gerber. And Helga didn't seem like the kind of person who would enjoy being in another skirmish like that one.

"I know, hon. Honestly, I was just thinking... maybe that Alice chick is somebody we should be looking at more closely." She raised an eyebrow playfully, and I had to admit, I was intrigued.

"Go on. I'm listening."

"I'm thinking the whole reason she went to the police about Seth has a lot more to do with her than him. She was obviously trying to deflect attention away from herself."

I nodded. "Agreed."

"Didn't you say the police had been hounding her lately, ever since that Allen guy died? Her husband?"

I nodded again. "Yes, that's right. But of course, whether she's guilty or innocent, her reaction could look exactly the same. Couldn't it?"

Helga knit her brow, considering this. "Well, I have to admit, that does seem possible. But does it seem *likely*?"

"I don't know. My head's all full of fluff about all of this, Helga. I'm just now sleeping better after the whole fiasco with Seth being arrested. I'd rather just put this whole thing behind us. Completely."

"But will you be able to put any of it behind you until someone is arrested? Someone who's actually guilty this time?"

I sighed. "Helga, I have no idea when or how this whole thing ends for us. Sure, it'd be over for everybody if they'd figure out who killed Allen and put that person behind bars, instead of putting innocent people behind bars. But I'm not sure the police know any more about who did this than we do."

"Which is precisely where I started this conversation, Maggie. I think you and I—and maybe Seth—could put our heads together and get the right person snagged for this."

"Let's not get Seth involved if we can help it."

"Wait!" came a voice from down the hall. "'Let's not get Seth involved' in what, exactly?"

As we both heard footsteps coming up the hallway from the back of the apartment, Helga looked confused.

"Is Seth here? With you?"

At that moment, Seth showed up at my kitchen table, smiling his adorable lopsided smile. He knew Helga was a sucker for that smile, and he was laying it on thick. I tried not to laugh. Helga was melting before my very eyes. She pushed back her chair and stood, arms outstretched to engulf Seth in one of her big bear hugs. He snorted with laughter as she went from hugging him to tickling his midsection. She knew he was ridiculously ticklish, and frankly, I wasn't going to be the one to stop her. It was doing my heart a world of good to even hear Seth laughing at anything. And I knew he genuinely liked and appreciated Helga. She didn't have that same fear and clinginess that a mom has when her kid is in any sort of danger. She had just enough distance from this situation to maintain her sense of humor and engage Seth in it.

"Seth! So good to see you, dude!"

"Ah, Helga, quit tickling me! I was just about to say I'm glad to see you too, but now, I don't know. *Hey!* I said quit it!" He kept laughing, and as for asking her to quit tickling him, I could hear that his heart wasn't in it. I imagined it felt as good to him to be able to laugh again as it felt to me to hear it. Around Helga, he was just a big kid.

Once the silliness settled down, Seth joined us at the table. "So, why were you guys talking about me? What did I do now?" He grinned.

"I was just telling your mother that we should join forces again and figure this thing out with this Allen guy and his wife, Alice."

"Because joining forces last time worked out *so* well for us, right?"

"Aw, geez, now you're both getting on my case about that! A girl can't catch a break anymore." She smiled, but I could tell she hadn't anticipated any sort of negative reaction.

"Helga, we're mostly joking. I don't mind sitting here with you and talking about what we think might have happened, but there is no way I'm going to stoop to the same level of participation that happened with Lee Gerber and Brenda's murders."

"I know. I don't want that, either. But we can at least sit here and just talk about it, right? You know, just bouncing ideas around?"

"That's how it started with Gerber. And then, just bouncing ideas around turned into getting out the white board and the dry erase markers and then that turned into charts and schemes and then *that* turned into breaking into the editor's office and desk. And then *that* turned into getting almost knifed to death by a psycho."

It was one of those rare moments when Helga didn't have anything clever to say. No retort. She just kind of blinked at us from across the table. I didn't like it. I wanted her to say the sassy stuff we were all used to. But at least she could see the wisdom in not getting involved again like we did last time.

"What do you think Alice is up to?" she said. "What do you think she was trying to accomplish by pointing a finger at Seth? If she is really the murderer, then the answer is obvious, right? She was trying to get the cops to look at Seth as a possible suspect instead of her. But if she's not the murderer, if she's not guilty, then why? Is it still the same reason? Still just to deflect that attention? Were they *really* sniffing that far up her skirt?"

Seth snorted. He'd always had a soft spot for Helga's colorful language, probably because Helga seemed like an old crazy cat lady to Seth. She was barely sixty, but of course, to someone Seth's age, that might as well be prehistoric, or dead.

"I think so," I answered. "She really seemed nervous about having to go in for another interview the last time I had lunch with her. I didn't think much of it at the time. After all, I know I'd feel the same way if that sort of thing happened to me. You know, it kind of *was* the same when they arrested Seth—which, yes, I know, is more than a little ironic, now that I think about it.

"But honestly, Helga, how would any of us act if we were in her shoes and we were completely innocent? We'd probably act exactly the same way."

"We'd implicate other people who didn't do it?" Seth piped in, sounding suitably offended.

"No, no, of course not," I replied. "I didn't mean that part. I just meant that we'd try to get the police off our scent, especially if it's the wrong scent. I certainly don't approve of her methods, and I most certainly don't think any of us would do that. You know, we didn't do that sort of thing when you were in the police station's holding cell, Seth. We did things by the book. We did things the right way. You know that's not what I meant, right?"

He nodded. "Of course. But it just didn't sound right."

"So," Helga said, leaning over the table to get a little closer to us. "So, what do we do next?"

"We don't *do* anything, Helga!" I chimed in. "That's what I've been trying to say all this time."

"Oh, that's not what I meant, chickie. You know that. But, can't we at least talk to her?"

"To who? Alice?" I hoped I sounded as incredulous as I felt.

"Yeah, why not? Just talk to her. You know—like you've already been doing by meeting with her for coffee or lunch."

"No no no, Helga. That's not happening any time soon."

"Why not?"

"You do remember that Alice is the reason Seth ended up in that holding cell in the first place, right? She's not my best friend in the world right now, Helga."

Seth sat across from us. He was avoiding eye contact with either of us, though. I'd struck a nerve, and until now I hadn't realized that, even though Seth seemed back to his old self, he was still working through his brush with the law. And it had come directly at the hands of Alice.

"All the more reason why we should want to talk to her!"

"Helga, you're not thinking clearly. Alice obviously knows *I* know she was involved in Seth's arrest. There is no way she would meet with me ever again. And, honestly, there is no way I would *want* to meet with her ever again. This discussion is over. Let's find some other sleuth game to play."

CHAPTER 18

ALL I KEPT THINKING WAS, *What in the world am I doing here?* Despite all my protestations the other day, Helga had talked me into sitting here in her puke-green Nissan Cube—quite possibly the most noticeable and most easily identifiable car on the planet thanks to its weird body shape and custom paint job—a half block down from Alice's house. Why were we doing this, on a cold, dreary Saturday morning when I had a bajillion other things I would rather be doing? Because Helga had wooed me into it, and I finally had given up and let her have her way. So, I had set my alarm and gotten up way too early to meet Helga outside my apartment building, where she picked me up in that ridiculous green car of hers. We had stopped at the local coffee shop, where I picked up a pastry and the caffeine I was going to need to survive this outrageous morning with Helga, and now we sat quietly in her conspicuous car, sipping lattes and not saying much. Granted, most of the reason I wasn't saying much was because I wasn't completely awake yet. If Helga had tried to talk to me in that first half hour, I would have bitten her head off. Even strong caffeine takes a little while to kick in.

"Maggie," she finally said, and I flinched, jerking fully awake and bolting upright in the passenger seat.

"I'm awake! I'm awake!"

She snickered. "I know you're awake, sweets. Just wanted to ask you a question, if that's all right."

"Sure. Of course. Go ahead." I can admit now that I secretly hoped her question was, "Shouldn't we just go back home and go to bed?" But I had a feeling that wasn't going to be her question.

"Okay, here's my thought. We're sitting here waiting for Alice to come out of her house and go somewhere, right?"

"Right."

So far, I was with her. If she kept her questions this simple, I could almost take a quick nap in between answers.

"Well, we're assuming she's actually going to, like, *leave* her house sometime soon, right?"

"Right," I answered again. So far, so good.

"But, what if she decides to stay home today? Like, all day?"

"You mean, like I do when I'm not on a stakeout with an idiot at the crack of dawn on a Saturday morning?"

"I sense some sarcasm there, missy. And it's not the crack of dawn. It's after eight o clock. Not cool. Definitely not cool."

I smiled and sipped more of the latte. "Moi?" I sipped still more of the latte, trying to hide my growing smile behind the cup.

"Hey! Keep up here, will ya?"

"So far, Helga, I'm right there with you. What's the next step in your thought process here?"

"The next step is to ask you again, more seriously this time, what if Alice doesn't go anywhere—"

"Wait, do you mean you don't know for sure that Alice is going to leave her house today, at all?"

I had assumed since Helga had talked me into this that she had already figured out Alice's lifestyle patterns and expected her to leave the house today on cue. But, now that I thought about it, Helga hadn't given me any indication that she knew any more than I did about Alice's daily patterns of personal behavior. And, as was becoming painfully obvious, I didn't know one damn thing about those patterns, either.

I looked over to see Helga shaking her head, trying to look both sheepish and apologetic. "Well, to be honest, no, not really. I just—"

"You just what?"

"I just assumed that she had places to go, people to see. Stuff like that."

"Why would you assume that? I'm not even sure she has an outside job. I think she was a housewife while Allen was alive."

Helga shook her head and looked down at her nearly empty coffee cup. "Yeah, well, I hadn't really considered that possibility. I assumed she had an outside job and would be going there this morning. You know, like a lot of people do."

"*You're* not going to a job today, Helga. It's Saturday. And *I'm* not going to a job today, either. I freelance. I just assumed you'd looked into this. You know—that you already knew something and were basing our plans today on what you knew about her schedule."

"Hell no! Why would I know more about her personal schedule than you? You were the one who used to meet her for lunch and shit and talk about your lives, or whatever you guys used to talk about when you met together."

She sounded frustrated. Ha, I wished she could have imagined how I felt.

"Helga, how did we end up here, sitting in this silly car of yours on a cold Saturday morning, sipping expensive coffee and waiting for one particular person to come out of her house and go somewhere, just so we can follow her?"

"I think it happened because I'm secretly an asshole."

"Secretly?"

"Hey!"

"Well, let's face it. This is the most ill-conceived plan I have ever participated in, and I've been involved in a few doozies in my time. Mostly with you." I guzzled the last of the latte and put the empty cup back into the cup holder on my side of the car.

"I'm sorry, toots. Really I am. I guess I just assumed you knew more than you do."

I chuckled. "Never underestimate how little I actually know, Helga. About anything. It will get you into trouble every single time, I assure you."

"Apparently!" Now she was the one laughing. "Then again, you hang out with *me*, so that should have been my first red flag. Right?"

"So, girlie. Now what?" I cringed at my use of the word "girlie." Any time I hung around Helga for too long, I started to pick up on her habit of calling everybody by odd little nicknames.

"Now we, um, well, to be honest, I hadn't planned on anything except seeing her get in her car and drive off. Then, of course, we were going to drive off after her and see where she went."

"Brilliant plan. And original."

She smirked. "Thanks."

"But you already said you expected her to get in her car and drive off to work. So, what would have happened then? We'd follow her to her place of employment, and then we'd, what? Stay in the parking lot all day in your obvious car, parked next to her car? Or were we going to follow her inside and try to not be seen? Because I don't see either of those ideas panning out all that well."

"Okay, fair enough. I hadn't really thought that part through."

"That part? It's kind of only the *first* part. I can't believe this was your whole plan. Eight hours of sitting in your car sipping lattes and eventually having to pee really bad."

She sniffed. "Well, okay, I screwed up everything in a colossal way. We should probably just start over."

I almost snorted coffee out my nose. "Start over doing what? Sleeping, I hope. Because if you want to put this Cube in drive and just take me right back home, I would be the last one to complain." On any other normal Saturday, I wouldn't even be up yet. Maybe I could convince myself this was all a bad dream and get the rest of my sleep somehow.

There was an autumn chill in the air. I shivered, realizing that sitting in this car was no fun at all and remembering just how comfy and warm I had been, snuggled up in my quilts when the alarm had gone off more than an hour ago.

Helga shrugged. "I don't know. Maybe we sit here a little while since we're already here, just in case she really does come out to go somewhere. At least we're pretty sure it wouldn't be to a boring old job. She might be going somewhere important. Somewhere significant."

I shook my head. "Helga, no. Without a plan, without some sort of leading, we have no reason to sit out here. What would we expect Alice to do? Come out, get in her car, and drive to the place where she buys all her poisons? Get real. Even if she came out of her house right now and even if she got into her car to go somewhere that wasn't a boring desk job, the odds of her doing something or going somewhere that might actually implicate her in her husband's murder are slim to none. Time to call it a day."

Helga started to nod slowly. I felt bad being the bearer of bad news, but I told myself that I was actually the bearer of realistic expectations. Sitting here any longer would mean more time we had wasted today when we could have been doing something more productive. And, right about now, everything on the planet looked more productive than sitting in Helga's car in a cul-de-sac sipping lattes in the cold.

Helga put her latte cup back into her own cup holder and turned her key in the ignition. The crazy little Cube car whirred to life, and I sighed. It looked like I was going to get that sleep I wanted after all.

And, just as I was relaxing into the passenger seat and feeling happy about this turn of events, my cell phone rang. I grabbed it out of my coat pocket—I had wisely left the black hole purse at home—and looked at the screen. It was Seth, so I swiped it across and answered.

"Seth! Hi! What's up, buddy? It's a little early for you to be up and calling me, isn't it?" I glanced at the phone, pulling it away from my face. It was 8:24—way too early for either Seth or me, and he knew it. So, why would he be calling me at this ungodly hour?

"Mom! Mom!"

"What? What?"

"Do you know where Frank is?"

"What?"

"Frank! Do you know where he is?"

"You mean, where he is right now?"

"*Yes!* Right now! Where did he go?"

"Geez, Seth, I don't know where Frank is. I haven't seen him since the day he—the day you—well, you know, when the two of you got into that fight at baseball practice. Why?"

"He's gone."

"What?"

"He's gone! Frank is gone!"

"What do you mean, he's gone? You just asked me where he is, like you don't know yourself." It was way too early in the morning for this kinda of baloney. Wasn't there anybody in my life who could think straight, reason straight, and talk straight?

"No, I mean he's *gone*. Like, left town gone."

"Wait—how do you know this? Where are you?"

"I'm over at Frank's place. But it's completely empty. There aren't even any curtains on the windows anymore, and when I peeked inside the front window on the first floor, I could see that the whole first floor is empty. Like he moved out or something."

"He—he moved?"

"It sure looks that way to me. What else would explain why his house is completely empty? And what else would explain why you haven't heard from him in days?"

"Well, I'm sure *something* could explain it. Because that just doesn't make sense that he would skip town like that. Are you sure you're at the right house?"

"Yes, I'm sure!"

"He wouldn't skip town," I repeated.

"Unless—"

"Hey, wait! What are you doing over at Frank's house? And so early on a Saturday morning, too?"

I was starting to think I was hallucinating. Nothing about this day so far was making a lick of sense, and it wasn't even nine o'clock in the morning yet.

"Me? I couldn't sleep last night, thinking about how wrong I was about Frank, about how *Alice* had done this to me, to us, and not Frank. And yet I tried to beat the guy up at baseball practice, like he had actually done something wrong. And, I'm pretty sure he didn't."

"Pretty sure?"

"Well, I *was* pretty sure until I came here to his house this morning to apologize. I tossed and turned all night thinking about it, and I knew I would have to come over here first thing so I could straighten this mess out with him. So, so you two could go back to being happy."

"Oh, Seth."

"And then I get here, only to find he's left. Left town, I bet! So now I'm completely confused. It sure doesn't look good to me to see that he just picked up stakes and left town in the middle of the night."

"How do you know it was the middle of the night?"

"Well, okay, I don't know. It's just an expression. It sure sounds like he didn't bother to tell you he was going away. Did he?"

I sighed. "No, Seth, you're right about that part. He didn't say anything to me at all."

"So, the jerk gets us all to believe he's innocent and gets into our good graces and everything, and we end up finding out the hard way that he's packed up and left. And yeah, maybe it wasn't in the middle of the night. Heck, I don't know about you but I haven't heard or seen him since that baseball practice, either. That means he could have a three-day head start."

"Head start?" I still wasn't thinking clearly, and having this new situation thrown at me was just confounding what little clear-headed reasoning I might have had. In addition to all this, I was still aware of Helga sitting next to me in the driver's seat, sipping that eternal latte of hers and looking at me quizzically, hearing only my side of this conversation and probably wondering what fresh hell I was about to unleash on our ever-growing list of unrelated, random facts about this case and this investigation.

"Yeah! It seems obvious now that Frank is gone, and that he's on the run from the law. That he killed Allen!"

"What?"

"You heard me."

"So now you're back on the Frank-as-the-killer kick?" I closed my eyes, sensing Helga next to me, filling in some of the gaps of the half conversation she was privy to.

"Mom, I don't care what you think about Frank, or how you still might feel about him. You've got to start facing facts here. The man you're dating—or, at least, the man you *thought* you were dating—has left town, has packed up all of his belongings and left, and he hasn't even bothered to tell you about it. It's not even just that he stopped dating you because you have an unreasonable son who doesn't like him. It's more than that."

"How do you know it's more than that, Seth? It might be *exactly* that. Frankly, I know a lot of guys who wouldn't have hung around after their girlfriend's grown son tried to beat the crap out of them in public."

"Mom, any normal guy wouldn't feel he had to pack up and leave town over it, though. He'd just break up with her."

"This is a small town, Seth. People talk."

"No, Mom, they don't. Not bad enough to leave town. It's just a breakup, after all. Right?" That doesn't make people pack up and leave."

"Well..."

He had a point. Still, as usual, Seth was going to extremes. I just didn't buy that moving away—if that's what had happened—automatically made Frank a murderer.

"It's not *that* small a town. Geez."

"Did you try calling him, Seth?"

"I don't have his phone number."

"He's part of your baseball team. I assumed you would have had each other's phone numbers."

"Nobody calls on the phone now. We text."

I tried not to chuckle at this, since, of course, Seth had just called me on the phone to have this conversation in the first place.

"But don't you text *to his phone number*?"

"Yeah, yeah, Mom, I know what you're thinking. We're having a phone conversation right now. And most people text to a phone number. But I only had Frank's Twitter handle and had made friends with him on Facebook. I never had a phone number for him. Allen, yes. Frank, no. I messaged him through Facebook."

"So, you had the phone number of a friend of your dad's but not a friend—a *boyfriend*—of mine. Okay."

"Don t get weird on me, Mom. Let's keep focused. Frank was here. Then Allen died. Allen was murdered. Poisoned. Now Frank is gone. And the two of you didn't have a fight to cause Frank to leave. And let's face it: I didn't beat the crap out of him. It wasn't even close. It's not like I was any sort of actual threat to ol' Frankie boy. So that's not why he left, either. The only thing that makes sense right now—to me, at least—is that he knew we were onto him and he left before we figured out too much more about what he did."

"Like, maybe *why*, for instance? Because that's the part that I can't seem to figure out right now, Seth. You're being ridiculous about this, and you're reading things into what happened because you already didn't like him."

"Mom!"

"Seth, let me try calling Frank and I'll get back to you. Okay?" He sighed into the phone, and then I heard it click. There was no point in calling him back until I had at least dialed Frank's number and given him a chance to explain himself. I held the phone away from my ear in order to swipe it back open and dial Frank's number. Helga swooped in immediately.

"So? What's going on? Something about Frank not being around or something?"

"Seth was over at Frank's house just now."

"But I thought they hated each other."

"Nah, it's just *Seth* who hates *Frank*. Frank doesn't really hate my kids, doesn't really have any issues with them, except that they hate him."

"So why was Seth over at Frank's house if he hates him?"

"Apparently he went over there to apologize for trying to beat him up at baseball practice the other day. And he got to Frank's house and found out that Frank seems to have moved out. All his furniture seems to be gone."

"Moved out, as in skipped town?" Helga's mouth dropped open. Nope, she wasn't jumping to any conclusions or anything. As usual. Just like Seth.

"Yes, you could call it that, I suppose. Anyway, Seth's already back on the Frank-is-the-murderer train. And it's apparently left the station, full steam ahead."

"Oh, great. Just what we need! Another suspect gumming up the works! Why on earth would Seth go back to thinking Frank had anything to do with any of this? *Alice* is the one who tried to frame him, not Frank."

I shook my head. "I don't have a clue, Helga. But until I get Frank on the phone and get an answer out of him, Seth's going to be on that anti-Frank train heading down the tracks at top speed."

And I was rapidly running out of train metaphors.

CHAPTER 19

HAD ALMOST GIVEN UP ON FRANK ANSWERING HIS PHONE when I heard a click. But, instead of hearing Frank's actual voice, I heard only his voice mail greeting, so I hung up. Figures. The last thing I needed right now was for Frank to *not* be answering his phone. I started to list in my head every *other* reason Frank might not have answered his phone, because I refused to believe that he had skipped town out of panic or guilt over Allen's death. Seth was the only one championing that misguided cause right now, and if I hadn't had him in my ear about it, I wouldn't for a second have thought Frank could have done this thing.

And, happily, Helga agreed with me. She was on her own guilt kick right now—Alice, of course—so, to her, Frank also seemed like a long shot. I was grateful for even small blessings at the moment, and solidarity with Helga was a big one. Still, I wasn't excited about calling Seth to tell him that Frank wasn't answering his phone. Seth wasn't going to hear that news with the same conclusion I came to.

"So, Helga, do I call Seth now and get it over with, or do I wait to see what happens with Alice here, if anything?"

"Geez, girlfriend, I don't know."

"Or do we simply both go back home and go back to bed?" I winked at her, and she broke into a smile.

"Good golly, you're really *not* a morning person, are you?"

I closed my eyes. "You have *no* idea."

"I don't know about that. I think I have a pretty *good* idea, as a matter of fact. I can see you flagging from here."

"So, which option do we choose? I vote for sleep, and I can call Seth later."

"You know he's going to call you back within the next five minutes, right? He's a guy, a *boy*. He doesn't have the patience to wait till you call him at lunchtime today, for crying out loud. In fact, I'm surprised he hasn't called back already."

"True. Still, I just don't want to get into this with him right now."

"Then don't. But you should at least call him with a Frank-phone-update. Just tell him you're going back to bed and will call him again later. That way, he won't be building up a huge head of steam until he gets to talk to you."

"Maybe you're right."

"You know I am. Even a little bit of information—coupled with you acting casual and unconcerned—might actually give him some time to get adjusted to the fact that Frank didn't answer his phone. Not a big deal most of the time, but there is no way on God's green earth that somebody like Seth is going to let that go."

"True. You do know how he can get."

"For a slacker, he has his intense moments, yup." She nudged me in the ribs, and I smiled again.

"I know. Right? The kid's priorities are always pretty obvious. At least to me they are."

"You're his mom. You know him pretty well, even if he doesn't agree that you do."

"I just wish I could get him to see Frank the way I see Frank."

"He will, hon. Just give him time."

"Hey, I've got all the time in the world. But I'm afraid that Seth hears a clock ticking after what happened with Alice and the jail cell experience. He wants to get this settled as soon as possible, if only to avoid having any other innocent person thrown behind bars like he was."

"But pointing the finger at someone like Frank doesn't make sense, either. He's just doing that out of a combination of wanting to find the culprit and hating your boyfriend. Not a healthy combination. And, it's going to get the wrong person arrested again."

"I know. I'm with ya, Helga. I just wish Seth was."

"Again, give him time. We'll pursue Alice—quietly and without her knowledge—and you can pursue any sort of conversation with Frank to straighten things out. Like, why all of his furniture is suddenly missing."

I frowned. I was trying hard not to think about what Seth had found—or *not* found—when he went over to Frank's house. Maybe he'd been at the wrong house. But what if he *had* been at Frank's house when he called? What had Frank done with all his furniture? Had he simply moved somewhere else in town? That would be the simplest explanation—or, rather, the safest one, as far as I was concerned—but I just couldn't see him moving so fast and not even mentioning it to me in passing. Then again, we hadn't spoken or had much contact at all in the past four days. So it was completely possible that he *had* picked up and moved to a different house in town in that period of time. He was only renting the house he'd been in, so moving wouldn't have to be a huge inconvenience if he had found a place he liked better. I clung to this explanation as the best one to present to Seth. But, until Frank actually answered his phone and talked to me—and answered some of these growing questions—I wouldn't be able to calm Seth down or get him off the Frank warpath. And, that was bothering me more than I cared to admit.

"Helga, I think I don't really want to sit here staking out Alice's house anymore today. Maybe we should just—"

And just at that moment, Helga shushed me and waved her hand in front of my face. She was looking intently out the windshield, and when I looked out, I saw Alice coming out of her house, her purse slung over one arm, a jacket on but unbuttoned. She locked her front door—obviously a deadbolt lock—and put the keys in her other hand. She walked directly to her car, unlocked it with the fob, which made a quick *boop* noise as she pointed it at the car door, and quickly got in, closing the door.

Helga and I watched her intently, as if we had never seen someone start a car or maneuver out of a parallel parking space before. Alice backed out of that space, and then the backup lights went off and she had put her car into drive.

"Helga," I whispered as loudly as I dared, though we had the car windows closed and there was no way Alice could have heard us.

"What?" she whispered back.

"Turn on your car. We need to follow her!"

Helga snapped out of it and clicked into action. She started her car, and I waved my hand low across the front console. She turned to look at me, perplexed.

"What?"

"Not yet. Wait a few seconds. If you're right behind her, in this ridiculously obvious car, she'll notice right away that she's being followed."

"Right. Maybe we should have brought your car."

I had been thinking the same thing all morning. My silver Cobalt was the most nondescript, common car on the face of the planet right now, and nobody would have noticed being followed by one. Chances were good that she would have been followed by three or four of them, out of sheer coincidence. Adding mine to the little silver sedan parade wouldn't have made much difference in her rearview mirror. This puke-green, square monstrosity was going to stick out like a sore thumb.

"Okay, now!" I announced, and Helga threw the Cube into drive and took off in a slow, O.J.–Simpsonesque car chase of glacial speeds. Alice herself was driving a bright red Honda of some variety—the model may have been a common one, but the color would make tailing her a little bit easier.

I found I was tapping the dashboard nervously, and Helga herself was clicking her tongue and tapping the steering wheel.

"Is this far enough back, do you think?"

"Gosh, I don't know, Helga. At least right now we're on somewhat major roads through town. Looks like we've got the same car behind us that's been there since we pulled out into traffic to begin with. That's a good sign, I think, that she won't easily figure out we're following her. I hope."

"Where do you think she's going?" Helga asked.

"I haven't got a clue. And of course, we have to assume that this isn't going to lead anywhere important, right? I mean, what are the odds that we'll happen to start following Alice the same morning she decides to do something really incriminating?"

"Slim to none. I know, I know. Still, we have to try. We're here now, right?"

"Yeah, of course. It's happening now, and we're here, so we do this thing. But if she ends up going to the craft store or the gas station and then heads home, maybe we don't do this again for a while. Deal?"

Helga sighed, turning left three cars behind Alice and trying to drive as inconspicuously as possible. Smooth and steady.

"Agreed. Geez, where *is* this woman going?"

We had passed several shopping centers and the mall by now, but Alice hadn't slowed down or considered stopping or pulling into any one of them. She did, though, seem to know where she was going. No false starts. No hesitations at any intersection so far.

"I haven't been to this side of town in at least a week," I said casually as Helga continued to drive.

"I'm not sure *when* I've been on this end of town, ever. What's over here, exactly?"

Alice turned right into a small residential section known for more renters than homeowners. The houses around here were fairly well kept, especially for rentals, but they were nothing special, really.

I knew this because this was the part of town where Frank lived.

"You mean, besides Frank's house?"

"Wait... what?"

Helga fought hard to keep driving steadily and to keep a close eye on where Alice's car was as she turned her head to face me.

"Besides Frank's house," I repeated, clenching my jaw tightly and trying not to find any of this oddly ironic. Which was becoming difficult.

"You're shittin' me, right? Frank doesn't live around here, does he?" She kept her eyes on the road as best she could, turning yet again to keep up with Alice. Unfortunately, the stream of the same cars that had been parading along with us most of this time had thinned out to only two, and neither of these had been right behind us when we started out. *And*, our cushion of cars between us and Alice's car ahead of us was now down to one. *And*, here we were in the bright green Cube, probably the only car like it in the entire county.

"Yes, he sure does," I said dryly, waiting to see if Alice was going to start turning right onto Frank's str—

Shit. Her blinker was on.

"Don't forget this right turn up here," I said, pointing. "You know, right onto *Frank's street*." I sighed, frustrated, confused, and a little bit pissed off, though I didn't quite have a target for my frustration just yet. I had a few suspicions about where this was headed, but I was trying desperately not to think that way yet. Not until I absolutely had to. And I was beginning to get pissed at Seth for putting these ideas about Frank into my head in the first place because now I found that I couldn't help myself. I was making connections that included Frank, and it was thoroughly unpleasant.

"Oh, good grief, Maggie! This is Frank's street?"

I sighed again, nodding, though her eyes were completely focused on the road ahead of her, and on Alice's car, which now turned on its blinker.

"Yeah, afraid so."

"And don't tell me she's about to pull into—"

"Frank's driveway. Yup."

Helga instinctively slammed on the brakes and pulled off to the side of the road, three houses up from Frank's driveway. We watched in stunned disbelief as Alice's car smoothly turned in to Frank's driveway. She parked and got out quietly, looking around her in what I could only describe as a furtive manner. She wanted to see if anyone was watching her. And that alone made me nervous. Helga and I looked at each other and then silently turned back to watch what Alice was going to do next. She walked up the little cement walkway to the front door and then peered as best she could through the small window at the top of the door. It was a little too high for her to see through, though, so she stepped off the cement walkway and instead went to the front bay window. She shielded her eyes and looked in, first a little bit left, then right, scouring the room for who knew what.

"I wonder if Seth was right," Helga said quietly.

"You mean, about the house being empty?"

"Yeah."

"Could be. Frank's car isn't in the driveway, for one thing. And he didn't answer his phone, of course. Anything's possible, as far as I'm concerned. I'm majorly freaking out right now."

"You look calm, cool, and collected," Helga offered, smiling at me in a way that told me she was trying to comfort me. I let it go. No time to overthink any of this. I had a sinking feeling there would be plenty of time for that later.

"Thanks. I'm starting to feel like crap, though, if you want to know the truth. I wish she would hurry up and either go in or go home. I'm dying to go up there myself and look in that window."

"So, you don't have a key to Frank's place?" She sounded disappointed. Frankly, right now, I felt disappointed myself.

"Nope. And now I wish I did. But no, we haven't gotten to that stage yet."

"The key exchange stage? Or the staying at each other's houses stage?"

I realized I hadn't shared much of my relationship with Frank with Helga up until this point. Now that I thought about it, I hadn't shared much of the relationship with anyone. Except perhaps Seth, since he knew Frank from the baseball team. And look where all that sharing had gotten me.

"Either one. I mean, neither one. We're dating, and I guess I'd say we're fairly serious in some ways, but not that way."

This was starting to feel more than a little awkward, not the least because of what we were watching out that windshield right now. Alice was done scouring the inside of the front room, and she stood up straight, backed away from the bay window, and stepped back onto the cement walkway. Her hands fell to her sides—she hadn't brought her purse with her up to the house, I now noticed—and she sighed heavily. We didn't *hear* her sigh, of course, but we saw it clearly. She looked exasperated. Helga motioned to me to scooch down into the seat a little bit, and I did. The last thing we needed right now was to have to explain ourselves to Alice. She'd know right away that we were spying on her. And even though it was starting to look like we had good reason to spy on her, I wasn't ready to deal with the fallout of having been caught in the act. I was going to need a little more time to process the things I was seeing and hearing this morning. And a little more sleep.

Just then Alice turned and headed back to her car. I scrunched as far down into the seat as I could, to avoid being seen. Then again, Helga and I were scrunching down in the most recognizable car around, so it was probably a losing battle, but we couldn't help it. We were scrunching like a couple of badasses.

She got into her car, started it up, and backed out of Frank's driveway slowly. Much as she had backed out of the parking space at her house, she came within a handful of feet of the front bumper of Helga's bright green Cube. And just as I expected to see her car then go into drive and to see her pull away, she instead kept backing up, steering the car around the front of Helga's car and back still further, till she was exactly next to it. She tapped the horn.

Both Helga and I eased upward in our seats a little bit to see what Alice was doing. She had rolled down the front passenger window and was frowning at us, right at us, and it was clear that continuing to scrunch down in the seat to avoid detection was a little ridiculous. Slowly, we both inched up in our seats until we were sitting normally again. Helga smiled a cheesy smile at her, and I leaned over and waved a small, pathetic, sheepish little wave before making eye contact with her.

"What are *you* doing here?" she said loudly, glaring right at me.

"*Me?*" I countered, finding my voice and realizing that I had as much right, if not more, to be here at my boyfriend's house as she did. "What am *I* doing here? Seriously? What are *you* doing here? This is my boyfriend Frank's house!"

Helga started nodding furiously, and I almost laughed, except that I still wasn't sure what the heck was going on here or what reason Alice had to be here in the first place.

"Your *boyfriend*?"

"Yes! Frank is my boyfriend. You know that!"

"I do?"

"Yes, I know I must have mentioned him one of the times you and I met for coffee or lunch, Alice."

I was really starting to hit my stride now, upset and growing angrier by the minute.

"I'm not sure you ever mentioned his name, no. And anyway, I certainly never put two and two together."

She was yelling to be heard clearly, and I too was yammering a little more loudly than I wanted to, just so Alice could hear me. Helga sat between us in the driver's seat, leaning back as far as she could so Alice and I could see each other.

I was still fuming. "That's not my fault, is it? And it certainly doesn't add to the situation to think you're here at Frank's house for some other reason that doesn't involve me in the slightest."

Helga reached over to pat my leg. It was obvious she didn't want to interfere with this conversation, though she was literally right in the middle of things.

"That's not the biggest question right now, Maggie! I want to know why you two must have been following me since I left my house!"

Helga couldn't help herself (which was not a surprise) and jumped into the conversation. "How do you know we were following you?"

"Because nobody else on the *planet* has a car like that! How dumb do you two think I am?"

Helga opened her mouth as if she was going to answer the question, but I reached over and put a firm hand on her shoulder.

"Rhetorical, Helga. Don't answer."

She turned to me, and I shook my head. She clamped her mouth closed and went back to simply sitting between us like she was a volleyball net during a heated match.

"Okay, yeah, we've been following you. So what? That's not a crime, the last time I checked!"

"Then I'm not sure when the last time you checked was, because I think it kind of *is* a crime to stalk someone like this."

I was half expecting one of us to say, "I know you are, but what am I?" This whole situation was stupid and surreal, and I wasn't sure what to do next.

Alice started to roll the window back up, and, without thinking, I yelled, "Wait!"

She stopped and the window sat halfway up. But, she didn't look at me anymore. "What?"

"Why *are* you here? After what you did to Seth, what could you possibly need from my boyfriend?"

She shook her head. "I said I didn't know he was your boyfriend. And what do you mean, what I did to Seth?"

"What are you doing here? What do you have against me and my son? He was traumatized by that night in jail."

"I don't have to explain anything to you. Or to your son. Or explain anything about your *boyfriend*. Now, leave me alone and stop following me."

She hit the button to roll up the window the rest of the way, put the car into drive, and took off down the quiet residential street. Helga made a move to do the same, but I shook my head and touched her arm.

"No, let's not follow her. Wherever she's going, it won't give us any more information today than we just got from following her here. Right now I want you to pull into Frank's driveway so I can take a look in that front window for myself. I need to see if what Seth told me on the phone is true."

Helga nodded and threw the Cube into drive. "You got it, boss lady. Good thinking."

CHAPTER 20

THERE WAS ABSOLUTELY NOTHING IN FRANK'S LIVING ROOM. Just as Seth had told me on the phone. Nothing on the walls. No furniture. No rugs. Nada. Not even the kind of stuff you leave behind when you move—little candy wrappers or bits of stuff that falls out of the couch cushions or from in between tables and the wall. None of that stuff. It was as if he had never even lived there. I shuddered as I pulled away from the window, watching Helga shake her head slowly in disbelief.

"Now what?" she asked, folding her arms across her chest.

"Now maybe I call Seth and just suck it up. I think it's time we pack it in and talk to Seth together. He needs to know that we followed Alice here. That she came here looking for Frank. Or, at least, looking for *something*. I have no idea what she was hoping to find, but it's clear she didn't find it. Or, that she didn't find *him*. Either way, though, the fact that this is where she came makes me wonder what's going on."

"Maggie, we've got to consider something else here, though, too."

"What?"

"First, let's go back to the car and sit inside and talk. It's cold out here. A lot warmer in my car where the wind isn't blowing up my ass."

She had a point. I was shivering, and it wasn't really because of how I felt. Autumn weather had shown up with a vengeance... and me without a jacket. So, back to the Cube we went, and once we were inside and felt a little more comfortable, we continued.

"What else do we need to consider here, Helga?"

"That Alice came right out and said to us that she knew we were following her."

"Because of your car?"

"Yeah, because of my car. But, the point is, she knew the whole time we were driving here that we were behind her."

"And your point is?" I wasn't following her reasoning here. Yet.

"If she knew we were behind her, no matter where she went, then of course she knew we would find out where she was going once she got there."

"Meaning she knew we'd see her here at Frank's house."

"Precisely. That we'd see her show up here."

"But she also just said that she didn't have any idea that Frank was my boyfriend."

"Do you believe her? Does it seem far-fetched that she didn't have a clue that you were dating Frank?"

"You know, Helga, I wish I could remember one way or the other whether I ever mentioned Frank being my boyfriend."

"What about at the ball games, with Seth? The whole key here is that Seth and Frank and Allen were all on the same baseball team. Right?" She squinted her eyes at me, wondering where things were going from here, just like I was wondering.

"Yeah, that's true, Helga, but Alice never came to the baseball games herself. So she never would have seen me and Frank together at all. Unless I mentioned Frank by name and made that baseball team connection for her, she might not have known about this until today."

"I see where you're going with this. I think."

"And, of course, even though she knew she was being followed, she probably didn't know *who* was following her. Right? Granted, you have quite a distinctive car, and it's almost impossible to miss it on the street around here. But, did Alice know whose car it is? I doubt it. You don't know her, do you?"

"No! And frankly, I'm pretty sure I don't want to know her." Helga rolled down her window and spit out onto the street. Then she rolled it back up and turned back to face me. "Damned bitch. Sorry, Maggie, but that's how I feel about that woman. She's made your life and your son's life a living hell these past few weeks. She's spit on your friendship, and if that makes me think she's guilty, then so be it. In my eyes, she's as guilty as the day is long."

"Well, thanks for the vote of confidence, Helga. Truly. But, let me stick to my point before I forget where I was going with this." She laughed. "My point is this: Just because she noticed a bright green Cube following her all the way from her house to Frank's house doesn't mean she knows who was *in* that car."

"Meaning you. Fair enough. So why is this information important?"

"Because I was initially worried—when she told us she knew she was being followed—that she had come here on purpose once she knew she was being followed."

"Oh, I see what you mean! You were wondering if she thought, 'Gee, I'm being followed. Maybe I'll take these jokers on a wild goose chase. I think I'll go to Frank's house.'"

"Precisely."

"But now you don't think that's possible? You don't think she did that on purpose?"

"Nope."

"Why not?"

"Because I'm pretty sure she really didn't know who was following her. Just that *somebody* was following her."

"So, now you think she just went ahead with her plans to go to Frank's house? Not caring whether she was being followed or not? Even if she didn't really know who it was?"

"Yeah, that's the best I can come up with. That she left the house intending to go to Frank's house, saw that she was being followed at some point, and then continued on with her goal of going to Frank's house anyway."

"Because...?"

"Because she didn't do something innocuous like lead us to the Walmart or to a gas station or something. She either didn't care or didn't think it mattered if she went to Frank's house."

"But there's got to be something fishy going on here with those two. She goes to Frank's house... and you're not even sure that she knows Frank. And then we see for ourselves what Seth told you earlier today—that, for some unexplained reason, Frank's stuff is all completely missing from his house. And he's not answering his phone. It's like the guy has vanished."

I tried not to sound as unnerved as I felt. "Yeah, kinda weird. I agree with you on that."

"You see this the same way I do, yes? That these two people are officially up to something. Right?"

She had leaned in as she was saying this, and I was trying to find this humorous rather than claustrophobia-inducing.

"Honestly, Helga, I don't know anymore. Yeah, my gut says there is something going on with the two of them, and that somehow, some way, it's connected to Allen's murder, but I'll be dipped if I can figure out what the connection is. Any ideas?"

"Beats me, chickie. But I wonder if Mr. Frank will answer his damned phone now. Have you tried to call him again?"

"No, as a matter of fact. Time to hit the ol' redial and see if he answers this time."

I pulled out my phone and swiped it. I called Frank's number and it rang four times—again—before that blasted voice mail kicked in. I left a message this time, though. The first time I wasn't thinking clearly enough, but I'd hoped Frank would see my missed call and call me back. But a lot had changed in the past hour since that first phone call. The familiar *beep* of the voice mail came over the phone, and I took in a deep breath and let him have it.

"Frank! Where the *heck* are you, dude? I'm sitting here with my friend Helga, outside your house. First of all, you're not answering your phone. Second, your house is *empty*. Where have you gone? Where is your furniture? Where—"

I saw Helga out of the corner of my eye. She was rolling her hands around each other in a sort of "go on, go on, keep it moving!" gesture. I was rambling. I needed to get to the point before the voice mail cut me off.

"Where are *you*? Please call me. In addition to being a little bit pissed at you, Frank—yes, I admit it, I'm pissed—I'm also just *worried* about you. Are you okay? Did you—"

And with that, I heard a *boop* and the voice mail cut out.

I turned off the phone and tossed it onto my lap.

"Voice mail too short?" Helga asked.

"Yeah, of course." I was beyond frustrated now. It wasn't even noon and my whole day had turned into one colossal joke. By now I had learned that it was entirely likely that my boyfriend had broken up with me, and that he had done it mostly by moving out of town under cover of darkness (or some reasonable approximation of that idea), without saying a thing to me. I had also learned that somehow, some way, Alice was involved with Frank. Maybe she hadn't known that he had moved out of town, either—she looked a little perplexed when she looked into that window and saw nothing in his living room, just as we had—but she'd known where he lived and seemed to get herself there by car without getting lost or even taking a wrong turn. Did she use a GPS to get there so easily, or had she known Frank's place of residence before this morning?

I started to feel sick to my stomach thinking about all the nasty possibilities between the two of them. No matter how I looked at this situation, I came in last place. Add on the phone call from Seth, and his current hatred of both Alice and Frank, and I was way too close to puking right here in Helga's car. I was glad Helga was here with me, but not very glad that I felt like puking in her puke-green car. I hit the button to bring down my passenger side window, stuck my head out, closed my eyes, and took a big, calming breath of fresh, cool air.

"You okay, girlfriend?" Helga asked. I kept my head out the window, kept my eyes closed, and gave Helga a silent thumbs-up behind me. "Good. I'm a bit worried about you. There's a lot going on here today, and it all seems like bad news for you, chickie. Are you sure you're okay?"

I nodded but said nothing. I wasn't sure I *was* okay, but I had to fake it till I could make it, to coin a phrase.

"Let's just get out of here, Helga. I don't ever want to see this house again. We know stuff about both Alice and Frank that we didn't want to know, but that I'm glad we now know. So now, it's time to get our asses out of here. Take me home."

I leaned back into the car and rolled the window up. We fastened our seat belts and I slumped a little bit in the seat. I didn't want to see the world go by while she was driving.

"We'll get you out of here, my dear friend. You've had quite a morning."

"That's the understatement of the year, isn't it? Yeah, let's just get me home. I want to sit on my couch, hug my silly dog, and not think about any of this anymore."

Helga started the Cube and pulled out of the driveway and onto the road, heading back to my apartment. I kept my eyes closed and tried hard not to overthink everything that had already happened today. I'd deal with Seth and even Frank later, maybe tomorrow. Maybe never, as far as Frank was concerned. I had this overwhelming urge to turn off my phone, once I realized that both Seth and Frank might call me back today. Seth was definitely going to call me back because he wasn't going to let this whole thing with Frank's empty house go for long without finding out what I had heard from Frank.

Of course, I could still hear from Frank. It seemed less likely with every passing minute that I would get a return call from him, but I had to allow for the possibility. I wasn't even sure I wanted to get that call anymore. Either way, I had to believe he would call me back. Eventually.

And until that time, I was going to have to suffer with worry and confusion.

The part that made me nervous, though, was that Seth might have been right: that Frank was somehow involved in Allen's death—his *murder*. And adding on Alice now made me even more nervous. It was entirely possible that Alice and Frank had collaborated to do Allen in. *Why* they would have done such a thing was beyond my comprehension in my current state, though. I couldn't see a reason for Frank to get involved in this, unless—

"Hey, chickie, you don't think Frank and Alice are having an affair, do you?"

I barely got the window down in time before I puked up my entire breakfast out the side of that conspicuous puke-green Cube.

CHAPTeR 21

I WOKE UP FROM MY UNSCHEDULED BUT INCREDIBLY NECESSARY NAP with a profound sense of disorientation. I barely knew where I was (on my sofa with Vlad tucked up near my chin), let alone *when* I was (sometime early in the afternoon of the same day) or how (Helga had gotten me home safely and left quietly). My head was throbbing and my eyes refused to focus properly. If I had been a drinker, I would have assumed this was a hangover. But I'd been born a goody-two-shoes and had never strayed from that basic personality trait in all my years of childhood, adolescence, and now adulthood and middle age. Sure, I had a brief time not long after the divorce where I contemplated a life of alcohol and misery in order to drown the memory of what George had done to me and our marriage, but those feelings were mercifully short lived as I began to see life unfolding anew before me. A life I wouldn't have anticipated but which I nevertheless welcomed with open arms.

And so, the life in a bottle I had contemplated had never actually happened. So, as I lay on my couch trying to wake up fully, with Vlad still scrunched up near my head, I found enough clearheadedness to thank God I had never fallen into that situation. Because, honestly? I felt like shit right now. Hard to believe people got drunk and felt like this on purpose—some of them more than once. And I suspected a real hangover felt a lot worse than this.

I pushed Vlad away from my head and he groaned a little doggy groan before stretching and dumping himself right off the couch onto the floor.

"Sorry, buddy. I gotta sit up before my head explodes." I could almost feel the pressure inside my skull. I pushed myself into a sitting position and sighed. Vlad whimpered from the floor, in his way that asked if he could just jump right back up here with me.

"Hey, buddy, let's give it a rest, okay? Not ready to deal with more doggy breath right now." I shooed him away with a wave of my hand, and he snorted—understanding the universal sign for "go away"—and padded toward the kitchen where his bowl of dry dog food awaited.

Closing my eyes and inhaling deeply seemed to center my thoughts. I wondered if any calls had come in while I was zonked out on the couch. There sat my phone on the coffee table in front of me. But surely I would have heard calls come in, what with the phone only a few inches from my face for the past several hours. And just how long had I been asleep, anyway? I grabbed the phone off the coffee table and swiped to the welcome screen. It was 1:15 p.m. I'd been asleep for several hours, then. I also noticed that I had indeed missed a few calls. One from Seth. I'd wait to call him back, though. I still wasn't sure where anything stood and still wasn't sure I wanted to deal with Seth's firm opinions about Frank until I knew more. Another call from Helga. I'd expected a call from her, even if only to check up on me to see how I was doing. I probably looked a fright when she'd dropped me off this morning. I had avoided throwing up inside her car, but I must have looked like death warmed over on the car ride back here.

The third missed call was from Frank. Now I wasn't sure if I wanted to deal with that call first, or the one from Helga. I envisioned the return call to Helga and realized she would want information on anything that might have happened since this morning, so my decision was made for me. I'd call Frank first and find out just what the heck was up with him. And what was up with him *and Alice.* My head wasn't ready to think about anything involving both Frank and Alice, but I knew there was no way around some of the things I was thinking. The only way to get past this icky feeling was to confront it head on.

Besides, a call to Frank might just clear up everything. That would go a long way toward curing this pounding in my temples. And, if things were worse than I feared—or, as bad as I feared— then it was still better to know for sure, sooner rather than later. No sense in dragging out my own torture. *Suck it up, buttercup.*

I called Frank's number and heard it ring two times, almost losing my nerve, before he picked up. Why hadn't he left me a voice mail when he called? I had no idea what to expect.

"Maggie! Is that you?"

Why did people still ask this question, in the days of caller ID? "Of course it's me."

"Yes, yes, of course."

"Where have you been?"

"What do you mean?"

Oh, good grief. He was already trying to deflect. This wasn't going to be a fun conversation. Not that I expected it to be, but still...

"I mean, I've been trying to get a hold of you all day!" I blurted.

"I know. I saw the missed calls from this morning. But honestly, Maggie, you were calling mighty early on my day off. I'm no night owl, but I usually don't answer my phone before noon."

I sighed, closed my eyes, and rubbed between my eyebrows with two pinched fingers.

"I know it was a little early, but... but... I needed to talk to you."

"What about?"

He sounded so innocent, but hadn't I been specific enough in my voice mails? I'd laid it all out for him. How could he not know what I wanted to talk to him about?

"Frank, Helga and I drove over to your house this morning."

I decided to say as little as possible at first, in order to give Frank plenty of rope to hang himself.

"Oh... um... really?"

Hadn't he listened to my voice mail?

"Yes, really. Do you have something to tell me?"

"About?"

"About? *About?* About the empty house where you used to live!"

There was no disguising my astonishment at having to spell this out for him. He was going to make me drag him all the way through this entire conversation. Lovely.

"Oh. That."

"Yes. That!" I wasn't going to have much patience for this. In fact, most of my patience was already gone. And the rest of it was following right behind.

"I, uh, I had to move."

"Apparently." I wasn't going to make this easier on him, so I maintained my heightened level of offense and said as little as possible.

"The landlord told me that the bedbug situation he had with the last tenant before me had come back. I decided to just move ASAP, and he let me out of my lease."

Bedbugs? Ugh. If that were true, I'd have to think twice about letting Frank sit on my couch until I was sure his fabrics and clothing were all safe. Bedbugs. *Gross.*

"Wait," I said, as I thought about this a little longer. "How would the landlord know about a new infestation? You're renting a single family home. If you were in an apartment building, then maybe that would make sense."

"Well, sweetie, unbeknownst to me, he's had this problem off and on at this property but never told me."

"Well, that seems a little bit... illegal."

"You have no idea."

"How long have you known this?"

"Just two days ago he told me. I told him I was hiring a moving company ASAP, and that I wasn't going to sue him for breach of contract as long as he paid my moving expenses."

I was feeling a little itchy around the back of my neck. I kept thinking of those bedbugs.

"You're grossing me out, Frank."

"Sorry. But imagine how I felt! I hired the first company listed in the phone book and was out of there in a flash. It still gives me the creeps to think about it."

I had so many questions right now that I didn't know which one to ask first. My hesitation gave Frank the opportunity to keep talking, which was all right with me. I didn't really feel I had much to add to the conversation, stunned as I was about, well, everything.

"Anyway, I found a lovely place just outside of town. Smaller than the house, but beggars can't be choosers, right?"

"Y-yeah, yes, right. Glad you found something so fast."

"Well, it's not the best area of town, but it's just a little less nice than where I was. The old landlord said he'd give me back my whole security deposit, and the new landlord is all right with waiting for it at his end. I had my old landlord give him a call to explain that everything was his fault."

"Oh, that must have been helpful," I said quietly, mulling over everything I was hearing and trying to fit it into the odd-shaped mental box I had for stuff like this: stuff that wasn't adding up right.

"It was. You probably know yourself that landlords get suspicious when a prospective tenant needs to move in in a hurry."

He was right about that. Landlords could sniff out a lying statement about needing to move fast like a bloodhound. If Frank's ex-landlord had really been accommodating about talking to his new landlord, then he probably hadn't had any trouble getting a new lease. *A new lease on life*, I thought, with very little irony or humor.

"Uh-huh," I said, still letting my mind swirl with various other explanations that might have come out of Frank's mouth. What was that they said about Occam's razor? Was this indeed the simplest, most straightforward explanation? Anybody's guess. I would simply let it play out.

I decided not to hound Frank anymore on this point. Not now, at least. I wasn't in the mood to deal with him or to second-guess every little thing he was telling me. There would be plenty of time for that later. For now, I had this urge to talk to Alice, if only to get her version of events about going to Frank's house this morning. I could see both sides of this one, and right now neither side was one I wanted to back in a race. I secretly wished I didn't have Seth's negative views of Frank in my head. They were clouding my perception of everything Frank was telling me.

"Frank, listen, I feel like crap right now. I got up way too early this morning, and I took a nap when I got home a few hours ago and now I'm paying for it."

"How do you have to pay for taking a nap?"

I'd forgotten that Frank wouldn't know why I hated taking naps.

"I hate naps. I wake up disoriented and feel ten times worse than before I took the nap."

"Then why did you take it?"

"I couldn't keep my eyes open. It was either give in and take the nap or listen to the television ramble on with some stupid show in the background while I vegged out. I picked the nap. Still not sure that was the right choice."

"Sorry to hear it. Go wake up then, and we can talk later. Want to get together for dinner?"

I knew any assent to a dinner date would have me scrutinizing every word Frank said, every movement he made, but I also knew that, right now, that was precisely the kind of information I wanted from Frank. The kind of information he'd never give me willingly but that I could glean for myself just by observing. And, I was really good at observing when I wanted to be. Heck, that's what I got paid for, though it was usually nitpicking words on paper and not people across the table from me. Potato, potahto.

"Sure. I should have my act together by then and not feel like a piece of shit, like I do now."

"Great! I'll pick you up around six then?"

"That'll work. Thanks."

He ended the call and I brought the phone away from my ear. Now what? Should I call Alice? Should I contact Helga to see what bits of gossip or other information she had stumbled across since she'd dropped me off earlier? I was curious to hear just why Alice was skulking around Frank's house—correction: Frank's *former* house—this morning. I didn't usually believe in coincidences, so there had to be some sort of connection between her and Frank that I had been previously unaware of. And the fact that Frank hadn't mentioned knowing Alice separately from any connection to me gave me pause now, too. Yes, I'd have to find out what was going on. And asking first Alice, and then Frank would give me the opportunity to hear both of their stories. I could compare notes if I talked to Alice now and then had dinner with Frank later.

I picked up my phone again and swiped around to Alice's number, and she picked up on the second ring.

CHAPTER 22

I'M NOT ENTIRELY SURE WHY I'M EVEN TALKING TO YOU," Alice said. "It's not like I owe you any explanations about anything I do or say."

She sounded clipped. This was a far cry from her needing me as a friend such a short time ago. I didn't like the change. Not one bit.

"I know. I'm sorry about that. I just have to know why you were walking around my boyfriend's house this morning. I had no idea you knew Frank."

"I didn't. I mean, I don't. I still don't. Except, you know, through you. I doubt I've spoken more than a dozen words to the man directly."

This answer vexed me, too. And it made Alice seem like a stalker or something, if she was peeking in his windows but hadn't ever talked to him.

"Then, why? Don't torture me like this. I just need to know. I'm not sure who to trust at the moment."

"I have no idea if you can trust Frank or not, but I'm telling you the truth, Maggie. I have a very good reason for being outside that house this morning. Probably a better one than you do, if you want to know the truth."

Okay, that hurt. But perhaps she was right. I'd need to hear her out to assess that, though.

"Go on. I'm listening."

"I'm moving."

"What?"

"I said, I'm moving. Out of our house."

"Out of the house you owned with Allen?"

"What other house would I be moving out of?" She tried a small, quirky smile and I smiled in return.

"Yeah, I guess that's obvious. You got me there."

"Anyway, I'm desperate to get out of my house and into another one, preferably as far from our old house as I can get and still live in Brighton."

"Why?" I couldn't imagine that she had any qualms about living in the house because of too many fond, misty memories of her years with Allen. It had to be some other reason.

"People. It's the people. The neighbors. They're hassling me."

"What do you mean, hassling you? About what?"

"About Allen. They're all convinced I killed him. And they're starting to make my life a living hell."

I was appalled. "How so?"

"It started small. People parking in my usual spot out in front of the house, since we only have on-street parking on our block. Then it was taking mail out of my mailbox."

"That's a federal offense."

"Well, try proving someone actually did it and then see what happens. They're taking bills—utilities, mortgage—and I've missed some payments and now I'm even getting shut-off notices."

"Good grief. But still, how can you be sure it's all tied to Allen's death?"

"Because that's when it started. Couple it with neighbors who used to be nice no longer speaking to me or contacting me for anything and you have more than just a slightly awkward situation. Now it's turned into throwing rotten eggs on the front porch and playing loud music at all hours."

"Oh, Alice, I'm so sorry." I wasn't entirely sure all this could be traced to people thinking she'd murdered Allen, but it did sound like she had a few vandals in her neighborhood. In the back of my mind, though, I kept thinking of the trouble someone—maybe Alice—had caused Seth.

"And maybe that would have been all right," she continued, "if that's all it was. But yesterday someone keyed my driver's side door and painted 'MURDERER' on my windshield."

"Ugh."

"You have no idea. That was the last straw. Not only do I feel unwelcome there, now I feel unsafe."

"I guess I can't blame you for that. Nobody should feel unsafe in their own home."

"So, yesterday I contacted a real estate agent in town. I told the woman on the phone that I had to move as soon as humanly possible. She reminded me that choosing and closing on a house typically takes a few months, and I got totally discouraged about that. I can't imagine how bad things would get in that house of mine if I had to stay there a few more months. So, when I told her the situation, she agreed that I should get out as soon as possible. She suggested I rent for now, and she gave me a list of a few places in my price range. Places that were already empty and that would take a month-to-month lease so I wouldn't be stuck in there a full year if I wanted to own instead. And—"

I saw where she was going with this. "And Frank's empty house was on that list."

"Yeah. I checked out a few of the addresses she gave me yesterday afternoon but I didn't get to all of them. Plus, I hadn't found any that really tickled my fancy, so I figured I'd get an early start and keep looking today. This morning."

"Early this morning."

"Yes, very early this morning."

"*Incredibly* early this morning."

Alice chuckled. Perhaps there was a bit of this friendship left to salvage. But, of course, it would all depend on whether or not she was telling me the truth. And whether she had meant to get Seth thrown in jail. And I thought maybe I wouldn't know some of that for sure until after I'd had dinner with Frank, and maybe after I had talked to a few real estate agents to check out her story. That seemed a bit stalker-ish, but if I wasn't convinced after tonight's dinner with Frank, I would definitely go that far in order to get a few good answers. I couldn't just let this situation fester, with a friend and a boyfriend both in some sort of truth-limbo with me.

"Alice," I said, "listen. I gotta go and get a few things done around here. I'm sorry you have to move—or, at least, that you *feel* you have to move—and that I doubted your motives in going to Frank's house early this morning—"

"Very early this morning."

"*Incredibly* early this morning," I repeated and laughed out loud. "Yeah, of course. Incredibly early this morning. Anyway, forgive me the suspicion. It was early—"

"Incredibly early."

I snorted. "Incredibly early, and I'm not sure I was thinking all that straight. You gotta admit, it looked kind of weird to see one of my friends looking in the windows of my boyfriend's house—especially since I had no idea you knew each other or that you even knew where he lived."

"Oh, I totally get why you felt that way. I'm sure I would have made the same assumptions. I'm just sorry I can't offer any better explanations about why Frank's house is empty."

"Oh, that part I already know. I talked to Frank a little while ago. Bedbugs."

"Wait... what?"

"He said he had bedbugs in his place, a recurrence from a previous tenant. His landlord not only gave him permission to move out but helped him find a new place."

I realized what I'd said as soon as it was out of my mouth.

"Wait. *What?*" Alice repeated.

"Oh, I'm sorry, Alice! I don't mean to imply that you'd be moving into a rat hole."

"Well, I hadn't said I was going to take the place just yet. But the real estate agent hadn't mentioned anything about the place having bedbugs. I certainly hope that's the sort of thing they'd mention—or at least deal with before saying the place is available for rent!"

I was confused. "They told you it was for rent already?"

"That's precisely why I looked at the place! I specifically asked them to give me a list of places that were currently available, and I was clear that I needed to move sooner rather than later. They totally understood my situation."

"Could have just been a slip-up. Or maybe they're already dealing with the bedbug issue and it'll be ready fast."

"Have you ever had to deal with bedbugs?" Alice asked. She wrinkled her nose in disgust.

"No, not really. Why? Is it bad? Does it take a lot of time?"

"Allen and I used to rent a place in the town where we lived before this one. The guy in the upstairs apartment introduced bedbugs and the whole building got infested before the landlord figured it out. It was a nightmare to deal with. We all had to subject our places to these multiple treatments by the pest control guys. They had to take off all the outlet covers to spray inside, and they had to check every nook and cranny of every piece of furniture. Our dressers, our end tables, our couches, our kitchen cabinets. Everywhere. Plus, we had to throw every piece of clothing and fabric into the dryer on high heat to kill off the eggs. It was a—"

"A nightmare," I finished for her. "It sounds like a *complete* nightmare."

I shuddered. And suddenly every spot on my scalp itched. I was way too suggestible about things like bug infestations. And I was going to go check my own bed and mattress as soon as I got off the phone with Alice.

"Anyway, it's not the sort of thing you can easily correct in a day, or even a week. It takes multiple treatments spaced out over the course of several weeks in order to get rid of them. Even a small infestation of a few bugs needs to be taken really seriously so it doesn't spread."

I was starting to get the picture. And it wasn't a pretty one, even if it wasn't about bedbugs.

"I see."

"I don't mean to say Frank is lying, though. Oh, Maggie, I'm sorry. I guess that's exactly what it sounded like, didn't it?"

"No, it's okay. There could be some pieces of this puzzle that I'm missing right now. I'm having dinner with Frank later, so I plan to ask him a few questions about all this. Something's just not adding up."

Alice sighed. "I'm sorry, Maggie. Really. Maybe you misunderstood the situation, or maybe the real estate agent just accidentally included this address in my list without realizing it really wouldn't be available fast enough for me."

"Yeah, that's true. Well, we'll see what Frank says. Later."

She sighed again. "I'll let you get back to what you were doing then. I'm sorry about any misunderstanding this morning. You've been a really good friend to me just when I needed it, so I really don't want to jeopardize that in any way. If there's anything else I can do for you, don't hesitate to let me know. Okay?"

Suddenly I felt terrible that I'd let this conversation be all about me, when Alice was the one who felt she could no longer live in her own home! I had it easy compared to her. At least my neighbors weren't egging my front door or keying my car. They might object to Vlad's occasional barking, but that was so infrequent that they probably tended to forget I even had a dog in the first place.

I'd have to find a way to ask her about the investigation—about Seth.

"Alice, no, I'm the one who's sorry. You're stuck looking for a new place to live, right when you're still reeling from losing a husband and dealing with the fallout from his murder. I apologize for dumping any of this on you right now."

"It's okay, Maggie. Seriously."

"Let's do coffee sometime soon then. Okay? My treat."

It felt like a lame offer, considering, but it might just be a start.

"Okay, yes. Let's. I might need something normal like a little time at the coffee shop. Thanks."

There were still things I needed to know. I ended the call and sat there a moment, staring at my phone, wondering how this entire mess was ever going to be over. I was feeling more uncomfortable about Frank than I had before I'd answered the door. Things just weren't falling into their proper place and I was going to have to put on a stoic face this evening and find a way to engage Frank in normal conversation while I was sniffing out just what was going on. Because, no matter how I looked at this situation, something weird was going on. Something somebody didn't want me to find out. I just hoped that something wasn't murder. And that somebody wasn't Frank.

CHAPTER 23

I WAS USUALLY THE KIND OF WOMAN WHO ADORED being taken out to dinner. I hated cooking—always had—and loved when someone else not only did the cooking but also cleaned up after me. I'd come home from a lovely evening to a clean kitchen and clean dishes, after having eaten a meal a thousand times better than anything I could have made for myself at home. So, the fact that I was now dreading a dinner out—with someone I had until recently loved being alone with—well, that told me quite a bit about how things could change, and how fast. I knew, though, that I had to maintain a sense of cheerfulness at some base level throughout this dinner, so that I could glean as much information from Frank as possible before he clammed up on me. I'd been terse with him on the phone earlier and more than a little cranky. So I could probably get away with less cheerfulness than usual. But I couldn't sound too suspicious or my plan to piece all of this together on my own was going to fall apart fast. And right now, it was all I had going for me. I was taking a chance assuming Alice had been telling the truth, but her story about being harassed in her current neighborhood held a distinct ring of truth. On the other hand, Frank's explanation about bedbugs in his house, although certainly plausible for a rental unit, felt like a bit of a stretch. Occam's razor was apparently a double-edged blade in this case.

I walked into the Rusty Nail seafood restaurant a few minutes before six o'clock, having texted Frank earlier to tell him we could just meet there instead of having him pick me up. The thought of an awkward car ride over here, in the darkening atmosphere of his car, not being able to face each other properly, with Frank trying to pay attention to his driving, seemed like too much for me to handle today. Plus, the ride home together would be excruciating if things went south at dinner. Dinner itself would be enough awkwardness for one day.

A quick glance around the foyer showed me more people waiting for a table than I had expected, but no sign of Frank. He wasn't in the habit of being early for get-togethers, so it didn't surprise me that he wasn't here yet. Still, waiting was going to be the death of me. The last thing I needed was more time to mull over everything that had happened today. I shifted my weight to my other foot, sighed, and fished for my phone out of my purse. Took me a bit longer to find it than usual, since I had more junk in this blasted purse than ever, but finally I grabbed it and brought it out of the purse, which I hoisted back onto my right shoulder.

Two swipes and I was checking my notifications on Facebook. What better way to mindlessly pass more time without having to think too much about an unpleasant—

"Maggie!"

There he was. Might as well get this uncomfortable evening over with.

He was coming straight at me, more eagerly and faster than I'd anticipated. Or was I just more sensitive to his every movement today? It felt like when we had first started dating—that internal scrutiny of every movement, every noise and word—only in reverse. In the beginning of the relationship, I was of course a bit giddy at all these things and loved to overanalyze each one with Helga, or anyone else who would listen to me gush about how wonderful Frank was. Now that same scrutiny felt a lot less exciting. And if I ever sat with Helga to scrutinize or overthink it, it wasn't going to be nearly as much fun anymore. Now it was going to involve wondering if Frank had a few tricks up his sleeve that he was purposely keeping from me. I hated this sort of relational garbage. Going through it in public, at a restaurant, was going to be one of my least favorite activities today. Or this week. Or even this month.

"Hi," I said weakly as he came up to me and lightly touched my elbow. He leaned over to kiss me and I subtly turned and offered him my cheek instead. He didn't seem fazed by this and pecked me on the cheek in an almost charming way.

"I called ahead and made sure they reserved a table for us," he said cheerily. In normal circumstances, it would have been a delight to start a date like this with Frank. Today, it was a little less delightful.

"Oh good," I said, almost meaning it.

We were shown to our table, bypassing several small groups of people waiting for tables who had obviously not reserved one in advance. We were seated at a lovely little booth toward the back, and I slid in to my side without waiting for Frank to do something chivalrous like pull out my chair for me. Since it was a booth, that wasn't going to happen anyway. He slid in to his side and sighed. The waitress handed us each a menu and asked for our drink order. I needed to stay sharp, so even though my emotions desperately wanted a rum and diet cola, heavy on that rum, please, I ordered just the diet cola and smiled wanly. Frank ordered a gin and tonic—his usual if he was drinking alcohol—and the waitress left us alone.

"Have you ever eaten here?" Frank asked. It was a good, neutral thing to say to start us off, so I let my guard down and relaxed.

"No, actually, I haven't. Been meaning to, but I just never found the opportunity." I glanced around the dining room, hoping to soak up some of the upbeat social vibe floating around me.

"I've heard the food's great," Frank said. "I haven't eaten here yet either, so we can christen it together." He smiled widely, and again, if it had been any other normal date night, I wouldn't have thought twice about that smile. But everything with Frank was now going to seem forced. I was going to run everything he said, everything he did, through a big filter of skepticism. I hated being like this—it reminded me too much of the days of my separation from George when I'd caught him cheating and then had to second-guess everything that happened and everywhere he went, or everywhere he said he went.

I disliked being put in that position a second time in my life. I thought I had chosen more wisely than that. Fool me once.

I HAD A HORRIBLE FLASHBACK to the night I got sick after we'd had dinner out together, so I figured I'd protect myself this time by ordering the very same food Frank did. That way, if there was someone back in the kitchen poisoning our food, trying to kill me, they might miss and kill Frank instead. Part of me wouldn't have minded that so much right now. I wasn't happy about the bedbug explanation, but I certainly wasn't going to call him on it in the middle of a public place like this. Not my style. And I suspected Frank knew that already. Perhaps that was precisely why he had chosen a dinner out. Certainly, if he had nothing to hide and his story was legitimate, he would have been more sensitive to the two of us eating out at a sit-down restaurant again so soon after the fiasco of last time. Then again, Frank was a fairly typical guy, so maybe he was just clueless. Not as clueless as George, maybe, but still clueless about things like decorum and tact.

I hadn't really seen that sort of thing from Frank, but deep down, how much did I really know about him? Not nearly as much as I wished I knew.

So, even though I really didn't like shrimp—something about the chewy texture—I ordered the shrimp scampi, as Frank had done, and I made myself eat it as if it were also my favorite food. I tried to think back to whether I had ever expressed my abject distaste for shrimp to Frank, but I couldn't remember it coming up in conversation before. I ate it fast, hoping to get past the texture and out the other side of this meal before I felt ill about it, and I said an eager yes to dessert when offered by the waiter as we finished up our entrées. I needed something to get the lingering aftertaste of shrimp out of my mouth.

"I'll have a slice of cheesecake," Frank said, seeming happy to see me ordering dessert. I had become one of those middle-aged females who never order dessert in a restaurant, who show amazing restraint by saying no to the cake cart—and who keep a private stash of Oreos in their kitchen cabinets behind the basil and oregano where no one would think to look for them. Yes, I was a sweets hypocrite, and I didn't even feel bad about it.

So, I was quite happy to hear Frank order dessert first, and to hear him order something I adored: cheesecake. I ordered my own slice, and some coffee, and sighed happily as the entrée plates were taken away so I wouldn't have to see the remains of my shrimp scampi staring at me on the table.

"I'm so glad you ordered dessert for a change," Frank started, but then frowned as he looked into my eyes. I felt a little bit choked up but chalked it up to nerves. Now we were going to have to start a conversation that would likely have to include those disgusting bedbugs, plus a few other things besides his empty house.

"Are you okay, Maggie?" I opened my mouth to answer, only to find that suddenly I was having trouble breathing. I blinked a few times to get rid of the tears I felt welling up in my eyes and brought my hands up to my throat, which now felt as if someone was squeezing it tight.

"I... I... I don't think so—" I managed to squeak out before my throat really began to tighten up. "Can't.. breathe..." I added and stood up, starting to panic. Frank also stood, so fast that his chair fell backwards onto the floor, bringing attention to us from all across the restaurant.

"She's—she's choking!" Frank said out loud, turning to look for someone to help. Even amid my rising panic at barely being able to breathe, I was also searching Frank's demeanor and behavior to see if it was in any way suspicious. Wow, I really had some major trust issues if I was in the middle of suffocating and still found brain space to nitpick Frank's facial features and gestures.

"Can't—breathe!" I gasped, so quietly I could barely hear it myself.

The waiter had come over, along with the maître d', and they were both standing around me with their mouths hanging open. But nobody was actually *doing* anything, for what seemed like hours. It was probably only about ten or fifteen seconds, though. Hard to tell, from my limited perspective.

Frank turned to the rest of the patrons in the restaurant and threw his hands into the air, waving them wildly. "She can't breathe! Somebody help us!"

I was starting to see flashes of white in my field of vision and my hearing got alternately sharp and focused and fuzzy and confused. From one corner of my sight I caught someone rushing to my side with her purse. She was looking at me with a face full of worry, but she had her free hand stuffed inside her purse, rummaging around for something I couldn't quite see.

Frank saw her, too. "What are you doing?" He seemed wary, but it was hard for me to tell. I saw bigger flashes of white light and was sure I would keel over any second. I fleetingly hoped I didn't hit my head on a table on the way down, and I was secretly relieved I hadn't worn a skirt. Knowing me, I'd land on the ground with my skirt up over my head.

Just as I was picturing that ungraceful image of myself, I saw this strange woman yank her hand out of her purse with something that looked like a thermometer or a pen or pencil or something. I had been assuming she was looking for her phone—she had that universal woman's look of frustration at her own messy purse, which even I could ascertain from within my precarious consciousness— and was going to produce her cell phone to call for help. It was as she wielded that pencil-like thing that I realized Frank would have gotten his own phone out to call for help, if the management hadn't done it already. I surprised myself at how lucid some of my thoughts were, even as I felt myself fading into unconsciousness, and later I would ask myself why I hadn't been wondering who had poisoned me a second time, in a second restaurant, when I was again alone with my boyfriend—the one I didn't really trust anymore.

For now, though, all that mattered was that this stranger was coming at me with what now appeared to be a sharp object, wielding it like a kitchen knife in a bad domestic squabble, and I was at her mercy because I could no longer control any body movements and was rapidly careening toward that floor, missing the edge of the table by mere inches.

CHAPTER 24

YOU WERE LUCKY," I HEARD FRANK SAYING as I was helped into the seat I'd been sitting in a little while ago, anticipating a lovely cheesecake for dessert.

"What?" I wasn't processing information at the correct speed just yet, despite being conscious again and sitting on a chair like a normal adult human being. At the very least, I didn't *feel* lucky. "How... how was I lucky, exactly?" I didn't bother to try to keep the snark out of my voice. Easy for Frank to say how lucky I was. He wasn't the one who felt like crap.

"Some nice woman at the next table was carrying an EpiPen."

"EpiPen?" I had a vague understanding of what an EpiPen was, but right about now I wasn't existing on the highest plane of coherence so it wasn't clicking in right.

"Yeah, an EpiPen. You use them for full-blown allergic reactions. Like the one you just had."

"But I'm not allergic to anything," I protested, taking a few deep breaths because they felt really good after the constricted air passages I'd had only a few moments earlier.

"Well," said the woman I vaguely recognized as the one who

had been leaning over me with what I now realized was that EpiPen just before I passed out. "Well," she continued, "you may not have been allergic to something before, but people do develop allergies later in life."

She smiled, which might have felt more helpful if she hadn't just referred to me as being "later in life." Then again, I felt a *lot* later in life at the moment than I'd felt when I came into the restaurant an hour ago.

"What do you think it was?" I asked, as if she might actually know.

"What did you have for dinner?" she asked, still smiling.

"Shrimp scampi."

She exchanged a knowing glance with Frank and nodded. "Shrimp. A relatively common food allergy—shellfish—as far as food allergies go. And you weren't allergic before?"

"Not—not that I know of, but I don't really like shrimp so I can't remember the last time I even ate it. Could have been years ago."

"What?" Frank said, leaning forward to take my hand, which I now realized felt clammy—no seafood pun intended—and sweaty. He held onto it tightly anyway. "You don't like shrimp?"

"No, I hate it. It's gross."

"Then, then why did you order it?" He looked genuinely confused, so I decided on the spur of the moment to fib a little bit. This was too public a place, with too many people around me, to say why I had really ordered the shrimp scampi. A little white lie wasn't going to hurt me. Well, wasn't going to hurt me any more than eating that shrimp scampi had hurt me.

"I wanted to order what you ordered. Wanted to learn to like more things that you like."

The woman with the EpiPen sighed, whispering a quaint little "aww" in our direction. The man behind her, whom I could only assume was her husband, also sighed. I thought I heard the waiter and the maître d', who were huddled around me like I was a quarterback in the big game, make appropriate approving noises, too.

But when I looked at Frank, he was just frowning. I couldn't decide if he looked confused or disapproving. Maybe a little of both.

But either way, he certainly wasn't buying whatever I was trying to sell. Not like the rest of the folks around us. He knew there was a lot more to what I had just said. We'd only been dating for a few months, sure, but I wasn't the kind of woman to change my food preferences, or anything else, just to please a man. I'd had enough of that sort of ridiculous behavior with George back when I was young and foolish. There was no way I was going to become *old* and foolish.

And Frank knew it. It was clear that once we were outside alone, where we could talk without all these people around us, he was going to press me on my supposed reason for eating the shrimp scampi. I had to think fast so I knew whether I would tell him the truth then or continue to lie my way through this. I had a feeling I would tell the truth. I wanted to get to the bottom of all this, and truth was the only way forward. I hoped Frank would give me truth in return.

"I... I think I feel a little better," I said, trying to sound convincing. Whether or not I was allergic to shellfish, the last place I wanted to be right now was in a seafood restaurant, surrounded by strangers, when I didn't feel all that great. "I think I'd like to go home and just go to bed. I'm... tired."

Now everyone was nodding their approval. I was relieved that I wasn't going to have to talk anyone into letting me leave.

"But maybe," said the EpiPen woman, "you should go to the emergency room and be checked out. In case there's something else going on here. I could be wrong about the allergy thing."

The last thing I wanted was apparently *not* the seafood restaurant, but rather the hospital emergency room. We'd be stuck there half the night just so some doctor could tell me that, lo and behold, I'm allergic to shellfish.

"Maybe I'll do that tomorrow," I said, trying to smile and look as cheerfully healthy as I could. "I'm really just tired right now. Wiped out. Would love to go home, get into my jammies, and curl up on the sofa." Another smile for good measure.

"After the emergency room. That would be my advice," the EpiPen woman said again.

"Okay, maybe you're right," I conceded, though I didn't really mean it. After all, I could leave the restaurant and go to my car and drive anywhere after I left here. There was no way she'd know whether I went to the emergency room or straight home to be with my dog.

The only person who would know for sure would be Frank, unless I could manage to talk him into going home himself instead of escorting me to the emergency room. And when I glanced over at him and saw the look on his face, I realized just how impossible that was going to be. I was either going to have to come clean about my misgivings concerning him or I was going to spend the night in the hospital for a stupid seafood allergy. Either way, I wasn't looking forward to leaving, even though staying here was rapidly becoming uncomfortable, too. Damned if I do, damned if I don't.

"Maggie," said Frank, still frowning, "will you let me drive you to the hospital? I think you need to go. I agree with this nice woman. She obviously knows a little bit about this sort of thing," he said, now pointing to the EpiPen she was still clutching in her hand. She looked at Frank and then turned to me and nodded seriously. I felt like a wayward child with a skinned knee.

"I do. Or, at least, I know enough to know there's a lot to know and you should be checked out by a doctor. Sooner rather than later."

I was starting to agree with them, but for all sorts of different reasons. Yes, I should get checked out by a doctor, but I wasn't so sure I agreed that it had to be immediately. I could stop at a local pharmacy on my way home and pick up an EpiPen on my own, couldn't I? Then I'd be safe at home. I could search the internet for all sorts of information on seafood allergies and EpiPens and everything else I probably didn't need to know. It might even be fun. Certainly more fun than what was going on right now.

"I can just pick up one of those things"—I waved at her EpiPen—"on my way home and then I should be fine. I don't even have any shellfish in the house. I really hate the stuff."

Frank frowned.

"Sorry, Frank. I do. I hate it. All of it. Which is probably why I didn't realize I was allergic."

The woman was now shaking her head. "You can't just pick up an EpiPen at the store. You could get some Benadryl. That could help in a pinch if you have a delayed reaction. But an EpiPen needs a prescription. Which is why you should be seen by a doctor. You might feel decent now, but what if you get home and continue to have some constriction of the throat—and you're alone and without an EpiPen?"

Now she was acting like she was my mother. And I already had a perfectly competent one of those, thank you very much. I made a mental note not to mention this to my mother for a while.

But now everyone was frowning at me. I'd never felt so judged in all my life. Well, except that time I got a perm in eighth grade and it ended up going frizzy on me and then my mom accidentally cut it into a mullet when she tried to fix it for me. That was one of the few times she really wasn't very competent. And it was the last time I let her cut my hair, too.

"Fine! I said, unable to take it any longer. "Fine! I'll go to the stupid emergency room!"

Frank smiled but raised one eyebrow in question.

"And I'll let you drive me there, Frank."

He smiled again.

"As long as you bring me back here afterward so I can get my car and drive myself home."

He smiled—and nodded. "You've got a deal. Now, Miss Smarty Pants, go get your purse. And your coat. We're busting out of this Popsicle stand."

I was reasonably certain it was going to be a long, long night.

CHAPTER 25

MOM, I SWEAR IF YOU DIDN'T HAVE BAD LUCK, you wouldn't have any luck at all."

"Thanks," I said from my comfortable spot on the sofa, Vlad tucked up next to me and enjoying his reprieve from a life of hard work and toil that mainly consisted of yipping at invisible adversaries and eating anything dropped onto the floor within his little doggy reach. I'd slept badly last night in the bed—what little time I spent there after leaving the hospital around four o'clock in the morning—and was grateful to give up around seven thirty to come out here to the sofa with my afghan, my bed pillow, and the TV remote. Seth had gotten up sometime after that point but I wasn't entirely sure when since I had been dipping in and out of a sleepy-conscious state since then myself. He hadn't even realized I had been gone most of the night and had quietly endured my story of high adventure (and seafood allergies) because I had been clear in the beginning that it was definitely an allergy and not another poisoning. But, even with the doctor's backup, I could sense the wariness in Seth's demeanor. He might not know enough to con-firm the doctor's diagnosis, but he knew a suspicious boyfriend of his mother's when he heard enough stories. And this was just another story in the ever-widening net that was entrapping poor Frank in the growing hatred of my two children.

"How are you feeling now? Can I get you anything?" His concern was touching, but I really couldn't think much about food right now. "Maybe just some ice water, sweetie. Is that okay?"

He shrugged and got up from the recliner. "Mom, really. A glass of ice water might be too much work? How much of a slacker do you think I am, exactly?" He grinned, and I smiled back. I was glad he hadn't gone back to his apartment yet. Introvert though I was, the company of my adult kids was something I always craved. This place would have felt mighty lonely if I were stuck here alone with just Vlad. No offense meant to dear little Vlad, of course, but sometimes a human being just wants human interaction and not dog spit all over her face.

Seth returned with the ice water and put it on the end table next to my end of the sofa. Vlad raised his head long enough to sniff for any aroma of food and, sensing none, dropped his chin back onto the couch cushions and let out a little snorting doggy sigh. *Rough life, buddy!*

"Didn't Grandpa have an allergy to shellfish?" Seth asked as he sat back down in the recliner.

"My dad? No. That was your paternal grand*mother*. Not genetically related to me."

"Oh, yeah. I didn't really think about that. Not related to you."

I sipped the ice water and let it slide down my throat. Felt good and soothing—and safe. I tried not to think about how it had felt to sense my throat slowly closing up last night, unsure what to do about it and thinking just before I blacked out that I might actually be dying. I could see why that other woman carried her EpiPen with her. I was certainly going to start carrying mine around with me at all times. Of course, the thought of trying to dig it out of the bottomless purse—and during an emergency, no less—felt a little daunting. I was going to have to find a way to straighten up that purse and put that EpiPen in an easy-to-find a spot inside the front of the purse. Maybe I would start carrying one of those gawd-awful purses with the individual pockets and zippered compartments for every little thing. A slot for every credit card. A little hook for my keys. A zippered section for those small packets of tissues. Another zippered section for coins and pens and sticks of gum. And one section on the outside of the purse for the new guy in town, the epic EpiPen. Oh, and of course, other Velcroed sections for things like Benadryl and ibuprofen and other life-saving Chiclets of modern man. Yes, and the Wonder Purse would also have a lovely adjustable strap and would come in various decorator colors, made of faux pleather and—

"Mom, are you okay?"

Seth's voice cut through my handbag hallucinations.

"What? Oh, yes. I'm fine, Seth. Just vegged out there for a minute. That's all."

"You were saying something about a new purse. Since when do you daydream about new purses?"

I snorted. "Since I now have to carry around life-saving devices and drugs in them, and might need to find them at the drop of a hat in an emergency. That's when."

"Right." It was clear he didn't like the idea of me being left alone with the purses he'd seen me carry over the years, trying to find such life-saving devices in a hurry.

"Seth, I'll be fine. Plenty of people have allergies like this. I don't even like shellfish, so this allergy should be fairly easy to manage. I'll just stay away from seafood restaurants. And, you know, ask about shared oil fryers and such whenever I go somewhere that serves shellfish. It's what Grandma Roberts used to do and it worked quite well for her."

He nodded, but he didn't look convinced. I tried to feel his frowning disapproval as a sort of love and concern rather than abject judgment and shaming. With adult children, it was hard to tell the difference sometimes, though. This was one of those times.

"But you'll be careful, right?"

I nodded, closing my eyes. "Yes, Seth. I'll be careful. I'll be painfully careful and will maintain a self-vigilance at all times. Okay?" I smiled sweetly, hoping to end this conversation so I could get back to mindless daydreaming about things other than purses and EpiPens.

"Okay, Mom. As long as you promise."

He got up from the recliner and headed into the kitchen. His offer to get me something was really just a thin disguise for his own bottomless pit of a stomach. I had no good sense of mealtimes today and hadn't thought to offer him anything myself. Sometimes a mom had to let her grown kids fend for themselves, even if it meant letting them forage in her fridge, another bottomless pit of fear and doom, much like my purses and Seth's stomach. God only knew what was buried at the back of that fridge that needed to be dealt with. But Seth could take care of himself in my kitchen. He'd become quite used to the rules of Mom's fridge: Grab things from the front. Avoid anything beyond the containers you can reach without pulling something forward from behind another container. I had a feeling his own fridge in his apartment looked similar. It was likely a genetic trait I'd passed down to him.

"Mom?" he called from the kitchen.

"The bread's still in the cupboard above the coffee maker."

"No, it's not that," he called again, and I heard cabinets being opened and closed. "It's about Frank."

"Yeah?" I tried to sound like I had no idea where this conversation was heading, but I knew quite well what was coming. Even though I didn't look forward to it, I was going to have to let it happen.

"Are you going to keep seeing him? After... everything?"

"Seth, nothing has changed after last night. This was a simple allergic reaction that would have happened whether Frank was there or not. I thought I made that perfectly clear."

"You did. I know. I know. But what about all the other stuff? It's not like he's the only guy on the planet, you know. You're not that hard up, are you?"

Ah, a mother loved nothing more than discussing her love life and her prospects for dating a normal guy with her grown son. This was just lovely.

"Seth."

"You know what I mean. You don't have to keep dating him just because you're dating him now. You can end this at any time."

"Yes, Seth, thanks. I know that already. But maybe I don't want to end this right now."

I wasn't sure why I was playing devil's advocate with myself against Seth. Most of me actually agreed with him. I would have been perfectly happy to say a quick *sayonara* to Frank and to move on with my life. Even if he had a notarized statement of his own innocence in this matter, I was getting so weary of having to deal with other people's drama, including his. Plus, bedbugs are just gross, and the thought that he was going to have to deal with all of his upholstery and linens and clothing now made me a little bit sick to my stomach. That wasn't his fault, I knew, but it was just another layer of dealing with everything I didn't want to deal with. I could control a little bit more of my life if I banished the likes of Frank.

I wished we had been able to talk about these things last night. It was the primary reason I had said yes to his offer of a dinner out, and it hadn't happened. While we'd been sitting in the emergency room last night, waiting for me to be called back, I considered bringing up the topic of Alice and also Allen's murder. There was a period of time when the waiting room at the hospital was essentially empty, and we could have had a fairly private conversation. But people were still passing through and hurrying about—such was the inherent nature of an emergency room—that I didn't want to start an awkward, uncomfortable conversation if we'd have to stop at a bad spot and hold our thoughts until I had been seen by the doctor and we were then allowed to leave. And, that had been the right choice at the time. We'd been alternately left alone and then surrounded by people for the many hours we spent there and we would have been interrupted more than once. And so, that important conversation hadn't happened yet.

If it had, perhaps I'd be sitting here with Seth discussing a post-Frank strategy for moving forward. That certainly would have made Seth happy. And Annie. And probably Helga, too, though I wasn't sure where she'd stand with things now that this allergic reaction had happened. She might have a response similar to Seth's—finding a way to continue a "what if?" scenario with Frank and blaming him for something that wasn't his fault. He was just in the wrong place at the wrong time last night, and the timing was such that a lot of people were going to want to blame him anyway. I would have to get used to that reaction. And, hadn't I entertained it for a short while myself last night, on the way to the emergency room? Yes, I had. And although I wasn't proud of it now, it felt organically right at the time. I couldn't blame family and friends for drawing the same knee-jerk reactions to what had happened. It hadn't been all that long since the poisoning that had sent me to that same hospital.

I wondered what Frank was doing today. He hadn't called since dropping me off here at the apartment around four thirty, but with the wonky schedule we'd kept last night, I couldn't blame him, could I? He was probably still asleep at home. I'd wait the rest of the day and see how things played out with him. Despite needing to have That Conversation with him soon, I wasn't eager enough to be the one to call first. I'd let him call me when he was ready. In the meantime, I would spend the time alone relaxing and recharging. I needed some time to sort through actions, reactions, and events of the past few weeks, so I might as well use the enforced downtime to do just that. If Frank didn't call today, I'd have time to breathe—literally—and to do a sort of mental pros-and-cons list regarding Frank.

"Mom?"

I blinked and looked at Seth, who was now back in the living room with a plate and glass. He'd made himself a tuna sandwich and had a tall glass of cold milk. I smiled. Some things never changed. This had been his favorite lunch since he was in fifth grade.

"I see you found lunch all right."

He looked at his plate. "Yeah, thanks. Are you sure I can't get you anything?"

I wrinkled my nose at the thought. "Somehow I'm still not very hungry, sweetie. But thanks for asking. Again."

He frowned at the sandwich and then looked up at me, shocked.

"Oh geez! Mom! Is tuna all right? It's fish. Sort of." He stepped back away from me, and burst out laughing.

"Seth, tuna is a fish. Not sort of a fish. But it's shellfish I'm allergic to. Shrimp. Lobster. Stuff like that. Regular ol' flaky fish is still fine. I'm fine around tuna fish."

He didn't seem convinced. I wondered if he remembered anything at all from high school biology class. Even I knew tuna wasn't in the same category as shellfish. Maybe I hadn't been clear enough about what I was allergic to.

"Are you sure?" he asked tentatively, coming forward again and slipping quietly up to the recliner, as if he was trying to sneak up on me and my allergy and get past us with this potentially harmful lunch.

I laughed. "Yes, Seth, I'm sure. I talked a lot with the doctor last night and got the lowdown on what's allowed and what would probably cause another reaction. Tuna is fine."

He sighed and sunk into the recliner, nearly spilling the milk and letting the sandwich topple off the plate.

"Careful!" I said, and he grinned, putting the glass onto the end table so he could hold the plate with the sandwich on it with two hands. I sat and watched him eat, enjoying just being a normal mom for a few minutes and letting Seth be a normal grown-up kid.

CHAPTER 26

Listen Maggie, I don't want to tax you right now. Are you sure this is all right?"

Frank looked overly concerned, and I wasn't sure how much of it was real and how much of it was a bit of an act for my benefit. That was the problem with situations like this—not that I had a whole lot of experience with situations like this or even knew what "situations like this" meant. You were forever second-guessing someone you should be able to trust implicitly. Things were going to have to change.

"It's fine, Frank. I'm fine. As long as you don't wave a handful of shrimp in my face or anything, I think I can have a normal conversation with you here in my own apartment." I sighed and shifted positions in the recliner, the footrest down, so I could get as comfortable as possible for this escapade we were about to have. I'd purposely made sure I sat in the small recliner—a decidedly one-person piece of furniture—so that Frank wouldn't have an opportunity to sit next to me and snuggle up too close. I wanted some distance—literal distance—in order to maintain some semblance of control over this situation, this entire conversation.

"Oh gosh, no, of course, I wouldn't—" He blushed and smiled. "Ah, I see. You were kidding. Very funny."

I blinked. "Of course I was kidding. You didn't think I was seriously worried about you waving shrimp around my apartment, did you?"

How had I hooked up with a boyfriend who couldn't keep up with my sense of humor? That wasn't even all that funny, and I'd left him in the dust. What was going on here?

"No, no, of course not. I just... well, I'm still a little shaken up about last night. I really didn't like seeing you like that. We were really worried."

"We?"

"Everyone in the restaurant. You know, everyone."

"Right. Well, sorry to scare you. Truly. I was too busy not being able to breathe to notice what everyone else was feeling."

"Naturally. But you're feeling better now?"

"Yeah, I think I'm back to normal. Seth made me some grilled cheese and chicken noodle soup for dinner a little while ago, and that really hit the spot. I hadn't thought I was all that hungry today until he made that for me. Gobbled it right up." I smiled, figuring a little small talk to start us off wouldn't hurt anything.

"Good. Glad you're eating again and feeling on the mend."

He was just far enough away that he couldn't reach over to pat my hand or anything else. And that was fine with me. I wanted to keep a completely clear head while we talked, and that included not being influenced by soothing pats on the knee or comforting hand-clutches. Better not to touch at all until this was all talked out.

"Listen, Frank, we need to talk about a few things. We need to get on the same page about some stuff." I bit my lip before saying anything more obvious. I'd wait to see what he said after each little point, just to give myself time to process whatever responses Frank had for everything I said. One small step for mankind. One giant leap for Maggie Velam.

"I suppose we do. So much has happened lately."

Understatement of the year, buddy, I thought. But I held my tongue and didn't actually say it. We hadn't yet hit the point where I needed to be wholly sarcastic and snippy. We might hit it soon, though. Anybody's guess how this was going to land.

"Yes, a lot. And I'm not so sure we're thinking the same things about those events. Plus, I have to tell you some stuff that happened with Alice the other day. And with Helga."

"Helga?" He frowned. He wasn't overly fond of Helga, and perhaps that should have been a big red flag earlier in the relationship. But I knew Helga was a polarizing person anyway. People either loved her or hated her. She was an extrovert's extrovert, and her brash, blunt nature often got her in trouble. It was the kind of trouble I found hilarious most of the time, though, so she and I had maintained an odd friendship over the years: her working at the desk of the Brighton *Bugle* and me stopping in to give or receive work projects associated with the paper or the small publishing house attached to it. The fact that Frank found her obnoxious wasn't necessarily a deal breaker but it certainly wasn't helping at the moment.

"Yeah, she and I did a little, well, *sleuthing* the other day."

Frank frowned even more. "I seem to remember a story you told me about the last time the two of you went *sleuthing*, as you call it. Didn't end so well, did it?"

"This was different. We were just... curious. About stuff."

"About who, exactly?"

"About Alice. Some stuff just wasn't adding up with her, and Helga and I decided to just, well, follow her last Saturday to see where she was going."

"You followed her?"

"Yeah. In Helga's car." Suddenly it sounded a little more bizarre than it had on the day we'd done it. "Okay, I know that makes us sound like a pair of stalkers, but it wasn't like that. Honest."

He raised an eyebrow. "It wasn't? How wasn't it like that?"

As far as I knew, Frank wasn't exactly friends with Alice, either, and it felt weird to hear him on the verge of defending her. I had anticipated quite a few problems in this conversation, a few spots where he and I would diverge in our interpretation of the events, but this hadn't been one of the spots I'd been worried about. Great. This entire conversation was already headed downhill and I had no idea how to stop it.

"She was acting weird. You know that! She was probably the one who got Seth thrown into jail, for goodness' sake! I needed to know if I could trust her. I thought she was my friend. I wasn't so sure she was anymore!"

I hadn't anticipated needing to defend my actions that day in Helga's car, so this was really throwing me off my game, big time. I had rehearsed the main salient points I had hoped to hit in this conversation and none of this was on the mental map I'd made for myself. Completely uncharted territory here, and not a place I wanted to be. But I would have to work my way backwards from this tangent to get us back to talking about Frank instead of Alice.

Maybe I could just start telling the story and hope Frank would give up and let me talk without questioning my motives. If anybody had unquestioned motives in this whole episode, it was me—not Frank, and not Alice. Time to focus and get back on track, away from Helga's traits or my own reasons for handling Saturday the way I had. The goal was to get Frank to explain himself about a few things. Not to scrutinize me and my choices about Alice.

I sighed and bravely looked Frank right in the eye.

"Frank, to be honest with you, I haven't liked a lot of what I've heard from you—and even from Alice—in the past few days. A lot of things don't add up. I'm not sure what to make of what both of you are saying."

He frowned. "Saying about what, exactly?"

"About what happened that day."

"About what day?"

I sighed, exasperated beyond belief. "*That* day. The day I followed Alice and she somehow led us right to your house. Your *empty* house. You know, the one that supposedly was suddenly overrun by bedbugs."

THE TELL-TALE HEART ATTACK **189**

"Are you saying I don't have bedbugs in that house?"

"Why are you still talking about it in the present tense? As if you still live there? I thought you just moved out." I crossed my arms over my chest and waited for what I was now assuming would be a fib, or an outright lie.

"Maggie, honestly, where is this coming from? These are accusations about strange stuff coming out of left field here."

"It's not that strange, not really. I just don't believe you about the bedbugs."

"Why would I lie about something like that? I had to move. I even gave you my new address. If you want, we can go over there and I can show you that all my furniture—furniture you would recognize—is in the new place."

He shook his head, looking for all the world like a legitimately confused guy. I wasn't sure just how confused he really was, though. I had a feeling I wasn't as confused as Frank was trying to look. Suddenly I remembered all those times I had been forced to question things my now-ex-husband George had said to me. Excuses he had forged, reasons he had given for being late for dinner or for some pretty young thing waving at him from across the room, at the grocery store or the movie theater or a restaurant. Young women who weren't smart enough or mature enough to realize that it wasn't a good idea to wave to your boyfriend when he was obviously out and about with his wife.

Ah, the discussions George and I had over the course of that year when we were hashing out just what was happening to our marriage, just what George was doing behind my back. I hadn't enjoyed the guessing game the first time around. I had promised myself back then that I wasn't going to go through anything like that ever again. That I wasn't going to let a man—any man—lead me by the nose through his sticky web of lies and excuses. And now, here I was asking myself if my boyfriend was telling me the truth about something. And although the story was vastly different and involved, of all things, bedbugs, the possible true explanations felt all too familiar. Were both Alice and Frank lying to me? Were they, in fact, seeing each other? The thought made my brain hurt—and my heart—but I had to admit that it wasn't outside the realm of possibility, ugly though it was to contemplate.

"Frank," I said softly, "listen. I have no idea why you'd want to make up a story about bedbugs and try to cover up why your house is now empty. I can come up with a few plausible explanations, though, that don't involve bedbugs at all."

"Then what *do* they involve?" His voice was quiet, and I wasn't sure how to read his tone, or his gestures.

"They involve you... being involved with Alice."

"Alice?" Now he was loud, and he started gesturing wildly. "You've got to be kidding me! You mean, am I seeing Alice? *Alice.* I—?"

"Are you?" I interrupted. "Are you? I've seen quite a bit in my day, and this certainly wouldn't be the stupidest explanation for both of you."

"Well, what did Alice tell you was going on?"

Had he really forgotten that I had told him this already, or was he asking me to state it all again so he could make sure that his story jived with hers? My brain hurt. The heart was on its own, though, because the brain was going to explode if this kept up much longer.

"Wait. You think that Alice and I—" He stopped and frowned all the harder.

"Yes, I do," I added before he could continue his sentence. "I definitely do. It's not all that far a stretch, though, is it?"

"Yes, it most certainly is!" He was doing a good job of sounding offended, and even though I wasn't entirely sure of my accusation, I figured I'd play this one out and see where it led. I could then move on to accusing him of other things, other lies. For as long as he would allow me to pester him like this. I didn't really know where his personal threshold of accusational torture fell, so I was in uncharted waters. And was feeling a little seasick over it.

"Listen, Helga and I follow Alice, and she leads us right to your house. Now, she *says* that it's because she's looking for a new place to live—that her neighbors are giving her grief—and that a real estate agent gave her your address. So, she was just scoping out empty houses and apartments. Sure, that makes sense. But seems awfully coincidental. Too coincidental."

"Just what is coincidental about it?" He folded his arms across his chest and was trying to look supremely offended. And, if I was wrong, then I supposed he was doing a decent job of it.

"That she landed at your house. The one place she went. The house that was only recently emptied of all its furniture. The house that you say has bedbugs."

"*Had* bedbugs. I can only assume the landlord took care of them by now. And that the place is inhabitable again."

"Why would you assume that? I did a little research online, Frank. Turns out it takes multiple treatments to get rid of bedbugs. Over the course of several weeks. There's no way any decent landlord would have that house listed as available for rent anywhere by now. Not so soon. No reputable pest control company could have completely gotten rid of the bedbugs by now."

Frank just looked at me blankly and I wasn't sure whether to press the subject any further right now. Maybe I should just let this sink in a little bit before hammering it home and insisting that he answer the implied question here. Maybe—

"That is just ridiculous!" Frank yelled, a little more loudly than I would have expected him to do in an argument. Not that we'd had many arguments up till this point. In fact, had we had any? Was he trying to intimidate me into just letting this one go?

"Just what's ridiculous about it? I told you, I did my research."

"Oh, well, your research might have been a little lacking, Maggie. Do you know when I moved out? When the house went empty?"

"Well, no, not exactly. But, I just assumed—"

"Ah, there's the problem!" he said, still too loudly. "You made some assumptions. Well, to be honest with you, I moved out of that bug-infested house two weeks earlier. Plenty of time for the landlord to treat the whole house for bedbugs. They apparently weren't all that bad—in terms of having someone come in and treat the place for them—so it took only the two treatments to get rid of them. No carpets to worry about, and I hadn't added curtains, so it was just the plastic mini-blinds on the windows. Once my own things were out, it was short work for the pest control company to come in and eradicate the bedbug population."

The extreme confidence in his voice threw me off a little bit. Was he telling the truth, and I had just been on a mission to point a finger wherever I could? His answer was quick, and thorough. But, of course, a good liar would have also done his own research on bedbugs so that his excuse would seem as believable as possible. It wouldn't do any good to come up with a brilliant excuse that couldn't pass muster if someone questioned it. Someone like me, for instance.

"Frank—"

"No, Maggie, if you get to throw out accusations like that, I get to respond. For one thing, I can't believe you've come up with this harebrained idea in the first place. It's not like Alice is telling you that we're seeing each other, right?" He hesitated. This apparently wasn't a rhetorical question and he was waiting for me to answer.

"Right," I said quietly.

"So, her story is that she needs to get out of her house because the neighborhood has turned against her. Can't say that I blame them, and it certainly does seem like a perfectly legitimate reason for her to have been at my *empty* house, the house I no longer live in, the house that my landlord has again listed as available now that the bedbugs have been dealt with. He gave me the opportunity to move out, and so I did. I found the whole idea of bedbugs distasteful enough that I preferred to move than to worry about them coming back in the future. And—"

"So why did you not tell me any of this when it happened, if you moved out two weeks ago?"

"Because honestly, if *I* find the thought of bedbugs more than a little creepy, I can only guess how gross and disgusting *you* would find them. I figured I'd get moved out and resettled at the new place and then tell you all about it. Once the bedbugs were no longer an issue for me. For us."

I sighed. I was confused. That brain-hurt thing kept coming back. And I just didn't like that I was taking two steps forward and then two steps back. Or maybe three. Was I actually in negative territory with Frank now? Because if he was telling the truth, and I had just spent a half hour accusing him of infidelity and lying, then I was going to have some major apologizing to do. At least I hadn't yet accused Alice of anything. Or, at least, not accused her of this.

"Frank," I said, trying to sound a little less harsh than I had a few moments earlier. How best to take a few steps back without completely unraveling everything I'd just said? Uncharted waters, to be sure.

I wished I was a better judge of character. I could find a missing comma in a manuscript at twenty paces, and I could tell you if that capital L was in the wrong font or the wrong type size, even without my glasses on. But I couldn't tell if my best friends, if my children, if my boyfriend, if my ex-husband were lying to me. Of course, the ex-husband lies had been the start of the downfall of my own character judgment techniques many years ago. Since then I'd learned to question my own thoughts about people I knew. And even—especially—people I didn't know all that well. Like Alice. And, in some respects, even like Frank. How long had I known Frank, after all? We'd met in the spring and started dating in early summer. So, really, only a handful of months. Certainly a good liar could fool someone—especially someone like me—for a handful of months before she found out.

"Frank, I need some space on this. I still don't feel a hundred percent yet after the hospital, and the last thing I need is any more stress in my life. About anything."

He frowned. "How is my having to deal with bedbugs a stressor for you? I purposely kept you out of the loop on this so that it *wouldn't* stress you out. I know you hate bugs."

"I know, I know. I'm partly being irrational here. But just allow me that tiny bit of irrationality, okay? I—I want to rest."

He exhaled loudly enough for it to be a form of communication, and I just looked at him sheepishly. I didn't want to talk about it—about anything—anymore, so I figured it best to stop feeding the conversation. He uncrossed his arms and sighed loudly. His unspoken signals were getting louder, and certainly were quite clear in their own way.

"Okay, " he said. "I get the hint. I'll leave you alone for now. Just give me a call when you're ready to be... friends again." He'd hesitated just enough between those words for me to notice it. I wasn't sure if I was supposed to notice it or whether he had just slipped and let the cat out of the bag. Was he dialing back our relationship from dating to friendship? All because I wanted some space and had asked him a few specific questions about his bedbug problem? What was wrong with everyone these days?

I nodded, still not wanting to stretch out this encounter any longer, and he turned toward the door. I slipped in behind him and came up to hug him from behind.

"Frank, I'm sorry. I just need some sleep so I can think straight. It's not you."

"Uh huh." He apparently wasn't buying my "it's not you" bit. And I wasn't sure I myself was buying it. Was it him? Or was it me? Clearly I wasn't going to know for sure until I had had a little more sleep. Or, probably, a lot more sleep. I could almost hear my bed calling to me.

Frank got to the door and opened it himself. He subtly broke free of my hug and hovered in the doorway now that the door was open. "I... I'll talk to you later then," he said, with every hint of familiarity withdrawn from his tone. I was just too far gone to care.

I'd deal with the fallout from this situation later. Not now.

"Bye, Frank," I offered, but he didn't turn around to face me.

"Bye, Maggie. Later then." And with that he was headed down the apartment building steps to the first floor. I stayed in the doorway for a few seconds, trying to figure out what to do next. I'd obviously seen way too many romantic movies (with far younger and prettier women as the stars) because I wondered if I should dash down the steps and into the street behind him, calling his name and watching him turn back to me, his own arms outstretched, running back to me with a huge smile on his face.

Yeah, that wasn't going to happen. I stepped back and closed the door firmly. That bed was practically yelling at me now. Time for sleep. And, I hoped, no dreams.

CHAPTER 27

GEEZ, WOMAN, WHAT IS WRONG WITH YOU? You can't seem to catch a break!" Helga was walking around the tall desk and countertop in the foyer of the Brighton *Bugle* office and headed straight for me. I let her come. Suddenly I felt as if I could use a big hug. I opened my arms to welcome her embrace and—

"Ow!" Helga had slapped me across the face. She'd caught me completely off guard and my hand flew to my smarting cheek. "Helga!"

"What?"

"What was that for? What's wrong with you?"

"What's wrong with *me*? You're asking what's wrong with me? I should be asking what's wrong with you, dearie." She threw her hands onto her hips and snorted. "Oh, wait. I already did."

"N-Nothing is wrong with me. I don't have any idea what you're talking about."

"You don't?"

"Well, besides the new allergy to shellfish. I suppose you've heard about that then."

"Yes! I called the house and talked to Seth. Scared the bejeebies outta me, woman. Do *not* scare me like that ever again." She headed for me again, and I flinched instinctively.

"Don't—"

"Aww, sweetie, I won't. Come here. Let me hug you proper." Now she came in for the hug, and it was a mighty tight one. She threw her arms around my neck and kissed me on the cheek. I grabbed her around the waist and was glad she wasn't really mad at me as I had first thought. Helga wasn't the kind of friend you wanted to have angry with you if you had any say in the matter. But a Helga hug was a thing of beauty, a bit of emotional sustenance she supplied, often just when you needed it.

I nearly broke down crying. A simple hug, from a trusted friend, and I was in tears.

"Sweetie, what's wrong?"

"Nothing. It's just—"

"Is it because I slapped you just now? I'm so sorry! I meant to just tap you on the cheek like this—" She reached for my face and I flinched again. "It *is* because I did that, isn't it?"

"No," I assured her, smiling and rubbing my cheek where she had slapped it earlier. "You didn't hit me that hard. And, if I was being honest, I'd agree with you about why! I don't really know what to think about my own behavior lately. I'm a basket case."

"Sweets, listen to your ol' Helga. No man is worth this sort of self-torture. None of them. And trust me, I should know. I've been through most of them personally!" She grinned, and I couldn't help smiling with her. Of course, I had no idea whether that sort of self-recrimination was actually true with Helga. She loved a tall tale, especially one about herself, and I hadn't ever seen her going on a date with any man in the handful of years I'd known her. But she was more than ten years older than I was, and I had no idea what her personal past love life looked like. She could have been a completely wild and crazy young woman back in her day. Back when I was married to George and raising two kids, back when my life was a lot further from any wild and crazy life Helga might have been living. Back when I didn't know Helga yet because I wasn't doing freelance work. Wasn't doing much beyond changing diapers and trying vainly to keep George happy. Ah, those were the good old days. Not.

"Helga, I'm fine, But I do think Frank kinda broke up with me when he was at my house last night."

"He did?" She immediately perked up and sounded excited by this news. It was the opposite of my own reaction when Frank had said it last night. Maybe I needed a change in perspective.

"I think so. He told me to call him when I was ready to be friends again."

She frowned. "And this is what he said to break up with you?"

"Yeah. Why?"

"Well, I'm just not so sure that's an official breakup."

"He kind of hesitated before he said 'friends.' He said 'ready to be... *friends* again.'" I hesitated the way Frank had last night. Helga kept frowning.

"Not convinced. Sure, it's open for that interpretation, but I think it could go either way. And trust me, I really want him to have broken up with you."

"Why the complete one-eighty about Frank?" I asked. "I thought you liked Frank." She lightly took my elbow and steered me to one of the chairs in the foyer. I sat and she took the seat next to me.

"To be honest, chickie, the way he treated you here at the end, these past few days—especially that day we were in my car and he didn't answer his phone for hours. Well, I just don't like the feel of it at all."

Now she had my attention. "What don't you like about it?"

"The whole bedbug story. Makes no sense to me. It feels like an elaborate lie to get you off his case about Alice."

"So you do think there's something going on between Frank and Alice?" I inched forward on the seat. This was precisely the reason I appreciated Helga so much as a friend. She never beat around the bush and you could count on her for a blunt, honest opinion about just about anything. Even if you hadn't initially asked for one. And especially if you had.

"You bet your bippy! Clearly that bitch is screwing him! And still trying to call herself your friend! Bad enough when a boyfriend cheats on you—that's a story as old as the hills, practically as old as I am—but to have a *friend* do this to you with your *boyfriend*? Well, honey, that's just way out there." She started to gesture off to the side, away from us, in a fairly exaggerated way. She was certainly getting her point across.

"Well, it's not like Alice is my best friend or anything—"

"Sweetie, she better not be! And not just because I'd like to apply for that job if it's currently open."

I smiled. Helga touched my elbow lightly again. I didn't realize how much I would appreciate a simple touch from a friend, and I sighed. I could feel the emotion welling up and fought it back down so that I wouldn't go to pieces here in the foyer of the *Bugle* office. I had to work with these people, even if most of the work was online now, and they didn't need to see me blubbering in their professional space.

"The job's yours, Helga. You got it on the first interview, if I remember correctly." I sniffled and smiled at her, and she leaned in to press her forehead against mine. Just for a moment. Just long enough for me to lose it and start snuffling loudly.

In perfect Helga fashion, she was up out of the chair in a flash and had zipped back around to the countertop, whipping a few tissues out of the box she kept there and coming back to tuck them into my fist. I dabbed at my eyes and sniffled in to keep from letting a runny nose lead to more embarrassment, But, no one was here out front besides us, so I took a deep breath and dabbed some more, then ran the tissue under my nose for good measure.

"What am I going to do, Helga?"

"For one thing, you're going to steer clear of both Alice and Frank."

I rose both eyebrows in question.

"For now. For your own good. Neither one of them desperately needs to hear from you in the next week. Let it simmer. Let *them* simmer. It won't kill 'em."

I nodded. It was simple wisdom, but it was wisdom I hadn't really been affording myself until hearing it from Helga. Again, I sometimes needed that outside, more objective perspective. If you could call a good friend's protective streak objective, that is.

"Okay, you're right. They can wait."

"But, I don't think lunch can wait. I'm starving. Wanna head out to Buster's?"

A greasy burger. Chili cheese fries. A large diet cola. It all sounded like the perfect antidote. Helga knew me too well. Or, maybe, just well enough.

"Let's go!" I said with as much enthusiasm as I could muster. "My treat!"

"Now yer talkin'!" she said and slipped her arm through mine.

CHAPTER 28

MY RESOLVE TO KEEP ALICE OUT OF MY LIFE lasted exactly two days. She called me two days after my lunch with Helga, sounding a little stressed and desperate. More like the Alice I had first met at the ball field. I felt my own resolve at holding her at arm's length slipping fast as the conversation went on. Clearly I had no will power. Clearly Helga was going to agree with this personal assessment, and would probably kick my ass or slap my face all over again.

"Maggie, I'm desperate!" Alice was saying, repeating herself in hopes of getting me to knuckle under. "You need to come over here right away!"

"Alice," I began, trying to sound as hesitant and reluctant as I could. "I don't know. I'm trying to clear my head about all the stuff that's been happening lately. I just want my life back."

I realized as soon as I'd said it that this wasn't the right thing to say to a recent widow. I could have kicked myself for my rude comment.

"Don't we all?" she said, clicking her tongue. She'd taken my comment exactly the way I had *not* intended it. Sometimes I could be a really shitty friend. This was one of those times. And, even though Helga would have told me it was for the best if Alice now walked away from our friendship, I wasn't exactly drowning in friendships in this town and wasn't ready to throw mine with Alice under the proverbial bus. Seth's little brush with the law had so-bered up more than one person I would have called friend. Nothing overt—that's not how people usually did this sort of thing. Just stuff like fewer invitations to get-togethers. The book club starting a new book and conveniently not telling me what it was. I could take the hints, and they hurt. So, proactively saying no to Alice's friendship before I knew for sure what was going on with her and Frank—if anything—seemed a bit extreme, Helga's warnings aside.

And I still meant to ask her whether she was involved in Seth's arrest.

Then again, I knew I had a tendency to see all sides of every is-sue, to my detriment, and this was was one of those times, wasn't it? Sometimes I hated myself for my constant waffling on every single issue in my life. Why couldn't I just make a decision and stick to it? Sure, I could commit to a semicolon here or the use of the serial comma there, but ask me to maintain my opinions about people and relationships and I was all over the map.

I realized that Alice had spoken again. I hadn't been listening. I'd been off in la-la land. Again.

"What?"

"Nothing, Maggie. Listen, if you have some problem with me—some *real* problem—I'd prefer it if you just let me know straight out. This bouncing back and forth between being friendly and giving me the cold shoulder has got to stop. I just don't have the heart for it. I've been through too much already."

She was right.

"You're right, Alice. Now, what's up? Why would you like me to come over? Why now?"

"I found something."

"Found what?" She was going to have to be a little more forth-coming than that if she was going to get me out of my house in this weather.

I looked out my living room window, phone still cradled against my ear. The dreary cold rain wasn't letting up—typical Brighton weather for this time of year—and the thought of dashing across the street to my car wasn't a pleasant one right now. I was warm and cozy and dry in here. Plus, if the temperature dropped, it would all freeze.

"A... a... a suicide note."

"A *what*?" I almost yelled into the phone and then caught myself before I did it again. "You found a *suicide note*?"

"Yes, that's what I just said."

I wasn't winning any brownie points in this conversation, that's for sure. I was either shutting her down or making her repeat herself even when I'd heard her clearly. Yay me.

"Yes," she repeated when I didn't answer her right away. More points for me.

"From... from Allen?"

"Who else would it be from?"

For a detail-oriented person, I sure was failing in the clue department. Although stuff like this merely fortified my choice to work behind the scenes with paper and a computer rather than to take up law enforcement as a hobby.

"Yes, yes, of course," I agreed. "Sorry. But, where? And why now?"

She sighed. "Because I'm finally going through Allen's things, and there it was in his top desk drawer."

My first thought was that Allen didn't strike me as the kind of guy who'd have his own desk in his house. She hadn't said "our desk" or "the desk," but had said "*his* top desk drawer." And, the fact that she was only opening this drawer now meant it wasn't the kind of drawer she typically used all that often. So, it wasn't a desk for paying bills and keeping the typical paperwork that comes with marriage and home ownership. All these thoughts zipped through my brain in the nanosecond it took me to respond.

"What does it say?"

"Not—not over the phone. It seems just, well, wrong. That's

why I'd like you to come over. I want to show it to you."

I fought the urge to ask her to just take a picture of the note and text it to me. Even to me that seemed callous and rude. One more short glance out the window. Sheets of rain coming down now. Great.

And I was going to be that good friend who went out in weather like this to help a friend who'd asked for help. And maybe not just because I needed friends. Maybe I was ridiculously curious about this suicide note, which would change everything I knew about this whole situation with Allen and the poisoned Sport-Aide.

ALICE MET ME AT THE DOOR. She'd been standing there watching me get out of my car, arms folded across her chest, looking fidgety. I wasn't sure how to interpret that, but I was going to pay a whole lot of attention to her movements and gestures. Not that I had any idea how to interpret such things, but maybe I could recount this to Helga if things seemed a little bit off. Then again, *everything* seemed a little bit off lately. I had no point of reference to judge anything anymore.

"Come in," Alice said hastily as I approached the door, my umbrella barely managing to keep up with the drenching rain. I wasn't sure why I was bothering with the umbrella at all. It had been locked in my car in the first place, and I had gotten halfway soaked just making the mad dash from the front door of the apartment building to my car to get over here. Trying to keep myself dry now was a wasted effort. I hopped onto the porch from the two steps leading there from the front sidewalk and immediately closed the umbrella, doing that rapid open–close thing to whisk as much of the rain off it as I could before bringing it inside Alice's house.

"Here," Alice said, reaching for the umbrella. "Let me take that from you," I stopped whooshing it open and closed and handed it to her. She let it drip onto the parquet floor just inside the door and held open the storm door for me. I lightly stepped in, glad to be completely out of this weather. She let the door close behind me and I stepped in all the way so she could shut the heavy steel door and lock it behind us.

"Thanks," I said, shaking myself a little to get some more water droplets off my jacket.

"Let me take that for you." I shrugged out of the jacket and handed it over. She hung it on a lovely coat rack just behind us, along with the umbrella, which she had closed up and snapped while I was trying to get the jacket off.

"Now," I said, clapping my hands together and trying to sound as much like nothing weird had happened between us as I could, "let's see that note."

She nodded solemnly. "It's in here," she said, motioning with her head and leading us toward what passed for a study in their small, quaint house. In it was a big desk that looked like an antique—maybe a family heirloom?—and several bookcases stuffed with books and various knickknacks and framed photos. But my eyes immediately went to the desk itself—not just the centerpiece of the room because of its wooden beauty but because it might now hold clues to what had really happened to Allen. The top drawer was open halfway, and I could see papers, pens, pencils, and other typical desk items peeking out from inside.

"It was in here?" I asked, pointing to the open drawer and walking toward it.

"Yes," she said. "It's right there. I took it out. It's on the blotter." She pointed to the single piece of paper sitting right out in the open, on that desk blotter, neat and tidy on the otherwise orderly, organized desktop. A mug full of pens and pencils sat just past the blotter, along with a banker's style desk lamp with a green glass shade, and a telephone on its base. Nothing else sullied the top of the desk. I walked toward the desk and peered down at the piece of paper.

"Don't touch it," Alice warned, but I had no intention of touching that thing. It was clearly evidence in an ongoing investigation, and hoped that it would exonerate anyone currently under suspicion—and a few people who had been under suspicion earlier but who had been cleared already. I never knew whether the police had completely given up on the idea of Seth being the murderer, and I worried daily that I would get another call telling me he was behind bars again. The thought that Allen might simply have killed himself sent thrilling trills of relief through me. I didn't dare say any of this to Alice, of course, since she was Allen's wife and wouldn't want to think about him having killed himself. What would that say about their marriage, about how unhappy he might have been with his life? So, I just looked down at the paper in morbid fascination.

Dear Alice,
    I know you'll never forgive me for this, but I can't take it any more. Good bye, cruel world.
                                                    Allen

He had signed it with a blue pen, probably a regular ballpoint pen.

My initial thought was that this was the most unimaginative suicide note in history. "Good bye cruel world"? Seriously? Did anyone actually write that in a suicide note? Wasn't that the stuff of melodrama? Or maybe Looney Tunes cartoons? I wasn't sure how to react, not with Alice standing right here over my shoulder, but clearly I had to say something. I couldn't just respond with a short "huh" and move on. She had asked me to come over here explicitly to see the note, to talk about it, and to come up with a few possible explanations for its existence. I wasn't sure I was going to be in any position to help her with any of those things based on my first gut reaction. But, I mustered the fortitude to turn around and face her. I shook my head slowly and said simply, "Wow."

It wasn't the best reaction, but it would probably get us started. I looked at her expression, trying to read where she stood on this. Just my luck, she had a ridiculously blank look on her face.

"I know, right?"

She'd found a way to interpret my own blank look (at least, I hoped it was a blank look, since I wasn't ready to project an interpretation of this note just yet) and my single-word response, so I clutched onto that and went forward. If I had to backtrack at some point, so be it. For now, onward...

"That's just... nuts. How long do you think it's been in that drawer?"

She frowned. "What?"

"You know, how long was it in there before you found it today?"

"Well," she said, stammering a little bit," I assume it's been in there since before Allen died."

She had misunderstood my question. Even when I agreed with her, I could find ways to be rude and embarrassing.

"No, I meant, how long ago do you think he wrote it? How long before... you know... before he..."

"Ohh, I see. Yes, I see." She wrinkled up her face in thought. "I don't have any idea. I really never go in this desk. Could have been here for quite a long time, or just before he... died. This was mostly Allen's desk. He did a lot of his accounting work in here."

"Do you have your own desk then?" I hoped she didn't view the question as either invasive or accusatory. I wasn't sure exactly how I meant it, but I had to ask. The curiosity about this new bit of evidence was killing me.

"Huh? Oh, no, I don't. We didn't really have the room for another desk anywhere and I didn't see a use for it. Allen was the one who wanted a full desktop computer, so it made sense for the desk to be mostly his. Plus, it belonged to his grandfather."

"The computer?"

She sighed and smiled. "No, the desk."

I smiled back, meaning it this time, "Oh, of course. The desk."

"So, we let Allen set up his big computer here, with those two ridiculous monitors, and I just used my laptop wherever I wanted to—on the couch, at the dining room table, in bed with me. I liked the flexibility. He just liked the big monitors."

"Why two? Most people are fine with just one. Aren't they?"

I myself had two monitors, but I did typesetting and proofreading work that often needed me to compare two documents side by side.

Putting one document on each monitor made that work infinitely easier. Why would a tax accountant like Allen need a computer with two monitors?

"Games. How that man loved his online games."

"Ohh, right!"

"I couldn't keep him away from Skyrim and Call of Duty. Anything where he could shoot stuff, blow stuff up—any of that garbage. He loved it all."

"Can you blow stuff up in Skyrim?" I asked. I knew Seth loved that game, and from what I'd seen of it myself—which was only bits and pieces whenever Seth had played it at my house, on my dual-monitor computer—it looked downright medieval. But I wasn't sure just how much the technology of that game's time period allowed for blowin' up stuff real good.

"Geez, I don't know, Maggie. The other games did, I think. Fallout or something like that? I just know that sometimes I'd walk by this office and hear all sorts of gory sounds coming from this blasted computer. He loved those games."

"And he played them with other guys? Other men? People?"

She nodded. "Yeah, every time he got the chance, it seemed. Tried not to let it interfere with stuff that needed to get done around here, but sometimes it did. I got used to it, that's all."

The gaming thing fit well with my preconceived notions about Allen. So, that really didn't surprise me. Nor did the two monitors now that Alice had explained it. Seth also had two monitors—mostly for his coding work—and I know he often used them for gaming. Even I had been known to play the occasional game of Minecraft on the larger of my two monitors, keeping email and work files open on the second monitor. If I had to wait for a file or email to come in, it was a good way to pass a few minutes here and there. But I never quite understood the people who spent hours upon hours in these MMO games, barely coming up for air and forgetting to eat meals or to get enough sleep. I let almost nothing stand in the way of a good meal or a good night's sleep. Creature comforts were my super power.

Time to segue into something else, something closer to the note.

Talking gaming wasn't going to get us anywhere right now.

"So, what do *you* make of the note, Alice?" What could it hurt to come right out and ask her what she thought? I just had to be sure not to project that I was going to piggyback off whatever she was thinking. It would be easier to draw her out about this if I at least pretended to agree with her, no matter what she was thinking. And, if by chance I actually did agree with her, well, so much the better.

"I don't honestly know what to think."

Great.

"Well," I said slowly, trying to scramble for a way to get her to open up a little more, "what was your very first reaction when you opened this drawer and saw that note inside?"

She walked past the desk and began to pace on the other side of the room, over near the bookcases. I watched her intently. Behind her the books stood silently on the shelves. As she paced, I glanced at the books. A lot of pulp fiction and mass market paperbacks. One entire shelf was Reader's Digest condensed books. I recognized those even from across the room. And I shuddered a little at the thought. My aunt proudly displayed all her Reader's Digest condensed books on shelves in her living room. She was sure they made her look well read and intelligent. I hadn't the heart to tell her otherwise. Instead, I had decided to be grateful she was buying books and not trashy supermarket tabloids like my other aunt.

Alice walked back and forth, passing the other bookshelf for the third time. This shelf had fewer books and more framed photos. I could see one that was probably a 5x7 picture of her and Allen, outdoors somewhere and fairly recent since both Alice and Allen looked a lot like they did now. Or, like Allen had looked until he'd died, anyway. I was glad I hadn't said that thought out loud. I was always stepping in it, wasn't I?

"My first reaction," Alice said, still pacing in front of those two bookcases, "was shock. Then for a second—just for a second—I thought it had to be a had joke. I mean, aren't we all convinced, even the cops, that Allen was murdered? This would undo all of that thinking. Then, after that thought, I was... well, I was sad.

Depressed, really. Because that meant so many other things were wrong. So many worse things. And I wouldn't have thought anything could have been worse than thinking Allen had been murdered. But, honestly, thinking Allen had deliberately ended his own life? Well, yeah, that's a lot worse. A lot."

She was pacing and looking at the rug beneath her feet. I didn't think she wanted any input from me right now—just someone to listen to her opine about her discovery—so I said nothing, but instead just watched her. After all, I was even more perplexed now about what to think of Alice and our friendship. If this note meant what we were both assuming it meant, then it changed everything, and I needed to adapt to this new reality—in terms of my friendship with Alice herself, and possibly in terms of my relationship with Frank, too.

She stopped walking and stood staring at her feet, her hands clasped behind her back. She closed her eyes, and suddenly it felt like a very private moment that I was intruding upon. I looked away from Alice and gazed at the right bookcase behind her instead. The photos in the frames. I'd look at those instead. The picture of the two of them. Next to that one a larger framed photo, their wedding picture. They looked so young together, and Allen looked almost trim in his dark suit. Alice was beaming in her lace white dress. I could see it clearly from here. The 8x10 was big enough to make out their happy faces. If this note was genuine, how had things between them—how had things for Allen himself—gotten so bad that he had decided to kill himself? It was sobering to the point of feeling suffocating. And if *I* felt this way, I could only imagine how Alice must be feeling. Even if she and Allen had drifted apart, if they hadn't been getting along in recent years, to think your husband hated his life so much that he chose to leave the world completely, rather than spend any more time in the house and the life you'd shared with him... Well, she had to be feeling absolutely awful.

"Alice, are you all right?" She was still staring at her feet, still with her hands behind her back. Now I was glad I'd come to her house. There was no telling for sure how she'd continue to react to this note.

"I'm... not sure."

I still chose to look mostly past her, at the photos on the shelf. One just below the wedding picture, on the shelf below that, caught my eye. From here I wasn't sure what I was seeing, but I couldn't be seeing what I *thought* I was seeing. This photo was smaller than the 5x7 of Allen and Alice. Maybe a 4x6 printout from a computer. But it was framed and sat there among the other photos, a little bit in front of ones that were older, sepia-toned family photos from previous generations. This one was newer, recent.

And, I could clearly see, even from here, that it was a picture of Frank.

CHAPTER 29

"A LICE... ALICCCCE?"

She looked up from the floor, where she had still been staring at her feet. "Yes?"

"Is... hey, is that a picture of... *Frank*?"

"What?" she said sharply, and she whipped her head around, looking directly at the photo. Of course, I was now pointing right at it, so that might have had something to do with why she could look right at it. But since I was sure she had been the one to put it there, and likely had done so after Allen had died, I wasn't entirely sure which was the real reason she was looking right at the same picture I was.

"Oh, yeah. Yeah, it is." She kept looking at the picture, which conveniently meant she didn't have to look at me. I was pretty sure that was on purpose.

"Huh," I said, trying to sound somewhere between catty and snarky, with a little hint of angry thrown in. "Now, who would have thought my recently single friend Alice would have a framed picture of my boyfriend on her bookshelf?"

"Maggie, I can explain," she said, finally turning to face me. She had an odd look on her face for someone who had just finished talking to me about her husband's suicide note. I instantaneously switched from feeling sorry for her to feeling a little more sorry for myself. Plus, I was a bit of a moron for not seeing what had dropped in my lap when Helga and I had seen Alice walking around right outside Frank's house. There was a lot of fishy stuff going on here, and I was going to find Nemo if it killed me.

"Go ahead, Alice," I said. I surprised myself with my ability to sound calm right now. I felt anything but calm. "Go right ahead and explain yourself. I can't wait to hear this one."

"I'm not going to lie to you, Maggie," she began.

"Well, good, since I'm pretty sure I'd be able to see right through a lie now, even if I'd missed all the clues handed to me before."

"Okay, here's the thing. Frank was nice to me after... after Allen died. I hadn't been expecting that. You know what I was going through. I was all alone. People were assuming I'd killed Allen."

"Did you?"

"Did I what?"

"Did you kill Allen?"

"What? No! Of course not! Why would you think that?"

"For all the reasons everybody else thought it, Alice! He wasn't happy, *you* weren't happy. Nobody in this house was happy!"

She stopped closer to me, but I was still behind the desk so she had to stop on the other side. "Just because people aren't happy doesn't mean one of them *killed* the other one! Honestly, Maggie! That's such a made-for-TV movie stereotype."

"So is dating your friend's boyfriend, but I don't see you denying that stereotype!"

Now we were yelling at each other. I didn't want things to escalate. I'd be no match for Alice in a cat fight. I was out of practice, for one thing, having participated in my last one back when George and I were married and I'd caught one of his bimbos in our house when I'd come home early and he'd left her there while he stepped out for more beer. It had been ugly, and I had been losing badly when George came back in and broke it up. I wasn't sure whether to be glad to see him then or not.

At any rate, here I was contemplating another cat fight, this time over a boyfriend I apparently barely knew. The more I thought about it—and I really only had a few seconds in which to think about anything, after all—the more I knew I didn't want to fight over this. Over Frank. He wasn't worth it.

"Listen, Alice, I don't really care what's going on between you and Frank, okay? I'm not that into him, if you want to know the truth. He seemed like a great guy at first, but lately he's been a little... I dunno..."

I was rapidly losing my train of thought. If I'd had one to begin with.

"A little sneaky?"

I looked up, and looked over at Alice. "What? What did you say?"

"He's been a little sneaky? Isn't that what you were going to say?"

"As a matter of fact, yes, I was. He *has* been a little sneaky lately. And he's come up with some downright outrageous stories to try to explain all sorts of things."

Alice nodded all the way through what I'd just said. "I know, right?"

"Wait, don't get all chummy with me, missy." Now I was pissed. "I have a funny feeling a lot of what he's been trying to explain away involves you, so don't pretend we're on the same side here."

She frowned and clucked her tongue. "But—but I think maybe we *are* on the same side, Maggie."

I wasn't the least bit interested in her excuses right now, but I found myself saying, "How do you figure that?" before I knew what I was doing. Apparently a small part of me *was* the least bit interested in her excuses right now. Sometimes I surprised even myself.

"Granted, Frank was really nice to me after Allen died. He believed in me—kind of like you believed in me—when nobody else wanted to take the chance. Eventually I just saw it as the two of you, as a couple, thinking the same things about me. Showing the same sort of interest. Like couples do. Sometimes couples are couples precisely because they think the same way about things."

"And about people?" I asked. Part of me was willing to hear her out. I had nothing to lose at this point. No matter what else, my romantic relationship with Frank was toast. But maybe there could be something to salvage of my friendship with Alice, depending on what she said next.

She nodded, looking as forlorn as a lost puppy out in the freezing rain. I fought the urge to go to her and hug her. I wasn't one hundred percent convinced yet. Yet.

"Yeah, and about people. At first I assumed you had just talked him into believing me, in believing in my innocence in Allen's murder. And I admit it, I grabbed for it."

"For what, exactly?"

"For another friend. For another friendly face. It didn't matter to me who he was or who he belonged to. I swear I wasn't interested in him for romantic reasons, Maggie. I wasn't. I just needed another friend. Any friend."

What she was saying held a ring of truth. But I had to remind myself that a murderer would likely be able to talk like this, too. Would have come up with alternate realities to impose on people in order to protect their film of innocence. In order to protect their false stories and alibis. I would have to decide if Alice was truly an innocent person caught in the middle, or if she was a guilty person, a murderer, well schooled in adapting to her environment in order to keep herself out of prison and free.

The small thing that decided this question for me was that, even if Alice *had* killed Allen, she wasn't a serial killer. She would have just killed Allen to get out of a bad, suffocating marriage. So, even if she was guilty of this crime, she was likely not well schooled in self-protection and would have slipped up by now.

Frank, on the other hand, had begun to feel slippery and a little too smooth for my liking. He was always there for me—including times I was discovering new allergies or being poisoned in restaurants. He was hiding big things from me, like moving out of his house. Who picks up and moves without saying anything to his girlfriend for weeks? His flimsy excuse about me not liking bugs was just that: a flimsy excuse.

"Alice," I said slowly. "I have just one question right now."

"Anything. What is it?"

"Why the picture of Frank?"

She smiled and exhaled, looking suddenly relieved. "Look!" she said, heading for the bookcase where the photo sat in its frame. "See?" She pointed right at the framed photo of Frank—and then moved a little bit to the left to reveal what I hadn't seen previously because she'd been standing in front of it: a matching framed photo the same size—of me. Right next to the one of Frank.

"Wait... what?"

"I printed out pictures of each of you. My only two real friends anymore. Sometimes I came in here and sat in the easy chair over there—" She pointed to a comfortable-looking old chair in the corner, a wing chair with a beautiful handmade afghan tossed over the back. "—and I'd look at all my precious pictures. Photos that made me happy. I had to add pictures of you two there. This one—" She pointed to the one of me. "This one I took at that one ball game. Remember?"

I nodded, trying not to get too emotional. Too much counter-information was coming my way right now.

"And... and this one of Frank. Remember? When we were first getting to know each other and you were trying to tell me which guy on the team Frank was. How the hell did I know? I never went to those games. So, you just—"

"—Emailed you that picture. I remember."

"I'm sorry. I printed them out and stuck 'em in frames to put in here. To remind me that I still had friends."

"You do."

"Well, one, at least. For now."

"For now, one is going to have to be good enough."

I smiled at her, hoping it would help smooth things over. I had a feeling she was telling the truth. Not just now, but all the way through this whole sordid episode with Allen's death. Certainly she hadn't been the one to up and move in the middle of the night (so to speak), and her story had always checked out. Even this one with the photos on the bookshelf. And I was perfectly happy to eat a little crow here if it meant getting to the bottom of what had really been happening lately.

"Alice, let me apologize right now, before things go any further, for not believing you about Frank and the photos over there. I was already feeling a little on edge about Frank, and I let my mind play into a fantasy for a few minutes. I'm... I'm sorry."

"It's okay, Maggie. Really. I think we're all a little bit paranoid right now. I know I am."

"Well, you have good reason to feel that way! You've had the cops on your tail for a while, and half the neighborhood, and... well, no need for you to apologize to me!"

We were now in that awkward territory where neither of us knew when to stop apologizing to the other. If I didn't shut one of us up soon, this was going to deteriorate into a bad Marx Brothers routine.

"Alice, let's just agree that we need to move past all this and go forward in our friendship."

"Fair enough, That'll work for me."

I put my hand out for us to shake on it, but she shook her head and came in for the hug. I wasn't ready, and we almost bonked heads before I figured out what she was doing and leaned to the opposite side and, hugged her back. We both laughed. The tension of the past few minutes was gone, and I, for one, was greatly relieved. Of course, that didn't get rid of the tension I was feeling regarding Frank. What in the wide world of sports was happening with that man? I broke free of Alice's hug and frowned.

"What's wrong?" she asked. My face was, as usual, an open book.

"Nothing. Well, nothing that has anything to do with you, of course. We're good. But Frank. I honestly don't know what to think about Frank. Something is definitely not right about that man, about our relationship."

Alice simply nodded. After all, what else could she do?

"So," she said, "what happens now?"

I had to admit that I didn't know the answer to that question. "I'm not really sure, to be perfectly honest with you. At some point—soon—I'm going to have to talk to Frank."

"You don't sound excited about that," she said, letting a small smile quirk up the corner of her mouth as she said it.

"Obviously I'm not," I agreed. "But it'll have to be done. Maybe I should call Frank now and get it over with."

"Are you going to do this over the phone with him? What would you even say?"

I frowned. "Not sure of that, either. But either way it all starts with a phone call, just to see where he is and what he's up to. But I think this has to be done in person, face to face."

I strode (more confidently than I felt) back to Alice's living room where I'd left the black hole I called my purse.

I opened it and shoved my arm in almost to the elbow, searching for that ever-slippery phone somewhere in the bottom. Alice had followed me and stood silently watching me fiddle with the contents of the purse. After what seemed an eternity, I felt the phone in my hand and clutched it tightly, bringing it out in a gesture of triumph that made Alice smile.

"Ta daaa!" I said, raising the phone high overhead. It didn't take much to make me proud these days. Small victories were sometimes the only victories I had left.

I swiped the phone and unlocked it, then hit the call button, scrolling down to Frank's number smoothly before pressing the talk button. Alice stood next to me expectantly, and I felt some pressure with her listening in. But maybe that was a good thing, to have someone else as a party to any conversation I had with Frank going forward.

Frank picked up on the third ring.

"Frank? Is that you?"

I was now officially guilty of doing the same thing I disliked when it happened to me. Who else would be answering Frank's phone?

"Hi, Maggie. Yes, of course it's me. What can I do for you?"

The enthusiasm in his voice was underwhelming. Gone were the days of giddy oohs and sighs over the phone line that were so loud they were audible on the other end. It was probably for the best. Maybe I'd feel better about it in the morning. I wasn't exactly sure *which* morning, but one of these mornings, I would probably feel better. Probably.

"Frank, listen, we have to talk."

"Trust me, I know we have to talk. I was waiting for your call."

"You have?"

"Well, the last time we talked, you said you needed some rest and needed some space. I've given you both by not contacting you and patiently waiting for you to contact me. And so, now, apparently, you have."

"I have."

"I trust this means you've gotten some rest and are ready to talk about some things."

I sighed. "Yes, Frank. It's long past time that we talked about... some things."

"I agree. Now, where and when? You choose."

My first thought was that I certainly wasn't going to choose a restaurant. No more public meetings at eateries with Frank. I'd learned that lesson the hard way. *Twice.* Even if there wasn't anything to tie those two experiences together, why tempt fate? I wasn't going to test the "third time's a charm!" saying any more than I had to. Besides, I hated clichés.

"Let's meet at your new place," I suggested. After all, I was curious about where Frank had chosen to live after leaving his house for a supposed bedbug problem.

There was a notable amount of silence from Frank's end of this conversation. After what seemed like ages, I spoke up again.

"Frank? You still there?"

"Yeah, um, yes, of course. You want to see my new place?"

"Sure. Why not? No time like the present." And, the present was always a good time for clichés.

"Well, there are boxes everywhere. I'm not really settled in yet. The place is a mess."

I'd known Frank for only a handful of months, but I already knew this much about him: his definition of a mess was a lot different from mine. He was the classic overachieving neat freak. Well, at least compared to me. So, I had a feeling even his newly-moved-in look was still tidier than my whole apartment on any given day.

"A mess? You don't expect me to buy that excuse, do you, Frank? You've seen my place. I'm sure yours is in nicer shape." I chuckled, loudly enough for him to hear me over the phone line. I wanted him to have heard what I said, but I wanted it to also sound light and cheerful, as if I were joking with him. I wasn't, but I was hoping he wouldn't pick up on that.

"Well, maybe so," he conceded. "But I still don't really want company over yet."

"Then where?" I continued, trying not to sound miffed. It would do no good to bait him this early. We were still making plans to talk at all. Being too transparent could end up backfiring on me if he chose not to meet.

"Let's meet... at my old place instead."

Now I was confused. "Your old place? But... you don't live there anymore."

"Yes, I know. But I still have one of my keys. We could go there and talk and could be sure no one would hear us."

"Wait. You moved out precisely because the place has bedbugs!"

"*Had* bedbugs. The landlord treated the whole place for them. It's fine now."

I glanced up and saw Alice frowning at me, shaking her head. She wasn't liking what she could hear.

"Frank, I don't know about that. It seems... weird. Plus, what would we do? Just stand there in the living room, talking into an echo in the empty space? Weird."

"The bar stools are still there, off the kitchen island. We could sit there and talk."

"Why not my place?" I offered. Alice nodded enthusiastically at this counter-suggestion.

"Well," Frank hedged, "to be honest with you, I never really liked that little dog of yours."

"Vlad. His name is Vlad." How could this man have been dating me for the past few months and not remember Vlad's name? The dog was practically all over him any time he came over to see me. I knew Frank wasn't all that crazy about dogs—he found them messy and inconvenient—but I never suspected he was this much against poor little obnoxious Vlad.

"Vlad. Right. Whatever. Anyway, he's always jumping up on me every time I walk in the door."

"He likes you," I said feebly. Granted, Vlad did that to nearly everyone, so that wasn't really the best explanation. Still, I had to try.

"Right. Anyway, with Vlad and his... eagerness... plus Seth, well, I just don't see your apartment as anything like neutral territory, Maggie."

He had a point. I shook my head for Alice's benefit, indicating that the apartment was going to be a no-go.

"I don't suppose you'd let me make everything up to you by taking you out to dinner..." Frank said, trailing off at the end as he realized that it sounded ridiculous. Because, well, it did.

"No offense, Frank, but I don't think I'll be eating in any sort of restaurant anytime soon. I'm not even tempted by the Burger King drive-thru lately."

Alice mouthed, "A restaurant?" with so much incredulity spread across her face that I had to curb the urge to laugh. I nodded and rolled my eyes, sticking out my tongue for good measure. She threw her hands over her mouth to stifle a giggle.

"Okay then," Frank continued, and I turned my attention back to the phone call. "Then where?"

I sighed again. This was taking too long, just to make arrangements for a single conversation. A conversation that probably wasn't going to go well anyway, if this phone conversation was any indication.

"You know what, Frank? Let's meet at your old place then. I have a feeling this won't take long anyway. We just need to clear the air. I'll meet you there in about thirty minutes. Is that all right?"

Alice was rolling her eyes at me now. Yes, she definitely didn't approve. But I had to put this behind me as soon as possible, and I was finding this conversation with Frank to be taxing all by itself. One of us wasn't going to be happy with the choice of location, so it might as well be me.

"Fine," he said. "See you then."

Click.

I took the phone away from my ear.

"Well, that's settled. I should leave now so I can get there a little bit ahead of Frank."

"Eww, Maggie. Bedbugs!"

"Yeah, I know. He said the landlord has taken care of them."

"But, isn't it back on the market? How will you get in if he's already moved out?"

"He still has one of his keys. Plus, to be honest, I have a copy myself. He made me one," I said, realizing it myself for the first time because I had never used it. "I could get there early and go inside to wait for him."

"Still, yuck. It gives me the creeps that I was going to look at that place myself. I was glad when you told me about the bedbugs because I'd never want to live in a place that had just gotten rid of them."

"Did you ever get to see the inside?"

"No. I wouldn't go in there once I knew. I'm still looking. And I think you guys should, well, stand outside and talk. Maybe in the driveway. Just in case the bedbugs are still there."

I looked out Alice's window in her living room. The rain was still pouring down in sheets.

"Alice, look outside. I'm not sure I want to stand in the rain with Frank and discuss how our relationship went south."

She looked out the window and frowned. "Oh, yeah. Well, maybe just sit in one of your cars then. Just avoid going into that house. The creepy factor would totally kick in for me if I had to go into a house where I knew they'd just had an exterminator."

"Then again," I countered, "that might be the best time to go in. The exterminator just got rid of them all. It's only later that they would have a chance to come back, right?"

I thought my logic was impeccable. I certainly didn't relish the thought of either standing in the rain to talk or cramming both of us into either of our cars, so close together. I wanted some space to move around—to move away from Frank—if the conversation got uncomfortable. I wasn't going to get that sitting in a car with him. The more I thought about it, the more the thought of meeting at Frank's old place seemed like the best one: not too comfortable, nice and roomy, and no other reason to be there except to talk. Yes, maybe this would work.

"Well, Alice, I'm going to get going. Sooner rather than later, right? Get this behind me, and all that."

She nodded reluctantly. "Sure. Now, what should I do about that note?"

"The note?"

"From Allen. The suicide note." She choked on that word, and I could certainly understand why.

I'd forgotten about the note, in all the hubbub about Frank and the photos in Allen's study. That had been the whole reason for my visit today.

"The note! Of course. Sorry. Maybe just hang onto it for now. Let me go talk to Frank and get this over with. Then I'll come back here and we can decide what to do next. But I think we'll have to turn that in to the police. Before I go," I added, "let me see that note again."

"Sure," she said and turned to go back into the office. I stared out the front window at the rain, which showed no signs of letting up. I felt about as dreary as the sky looked. After this was all over, I was going to go home, curl up under an afghan with Vlad, and take a long nap. Like, maybe, for the next few weeks.

"Here you go," Alice said as she came back into the living room. She handed me the note. I looked it over, front and back, though I didn't really know what I was looking for. My proofreader brain just liked to scrutinize words on paper. It was a bit of a curse sometimes, to always look at the printed page and want to decipher its secrets, to figure out where the mistakes were. Because there were always mistakes. Always. It came with the territory of being fallen human beings capable of making mistakes.

The only thing that kept standing out to me—besides his use of "any more" and "good bye" as two separate words—was the incredibly unimaginative nature of the note itself. Granted, I had a feeling that people about to commit suicide weren't trying to be overly flowery or creative when they wrote their loved ones those final notes. But still, this seemed trite, trivial, cliché. I'd seen better notes in cheap murder mysteries on television late at night.

"Anything?" Alice asked. I realized she was standing there, looking at me as if I held the keys to the kingdom in my hand. She'd been thinking that I wanted to look at the note so I could solve the problem and answer the question of what happened to Allen. I wished I could have helped her with that, but nothing about this was easy.

"Sorry, no," I admitted. "I just wanted to look at it one more time for now. I keep thinking there might be something here, some clue as to what really happened. But I don't know. I don't think so. I think it was wishful thinking. I'm sorry. I didn't mean to get your hopes up."

She touched my hand as I held it out to give the note back. She shook her head. "Take it. I don't really want it here in the house with me. It makes me feel... ill somehow."

"No, Alice, I can't take this. It's evidence. You need to keep this here until we can figure out what to do next. Give it to the police, as I said." I handed it back to her, and she sighed and took it from me. I didn't like forcing it on her, but there were larger issues to think about. Something still didn't seem right about it, and I wanted to know what the police would make of it once they saw it.

But all of that would have to wait. Right now I had to meet Frank at his old bedbug-ridden house on the other side of town.

"One more thing," I added. "I've got a tiny middle-aged bladder. Can I use your restroom before I leave?"

CHAPTER 30

BY THE TIME I PULLED INTO THE DRIVEWAY of Frank's old house, I was completely on edge. I had to peel my hands off the steering wheel and force myself to open the car door and get out. It had stopped raining, but the sky still looked ominous. It might start raining again at any time. I considered Alice's suggestion that we meet right here in the driveway instead of in the house, but her reasoning wouldn't have been mine. I was reasonably certain that the bedbug issue had been successfully eradicated, although remembering the look on Alice's face when she talked about them gave me the creeps now, too. I itched the back of my neck—a sort of psychosomatic reaction to the thought of bedbugs crawling anywhere on my body. Maybe the driveway was the better option. It was dreary and a bit chilly, but at least it wasn't actually raining anymore.

I locked the car and stood in the driveway. If he didn't get here soon, I'd go back inside the car and wait. Maybe I could use the cold temperatures to keep our conversation short. I could use the bedbugs as an excuse not to go inside, and then use the chilly air outside as an excuse not to talk very long. The plan seemed perfect. I relaxed a little, knowing I could get out of this anytime I wanted just by announcing that I was freezing cold. Of course, it would be best if we had each said our piece by the time that happened, so I wouldn't have to fret about any future conversations with Frank about these things. I already was assuming that he and I weren't going to be in each other's lives much after today. Of course, there was still next year's baseball season to think about, but I would worry about that next spring when the games started up again. Maybe Frank would have found yet another place to live, completely outside of town. Maybe he'd decide that baseball was no longer for him. Maybe—

"Hi," Frank said, interrupting my musing. I startled out of my reverie, looking up to see Frank staring at me, his hands thrust into his coat pockets. Somehow he'd driven up and gotten out of his car without me noticing. I looked around and saw his car parked out on the street rather than in the driveway behind me. I gulped and said nothing.

"Sorry," he said. "I didn't mean to surprise you. I figured you heard me coming."

"No. Sorry. Was just... lost in thought."

"So I see. Anyway, shall we go in?" He gestured expansively with one arm and kept the other inside his coat pocket. I shivered, reconsidering my idea of staying out here in the driveway.

"Well..." I began. Just then a low, faraway crack of thunder rumbled and I looked up just in time to feel a torrential rain start to hit my face. "Well," I said again, this time more loudly to be heard over the noise of the crashing rain. "Sure. I guess we'd better go inside, to get out of this rain!"

Frank nodded as he ran for the front door. By the time we both reached the porch he had whipped out his keys and was fiddling with them in the lock. I huddled up close behind him, and hoisted my gargantuan purse up higher on my shoulder so it wouldn't slip down yet again. I was technically under the awning but it was a small porch and the rain was coming down almost sideways now, continuing to get us both wet. The awning was apparently just for show. And not even a very good-looking show at that.

"Hurry!" I said. We're getting soaked!"

Frank's key turned in the lock, finally, and we were inside and out of the rain. Although I already knew the place was empty, it felt eerie, stark, and cold in here without any furniture to warm the place up. I threw my arms around myself, with my coat still buttoned up all the way, and shivered in reflex. My purse yet again slipped off my shoulder, and I caught it before it slid all the way off my arm. Instinctively, I opened it up to reveal the huge chasm full of stuff inside. My eye caught a glimpse of something large and white that hadn't been there before. I shoved my hand into the purse and brought out a single piece of paper, folded in half and now a little bit crumpled since it had been in my purse. It was Allen's supposed suicide note.

Frank was busy taking off his coat, not facing me, so I quietly took the paper out of my purse and unfolded it, putting my back to him in case he turned around and saw me. Alice must have slipped this into my purse while I was in the bathroom. Sometimes I hated my tiny bladder. I wholly understood her not wanting to have this note in her possession, but she was only making things worse for herself—and possibly for me—by planting this on me, no matter what her reasons were. I looked at it again, rereading the generic note, scrutinizing every word. What looked odd about this thing? What wasn't I seeing? Something was just not quite—

"Maggie? Are you okay?"

"Huh?" I said, refolding the note hastily and turning around at the same time. I had a way of looking guity about things even when I had no reason to, and I had a feeling this was one of those times.

"What have you got there?" Frank asked, pointing at the folded paper just as I was trying to surreptitiously slip it back into my purse.

"N-nothing," I said, sounding anything but convincing. He could easily see I was holding a piece of paper in my hands. "J-just a grocery list."

Nice save, Maggie, you idiot, I thought.

"A grocery list?" he said, frowning. He wasn't buying it. "Why would you need your grocery list now?"

He knew he'd caught me, and was calling me out on my fib. *Great.* I really sucked at subterfuge, and Frank knew me just well enough to see through my flimsy excuse. Still, I had to run with it as far as I could.

"B-because I'm going to stop at the store on the way home. I just remembered that I need to get more dog food for Vlad." I smiled, thinking that this might add a bit of legitimacy to my flagrant lie. From the look on Frank's face, though, it did no such thing. This didn't surprise me. My career as a spy was going nowhere fast.

"Whatever," he said, waving a hand and dismissing whatever I was trying to pull as if it didn't really matter anyway. And it probably didn't matter. I sighed and opened it back up for one more glance. It was, by all accounts, exactly what it seemed like: a note from Allen in which he briefly expressed his sorrow at the direction his life had gone. If he was anticipating killing himself soon, he might not be at his most eloquent. Of course, why anyone would kill themselves by drinking poisoned Sport-Aide was beyond me. If anything, that made his death look like anything but a suicide. Wouldn't he have simply done this at home, away from so many other people? Did he perhaps hope someone would save him? Would talk him out of it? Or something else? What could be the purpose of such a public suicide, one that would have definitely looked like murder?

"So, what exactly do you think we need to talk about?" Frank asked, sounding more miffed than I would have presumed since he himself said that we had to talk when I'd spoken to him on the phone. And, we'd met where he wanted to meet, too. He had no reason to sound this way. Except, perhaps, that I was intently staring at my grocery list as if it contained the secrets of the universe, obviously more intent on that piece of paper than I was on him.

"Hm?" I answered, barely registering the fact that he was also impatient for a response. I ran my finger over the text on the paper I was holding, looking at it closely for the first time. That is, looking at the *actual letters* closely for the first time. Something was trying to click in my brain, and I could almost feel it rising to the surface. Something was—

"Maggie? What is it?" Frank asked, his tone changing from annoyance to concern. I blinked and looked up at him, unsure what to say but knowing there was something ready to fly out of my mouth. Probably something inappropriate and embarrassing. That was clearly my *modus operandi.*

"Well, I don't really know," I admitted, quite truthfully. I looked back down at the note, moved my finger over the text, and just that fast my brain switched from confusion to clarity. *The text.* That was it. The note was typed—no, printed out from a printer—in Comic Sans. My arch nemesis! *Comic Sans!* The typeface that would come back to haunt me any time I'd gotten any communication from Frank. He had his email program set to use Comic Sans any time he composed an email. When we'd taken that trip to Cleveland in the spring, when we'd first started dating, Frank had printed out the directions in Comic Sans. I knew for a bloody fact that nobody in their right mind purposely used Comic Sans for *anything.* Certainly not for a suicide note—or even a grocery list.

I had a horrible feeling in the pit of my stomach as I looked up from the piece of paper I was holding to look at Frank. From this angle, he couldn't see what was really on the paper, but it was clear that he knew it wasn't a grocery list. He didn't know I had just been at Alice's house, either, so he'd have no way of knowing what I was holding. And, of course, just the choice of a font couldn't incriminate him completely. After all, why in the world would he want to see Allen dead? Why?

My mind tried to race through pros and cons of what I was now thinking. Alice had given me what I felt were convincing explanations for the photo of Frank on her shelf. There was indeed a picture of me right next to it. She'd been here at Frank's house—where we were standing now—because she was scouting out possible new places to live and Frank's house was on the market. She wasn't dating Frank. She couldn't be dating Frank. This couldn't just be the same old trite, clichéd motive, could it? Surely this wasn't a sick, twisted love triangle? Or, since it involved me, too, a love rectangle? Was that even a thing? Probably somewhere.

My mind couldn't keep up with what I was thinking. And, as I felt Frank get ready to ask me once again just what was going on, my phone rang from inside my purse. When had I put it in there again? I was sure it had been in my coat pocket. I flustered and thrust my hand into the purse that was slung over my arm. The note was in my other hand, now waving back and forth and flapping as I rooted in the purse for the ringing phone. Relieved, I found the phone on the third ring, whisked it out of the purse and swiped it to answer the call, even before I looked at who might be calling. It didn't matter: I needed the distraction of talking to someone else, someone other than Frank.

"Hello?" I said, a bit too loudly. I looked at Frank as I talked, and he just blinked at me, his expression blank. I didn't want to see him looking angry, of course, but not having any clue at all what he was thinking wasn't all that great, either.

"Maggie! Maggie, are you all right?" It was Alice.

"Of course. Why?" I had to remember to watch what I said when I responded to Alice right now. Frank was standing here hearing everything I said. I could only hope his hearing stunk as badly as mine did so that he couldn't tell who I was talking to.

"Get out of there now! I don't care where you are! Get back here, and most of all, *get away from Frank*!"

"Why?" I said, panic rising, trying to sound casual, as if this was a carefree call from my mother or even Helga.

"I found something! It's... I think it's Frank."

"You... what?" Rats. I couldn't say more with Frank standing here. And I had a feeling I couldn't easily excuse myself and head back outside. One glance out the curtainless window in front of me told me that wasn't going to work. The rain had started up again and was worse now, and visibility was poor. I could barely see the street at the end of the driveway. I'd be drenched in seconds if I went outside.

"*Frank*! He was... well..."

"Just. Say. It," I said quietly, trying not to grit my teeth or say Alice's name. I smiled at Frank, who continued to stare at me blankly. My goodness, that was unnerving.

"Allen did Frank's taxes this year."

Somehow, this hadn't been what I had been expecting to hear, and it was a bit anti-climactic. When I thought of devastating reasons for Alice to call and warn me about Frank, his tax returns really didn't enter into it. I'd heard of reasons to murder another person that were a bit sketchy, but botching someone's tax returns surely rated pretty low on that list.

"Why, whatever do you mean?" I said sweetly, feigning a light tone and hoping Frank wouldn't suspect we were actually talking about him. He still stared, but now he crossed his arms in front of his chest and stood with his feet a little bit apart, as if he were waiting for me to stop talking on the phone and get back to our conversation. I wasn't in that big a hurry to do that. Not just now.

"I mean," Alice continued, her voice rising in both pitch and volume. "I mean, from what I can see—and I admit I don't know all that much about tax returns, not compared to Allen, anyway—it looks like Frank was, well, let's just say his return looks a little shady."

"Really?" I asked, still painfully aware of how little I could really say out loud. "Whatever do you mean by that?"

Frank was now tapping a foot, impatient and clearly trying to communicate that to me so that I'd shut up and get off the phone. I held up an index finger and smiled weakly, trying to indicate that I would be just a moment or two longer. I had no idea how long I would really be on this particular phone call, though, and I hoped Alice would get to the point soon.

"I mean," Alice said again, "Frank was committing major tax fraud. Even I can see it here." She hesitated, and I could hear papers being rustled around on her end of the call. "I... I thought maybe I'd find something else in Allen's desk," she continued. I had a feeling I was going to get all the gory details right now, while I was standing here with Frank, and all I really needed was the Reader's Digest Condensed Version. If it was good enough for my aunt...

I coughed and held up that index finger again. But this time I said loudly—loudly enough for both Frank and Alice to hear me, "Just a minute, Frank. I'll wrap up this call."

I heard Alice stop rustling papers.

"Oh shit! You're with him right now!"

"Mm hmm," I said, pulling out my cheeriest, chipperest voice. I added a smile for Frank's benefit, but I was wondering how much longer he was willing to stand there waiting for me to shut up and get off the phone.

"Okay, okay, here's the thing," Alice said, understanding finally that she had to give me the short version. "Allen had a... sticky note on top of Frank's file, which was right there in his top middle drawer. He never keeps tax files there so I thought it was odd. I expected to find maybe another note or something, but not a tax file."

"Uh-huh?"

"It had a phone number on it. No name."

"A-and?"

Frank stepped forward one step. I flinched.

"And I called it to see who it was because the income and stuff listed on this return looks way off base. *Way* off base."

"A-and?" I said again, a little more loudly this time. She was doing a bad job at condensing the situation into bite-sized chunks for me.

"And it was the IRS fraud hotline. *Allen was going to go to the IRS about Frank's return.*"

"I—I don't know what to say," I said, which was the truth, no matter who was listening to me right now. "Why now?"

"It's *last year's* return!" Alice practically shouted over the phone. "Allen didn't *do* this one. Frank must have given Allen a copy of last year's return to go by or something. Or come to him for tax advice. Or... geez, Maggie, I don't know! I just know that Allen knew something about Frank's tax fraud. He always wrote himself notes about clients and put them on sticky notes like this. Usually it was stuff like 'Remember to get the rest of the receipts' or something like that."

I was absorbing what Alice was saying but I couldn't help sneaking a look over at Frank. He no longer looked impatient. Now he seemed to look worried. Or maybe upset. It was hard to tell since my own brain was doing back flips trying to keep up with what Alice was saying, and what it meant about the man who was standing here in front of me right now. I wasn't sure how much he suspected, but I had to be projecting fear because he looked like he was ready to take action. What kind of action? Anybody's guess, but he wasn't going to reach over here and pin a medal on my coat, that's for sure.

"Alice?"

"Yeah?"

"I think I gotta go now. I'll try to get back to you later about all this, okay?"

"Sure. Do you want me to—"

Click. I hung up the phone, suddenly nervous about whatever she might say next. Of course, I had a feeling I knew exactly what she would have said next. She would have told me to get the heck out of the vicinity of Frank and head straight to the police for the sake of my own safety.

Frank, on the other hand, was now fuming. Quietly, but he was still fuming. "Alice? You were talking to Alice?"

I had said her name without realizing it, and now Frank knew who I had been talking to. And, depending on what was really going on with Frank and Allen, he might now suspect that I suspected him of... *oh, shit.* I was in it deep now.

"Y-yeah," I said sheepishly. "I f-forgot my phone at her house."

"You mean the phone you're holding in your hand right now? The same phone she just called you on?"

And this is precisely when I realized I would suck at poker. I couldn't fib or bluff to save my life. I started to pray that, in fact, I wasn't currently in a situation where I had to think about actually saving my life, because if I was, I was in a lot of trouble.

"Oh, heh heh," I laughed nervously. "What do you know? I do have my phone! Gosh, I wonder what phone Alice has then. Must be someone else's."

Frank sighed and crossed his arms. "Must be. So, what happens now?"

I blinked. I certainly wasn't ready for that question. "I—I don't know. I guess I should go see what Alice needs, or if I can help her, um, identify that phone she's got that isn't hers. And isn't mine."

"Really?" He sounded singularly unimpressed. I couldn't blame him. My lying skills were certainly not improving as we went along.

"Yeah. Um, so, let's just call it a day, shall we?"

He stepped forward—just one step—and I flinched. I was telegraphing all sorts of fear issues, and he was picking up on all of them. One more step closer.

"Well, we haven't finished our little... talk." The slight hesitation freaked me out a little. Okay, a lot.

"We—we can finish it later. Maybe on the phone." I nodded at my own suggestion.

"You mean, on that phone right there?" He pointed at the cell phone in my hand. "That one. That phone that you supposedly left at Alice's house. Would that one work?"

"Frank, listen. I can explain."

"Explain what? That Alice didn't realize you had to actually have your phone in your hand to be talking to her over the phone? I never thought that woman was all that bright, but I wouldn't have pegged her as quite that stupid. Same with you, my dear."

He stepped forward one more step as he said that last word, and I felt my pulse pounding in my throat.

"Heh heh, well, she can be a b-bit of a s-scatterbrain at times. It's one of the things I l-love about her." I stepped backwards, and it began to look as if we were doing a slow-motion cha-cha, only a little too far apart. Then again, I was hoping we could get even farther apart. Like, now.

"And what about you? I wouldn't exactly call you a scatterbrain, Maggie. And yet even you didn't notice that you had your phone right in your hand and couldn't have left it at her house. You're slipping, Maggie. Admit it."

He stepped forward again, and I slid backwards. At his sides, his hands clenched into tight fists. My mind was scrambling to find a way out of this nightmare. I was alone in an empty house with a man who very likely killed another man over what he knew about his tax fraud. And if he'd been so careless as to think a tax accountant wouldn't be able to figure out a case of tax fraud when it was put right in front of him, well... how careless might he be now in trying to cover up that crime? He'd apparently already killed one person to keep his secret. Was I next?

My purse slid off my shoulder—again—and I clutched it to my chest. Here was a time when I wished I'd been proactive enough to carry something like Mace or pepper spray in this purse, instead of old packs of gum and dried-up Tide sticks. Not that I would have been able to find the pepper spray in the purse in any sort of reasonable amount of time. I'd be long dead before I could locate the thing.

"Maggie?"

"Yes?" I hadn't been paying attention for a nanosecond or two, and Frank had slipped a few paces closer. Now he was almost within striking distance if he wanted to swipe at me. I had to remember to date shorter guys who didn't have such long reaches. If a guy was short enough, I could theoretically have the edge here. But, dating a guy like Frank, who towered at a dizzying six foot four, I was doomed in a situation like this.

"Come here," he said. I'd let another few precious nanoseconds slip by, and I knew I'd have to stop running scenarios in my head and pay closer attention to what was actually going on.

"N-no, Frank. I'm leaving." I tried turning and zipping out of the house, but, of course, tall, lanky Frankie was right behind me and then had me by the shoulders. I dropped my purse and my phone and froze. The purse simply thunked at my feet, but the phone skittered away, halfway from me to the door, and the battery came off the back. I knew I should have gotten a case for the stupid thing.

"I don't think you are. Not until we settle a few things."

"Such as?" I had no idea why I had just asked him this. I was pretty sure I didn't want to know what he thought we should settle, and I was asking for trouble. Because apparently I didn't think I was in enough trouble yet.

"Oh, I think you know."

"I... I do?"

"Yes. And no matter what's going on between the two of us, I think we should be able to pull together in a situation like this."

"A situation? Like... this?" Where was he going with this?

"Yes. Are you thinking what I'm thinking?"

"I'm hoping not, no."

"Well, of course you don't want it to be true, but I can assure you that your instincts in this are exactly right." He still had a tight grip on my shoulders and had spun me around to face him.

"They are?"

"Yes! Yours and about half of her neighborhood's!"

"Wait... what?"

"Alice. You're onto her, too, aren't you?"

"Wait... *what*?"

"Alice. Sure, it's cliché, but in this case, it's also true."

"What's cliché? What's true?"

For a second I lost my paralyzing fear of Frank. Instead, I was confused, puzzled. He wasn't attacking me. He wasn't even threatening me. He was—well, I didn't really know what he was.

"Maggie, it's Alice. It's always been Alice. Surely you see that now. Cliché to think the wife did it, but sometimes it's a cliché for a reason. You see it, too, don't you?"

"I, um, I do?"

"Sure. But why did you also think it would be a good idea for you to tackle this alone and not let me in on it? What were you thinking?"

"Thinking?" I hedged, trying to catch up to Frank and also not look like a complete idiot. "I—I wasn't thinking—"

"Well, that's clear enough," he said, and smiled. Yes, he smiled!

And I couldn't handle it anymore. I dropped to my knees and then completely collapsed to the floor, putting my hands over my face and sobbing.

"Frank, I don't know what... I... oh, Lord, help me."

"Maggie!" He leaned down next to me and put his hands on my

shoulders again. This time it felt completely different, but I knew that was due to my own perspective and not because he was actually doing anything different. "Are you okay? What's wrong?"

"What's wrong?" I blubbered. "How can you ask me that?"

"Oh, I'm sorry, Maggie. Of course, Alice is your friend! I'm sorry, I didn't mean to be so... cavalier about it. I've suspected for a while, but you're just figuring it out. You're probably in shock." He started to rub my shoulders in a way I found strangely comforting, despite the fact that, minutes earlier, I thought he was going to strangle me with those same hands. I felt incredibly nauseated and hoped I wasn't going to throw up.

I closed my eyes and got my sobbing under control. Once I felt I could handle it, I opened my eyes and looked up at Frank. He had the most sincere look of concern on his face. I was stunned. Now I had to process what he'd said, what he'd implied about Alice. What about the suicide note? What about the tax fraud? What—

"Maggie, what should we do? Should we go to the police? Do we have anything concrete on Alice? Or just suspicions?"

"I... I don't know. I'm not thinking clearly." Another gross understatement by yours truly.

"Well, okay then," he said, rubbing my back now in a way that was obviously supposed to make me feel better. In reality, I still kind of wanted to throw up.

"Frank, I just need some time to think things through."

"Of course, of course," he said. "I was just worried there for a minute."

"About what?"

"About you! You sounded like you were buying Alice's bullshit when you were on the phone with her. It was making me mad to hear it. But then you got off the phone and I could see you felt the same way I do."

"So... um... what exactly do you have on Alice?" I figured I might as well ask him straight out before I settled on which side of this enormous fence I was going to come down on. And before I threw up all over his shoes.

"Well, let's start with the motive. She hated the guy. Poor Allen was so into the baseball team precisely to get away from Alice at least two or three times a week while the team was active."

"That doesn't mean she'd kill him."

"It does if she stands to inherit money and property."

"She does?" I asked myself how Frank could know something like this. Surely she hadn't come right out and told him.

"Sure she does. He told me all about it a few months ago. Once they realized they really weren't going to have kids of their own, he changed his will and left everything to her."

"Wait, what does that have to do with it? Hadn't he had her as the beneficiary before?"

"No. It was his brother and his wife and their kids. But when Alice had the cancer surgery last year, Allen decided to make sure she was well provided for."

"But that doesn't sound like Allen. And Alice had cancer surgery?"

"Sure, he was a bit of a jerk sometimes. Loud, brash, but funny as hell. And secretly, he wanted to do right by Alice. He knew she was never really all that happy with him. It was his way of telling her he loved her."

"And he told her he'd changed his policy?"

"Well, it certainly wouldn't do him any good to not tell her, if one of his goals was to improve his marriage, right?"

"Right," I agreed, sitting in a heap on the bare floor with my purse in my lap. "Right."

I opened the purse and took out the piece of folded paper.

"Frank," I said, hands shaking as I handed him the paper. "Alice called me today and asked me to come over to her house. She gave me this when I got there."

I let him read the suicide note and watched him carefully for any sort of odd reaction. When he finished, he dropped his hand to his side and clicked his tongue.

"That's ridiculous. Allen didn't kill himself."

If Frank had killed Allen, he probably wouldn't have said what he'd just said. In, fact, he would have embraced this as an alternate explanation for what happened to Allen. Still, I had to press a little more.

"I agree. The note, anyway, sounds too—"

"Too stupid! Even for Allen!" He threw the paper down and sighed.

"Yes, precisely. But..." I trailed off, not sure whether to mention what else I was thinking. But, I pressed on. Now or never, and for some reason, I didn't feel as if I was in any particular danger at the moment. "But look at the *font*."

He retrieved the paper from the floor in front of his feet and looked at it. "Yeah. It's Comic Sans. I'd recognize it anywhere."

"I know you would." I waited to see how he'd react to that.

"It's my favorite font. You know that."

"Yes, I do. And so does Alice. We used to joke about it."

"Why would you joke about someone's favorite font? That's just... weird."

"Well, sometimes women like to be catty about their men. Anyway, that's not the point. The point is—"

His eyes widened as it dawned on him. "Alice knows what my favorite font is."

"Yes."

"And she used it to... to make this fake suicide note."

"Yes," I sighed, closing my eyes and relaxing as he said it and connected the dots that even I hadn't really seen until now. "Yes, unfortunately, yes."

"Oh, no."

"Oh, yes."

"But, it's just a note from a computer, with a font I like. She didn't honestly think that would be enough to throw suspicion on me, did she?"

"Well," I fudged. "Not exactly. But it was a start."

"What does that mean?" His eyes were still wide and unblinking, his pupils dilated.

"She called me over to her house to show this to me today. And then warned me to be careful when I met you today. She warned me... not to meet you alone in this house. But she honestly also knew I wasn't about to meet you in a restaurant again." I smiled wanly, and Frank patted my hand.

"Sweetie, I'm sorry. We'll probably never be able to go out to eat ever again." He smiled, too.

"It's okay. Then she called while I was standing here—"

"On that phone she supposedly thought you'd left at her house?" He raised an eyebrow.

"Well, I admit, that was my own fib. And that's not why she called me. I was... well... I was half convinced she was right about you when I came here. Then she called and—"

"And what? What did she say?"

"She... she said she found the tax returns you gave to Allen so he could do your taxes for you this year."

I waited to see if he'd tense up or in some way react like a guilty person. He did no such thing. Instead, he simply nodded in agreement.

"Yeah, Allen did my taxes this year. I gave him returns for the two previous years, just like he asked for. I'm new in town so I was quite happy to find someone who knew what he was doing. I didn't mind throwing business his way. Figured he could use it if he was going to keep that wife of his in the lifestyle to which she'd become accustomed." He half smiled in a sheepish sort of way. My stomach did a little flip in response. I was either going to vomit or cry, and I wasn't entirely convinced that I wouldn't end up doing both at the same time. And that was going to be seriously awkward for both of us.

"Well..."

"So what do my tax returns have to do with Alice and Allen? I mean, beyond the obvious fact that I paid him to file my return for me this year? Why would Alice call you to tell you that?"

"Well, you hadn't mentioned to me that Allen had done your taxes."

"Maggie, I have no idea who did *your* taxes this year. Apparently I'd say we're not serious enough yet to know who does our tax returns." He grinned wide, thinking this very funny. But I wasn't in the mood to laugh at much of anything right now.

"She said she could tell you'd committed tax fraud, and that Allen knew about it."

"What?"

"Something about your old returns, not this year's. That Allen had figured it out and left himself a note to go to the IRS about you, or something. I don't know. By that point in the phone call, I was sweating bullets and hoping you couldn't tell how nervous I was."

"Oh, I could tell!" It was true. By then he was staring at me as if I was a science specimen and he was Jonas Salk.

"So, by the time I got off the phone with her, I was pretty sure you had k-k-killed Allen."

"What? You?"

I lowered my eyes. "I'm sorry, Frank. Truly. You and I haven't exactly been on good footing the past few weeks, and I guess I was just ripe for Alice's story. First the poisoning in the restaurant—"

"Which was simple food poisoning, as you remember."

I rolled my eyes. "Yes, I know that now. But I started adding this stuff up, with an unsolved murder hovering over everyone, and, well—"

"And you thought I killed Allen?" He sounded wounded, and I suppose he had every right.

"Not then. But then there was the shellfish incident—"

"That was a simple allergy! I couldn't have had anything to do with that!"

"I know that, too!" I said, feeling defensive. "But at the time it felt wrong."

"Of course it did! Allergies are bound to feel wrong. They *are* wrong."

"Then today she showed me the suicide note—"

"The *fake* suicide note," he reminded me.

"Yes, sorry. The fake suicide note. And it wasn't until I opened it again here and saw that it was in Comic Sans—"

"Oh, for crying out loud! It's a *font*!"

"Your *favorite* font."

"Yes, my favorite font," he conceded. "But honestly, Maggie."

"*Nobody admits their favorite font is Comic Sans!* Frank, you use that horrific font for everything!"

"And Alice knew," he said, ignoring my jibe about his favorite font being horrific. "And so she purposely printed it out in Comic Sans, knowing you're a font nerd and you'd eventually make the connection."

"Eventually," I admitted. "I didn't make it right away, though. Not while I was with her at her house."

"Maybe that's why she called you. Did she know you were here with me?"

I nodded. "Yeah. She told me not to come here."

"So she called you, hoping to talk about this added piece of 'evidence' against me."

I nodded again. Things were clicking into place in ways that made me feel even more like vomiting. I was starting to calculate how many steps it was from here to the bathroom on this floor. Too many.

"That bitch!" Frank said, and he scrambled and stood up. He started pacing the room. I stayed on the floor, feeling a little too dizzy to stand, even though it would have made my getaway to the bathroom easier if I began to feel even worse.

"I wonder what she planned to do if you wanted to take this further with the police. I mean, about the tax returns."

"I don't know. I'd have to talk to her about it."

"You're not going over there! Oh, no!"

"Trust me, Frank. I have no real intention of going back over there today."

"Or any day!" He paced a little more quickly, in a tighter circle around me. It was beginning to make me feel woozy.

"Let's just think this through and work out a plan."

"And to think she tried to seduce me that time she came to one of our games—"

I didn't have time to stand or to make it to the bathroom. A second after Frank spoke I had vomited all over the hardwood floors. The ones that probably sold the place at a higher rent for the landlord. They were going to have a devil of a time cleaning it up and getting rid of the stench. "Frank, take me home."

CHAPTER 31

GOT INTO FRANK'S CAR AND WAITED FOR HIM to come around to the other side and get in himself. He sat in the driver's seat, pulled the driver's side door closed, and sighed. Then he turned to look me straight in the eye.

"Are you okay? Because I can sit here a while till you're sure you're not going to throw up again."

"You mean, until I'm sure I'm not going to throw up in your *car*." I tried to smile but nothing was really all that funny right now.

"Well," he said sheepishly. "Yeah, that too. But honestly, are you all right?"

I sighed back. "I'll be fine. I'm just a little confused, and a *lot* disappointed and sad."

"Disappointed?"

"In Alice. In myself, for believing in her and thinking I was doing a good deed."

"A good deed, how?" He started the car but kept it in park, his hands gripping the wheel.

"Being her friend when no one else would be. Turns out all the other people were right, and I was being a fool."

"It's never foolish to reach out to someone in friendship," he said and took his right hand off the wheel to pat my knee. I smiled, appreciating the gesture more than he knew.

"Thanks. It'll take me a while to agree with you, but... thanks."

He put the car in drive and we headed toward my apartment. I wasn't sure if I needed a nice, long nap or a stiff drink. All I knew was that I was going to have to contact the police about Alice, and soon. I was glad I had Frank to support me in this, though, because I didn't relish the thought of ratting out Alice for what she'd done, even if it meant Allen would finally get the justice he deserved. It still wasn't going to be a pleasant experience for me.

"Frank?"

"Yeah?"

"Should we go straight to the police station first? You know, before taking me back to my place?"

He kept his eyes on the road but tightened his grip on the wheel. "Why now? Wouldn't you want to go home first since you're not feeling well?"

"Part of the reason I don't feel well is that this is now hanging over my head. Maybe if I get it over with—or, at least, get it started—then maybe I'll feel better. Or won't feel any worse."

I wasn't sure I bought my own line of reasoning, but it seemed right to go do this now. Waiting seemed almost like withholding evidence or being a cohort of Alice's, even though I hadn't tipped her off that we knew what she'd done.

"I dunno, Maggie. I don't like how pale you still look."

"Frank, it's almost winter. And even in the summer, I almost never go outside. I always look this pale." I tried to smile, but I knew it didn't look convincing. He seemed overly concerned, though, and I knew I'd have to work at it to convince him I could handle a trip to the police station.

"You just threw up in my old house!"

"I know, I know. And I'm really sorry about that. You were a good sport to get the paper towels out of your trunk and clean that up for me."

Truth be told, if I had had to clean up that mess myself, I would have gotten sick all over again. He really had gone above and beyond to take care of that. One call to the landlord to let them know what had happened, and he had just found a way to help me get it off my mind for the rest of the day.

"Maggie, I keep picturing you getting sick in the middle of the police station. Not cool. Where's your hurry?"

"Where's my hurry? Alice *killed* Allen! We can't just let what we know languish out there without doing something about it!" I reached inside my purse and found the folded-up paper, which was on top of all the rest of the junk and therefore easy to swipe. "We need to give them *this*. A fake suicide note? Seriously. We have evidence here in my hot little hands. We can't hang onto this. We have to turn it over, and we can't wait. 'Oh yes, officer. I was given this fake suicide note, but I was a *little* bit sleepy so I decided to go back to my apartment first to take a nap and binge-watch a couple of episodes of *Stranger Things* before coming down here to drop this off. Was that so wrong?'"

Frank rolled his eyes, which I could clearly see even though he kept looking at the road in front of him. "Maggieeeee..."

"Frannnnnk..."

"Look, we're closer to your apartment than we are the police station. Let's just stop there and let you freshen up a bit first."

He turned onto the street that would connect with my own in about three blocks. He was right about that, but mostly because he had kept driving toward my apartment and made choices in his driving while we were discussing where to go. Still, here we were in my neighborhood. Maybe it wouldn't hurt for me to change into something different. It was probably my imagination, but I could smell the ugly stench of having gotten sick, even if I'd missed my own clothing and hit the floor. I could brush my teeth, gargle a little bit, and freshen up. It had a fair amount of appeal.

"Fine," I said as he turned onto my street. "I'll tidy myself up a bit."

I CAME OUT OF THE BATHROOM feeling a lot better than when I went in. Frank was right to suggest it for me. Cool water on my face, some lovely minty toothpaste on my toothbrush, some refreshing mouthwash for good measure. I felt like I was back to normal again, and only a small part of me was dreading the impending trip to the police station to tell them what I now knew about Alice.

Switching off the bathroom light, I emerged into the hallway and could clearly see straight into the living room, where Frank was rifling through my purse. I stood frozen in one spot. His back was partially turned away from me, which meant I could see him but he couldn't really see me. I watched, still glued to the floor just outside the bathroom in my hallway, as he grabbed that folded piece of paper out of my purse, unfolded it, and held it up to the ceiling light, which he had turned on while I was in the bathroom. Instinctively, I knew it would be best to wait and watch for a few more seconds, or even minutes, to see what Frank was going to do next. I didn't have a good feeling about this at all.

As I watched, Frank took the fake suicide note—and I admit I was starting to wonder just how fake it was, and if it was fake, just who had created it—and crumpled it up in his fist until it was small enough to shove into his front jeans pocket. It took some doing, because paper doesn't ever want to cooperate and crumple small when you need it to, but as he shoved it as far down into the pocket as he could, he then looked furtively around my living room.

When his gaze swung back to the hallway, our eyes locked on each other. I was still unable to move, now from a sense of fear coupled with prudence. Besides, I had no back door out of my apartment. Just the front door, which was where Frank was currently standing, and various windows I could theoretically climb out as long as I didn't mind a twenty-foot drop to the ground below. At times like this a second-floor apartment no longer seemed like the safest option. Right now it could literally end up being the death of me.

"Maggie," Frank said. Simply. Almost blandly.

"Frank," I replied. Not quite as blandly. I couldn't seem to keep my voice from shaking and showing just how frightened I suddenly was.

I couldn't even bring myself to ask him what the heck he was doing, going through my purse and pocketing what I considered to be crucial evidence that we were supposed to now be bringing down to the police station. And yet I had to know.

"What are you doing?" I kept the question generic, trying not to let on exactly what I'd seen.

"What did you see?"

Well, there went that idea.

"Not much."

He let out the breath he'd been holding. "Oh, okay..."

"Just my boyfriend stealing police evidence out of my purse, crumpling it up, and stuffing it into his jeans. Not much more than that."

Yeah, one of these days my big mouth was going to get me into a lot of trouble. I was now thinking that day might be today.

"Now, Maggie. It's not the way it looks."

"What's not the way it looks? You filching the suicide note from my purse while I wasn't looking? Or you crumpling it up into a tiny ball? Or maybe you shoving it into your pocket before I got out of the bathroom? Which of those things isn't the way it looks, Frank?"

As I kept talking, I found myself getting more and more pissed off. Even though I knew this wasn't a good state of affairs for me, because Frank was so much taller and stronger than I was, I couldn't help myself. Sure, I was still pretty confused about everything. My brain had now bounced back and forth between thinking Alice was the killer and thinking Frank had been the one to do Allen in. Now he'd gotten me to think it was Alice less than an hour before, and here I was *yet again* thinking it was Frank instead.

"I had to get this away from you, Maggie. You're wrong to think the police need this stupid piece of paper. It's meaningless."

He stuffed his hand down into that front jeans pocket and brought out the balled-up fake suicide note. He waved it at me angrily. "This—this stupid piece of paper could get me into a lot of trouble, Maggie."

"How so?" I said, speaking up when I should probably try to stay silent. "It's fake, right? Alice just made it up to frame you, right? Or so you keep saying."

Good grief, I was an idiot.

"Yes, she's trying to frame me. This whole thing was her idea, but I wouldn't have gone along with it if she hadn't held that ridiculous tax return over my head!"

"Wait... so that's true? About your tax return and the tax fraud?"

Now my head was really spinning. And if I wasn't careful, I was going to lose my head in addition to my ability to just shut up.

"Of course it's true. What other reason would I have had to go in on this with Alice? I barely knew the woman before all this started!"

He was hopping mad now and losing his own grip on what was prudent to say. What a fun pair we were, both of us blurting out things we probably shouldn't be saying. At least, not to each other, and not now, alone in my apartment. I suddenly wished we had gone to the police station first, but now I could see clearly why Frank hadn't wanted to do that. Couldn't say that I blamed him. Murderers probably avoided police stations the way I avoided the gym.

"So... so... what you're saying is that you—"

"Yes."

"And Alice?"

"Yes!"

"Yes to what, exactly?" I wasn't even sure what I was asking him anymore. But he now seemed eager to tell me anything I wanted to know. Not that I really wanted to know any of this. I was starting to feel sick all over again.

"Yes to whatever it is you're thinking right now. Yes, she found out about my tax return. I figured Allen must have told her because how else would she know? She held it over my head."

He started tapping his foot on the carpet, which made nothing more than a muffled *whuff* sound but which still unnerved me as I continued to stand rooted in that hallway outside the bathroom.

I tried to do the physics calculations necessary to decide whether making a run for it would work. Right now Frank was physically standing between me and my front door. Unless he moved away, that escape route was out of the question. Could I even get to any of my windows here at the back of the apartment and get one open in time to get out of here? He'd run right after me if I tried that, and I'd lose time trying to get myself physically out the window backwards so that I could dangle my feet down, then hang on with my extended arms and perhaps drop down to the ground without breaking more than a few dozen bones in the process.

And of course, even if I did manage to get out of the apartment this way and hit the ground to excruciating pain, I'd be unable to walk or run away, and within minutes Frank could be down the front stairs of the apartment building and upon me. There was just no way this was going to work. I'd have to shut up now and try to talk my way out of this dilemma. And I didn't see that happening either. *Shit.*

"Frank—Frank, listen to me," I said, hoping to cast a preemptive strike in my favor. "I don't want to go to the police. Not anymore. Right now I just think maybe we should talk this out. You need to tell me how Alice did all this."

Maybe if I cast aspersions on Alice and let Frank implicate her in his ongoing rant, he might forget that I also now knew he was heavily involved in Allen's murder. I didn't hold out much hope for this plan, but it was really the only one I had. As a plan, it sucked. As my last hope, it also sucked.

He frowned and exhaled so loudly and so long that I wondered if he was going to pass out. I sure hoped he would, but of course he didn't.

"Alice? I don't want to talk about Alice! That woman is a nut case. A total whack job."

Great. There went my one remaining idea. I was fresh out of thoughts on how to proceed.

"What am I going to do about you now, Maggie?"

I was pretty sure this was a rhetorical question, but at any rate, I wisely chose not to answer it. Anything I suggested, no matter how well meaning (and self-serving), would probably not have lined up with what Frank wanted to do about me right now. His answers would have been vastly different from my own.

Frank then reached into his back right jeans pocket and pulled out a multi-tool, that omnipresent piece of gear that every man in my life seemed to need to carry around, except Seth. He was more the type to carry a USB stick in his pocket for the kind of emergencies he encountered in daily life. Frank's multi-tool was an impressive piece of utilitarian tech. The guy could have survived in the deepest, darkest part of the forest with this thing alone, and I already knew that. He fiddled with it a little bit, first pulling out the cork screw, then putting it back, then flipping out the bottle opener. He looked at that for a few long seconds (too long, if you asked me), and put that back as well.

Then, as if settling on something in his own mind, he brought out the knife. The ridiculously sharp knife. The reason multi-tools were no longer allowed on airplanes unless you stuffed them in your checked baggage. He slowly ran his finger down the back side of the blade, the safe side, looking at the multi-tool closely and avoiding looking at me. I assumed this was done to freak me out and not because he was in any way ashamed or worried about making eye contact with me. Whatever his intent was, though, he was indeed freaking me out.

It was time to answer that rhetorical question.

"Y-you don't need to do anything about me, Frank. I'm just fine standing here, for as long as you need me to stand here. Not going anywhere."

Now he looked up at me, a grim, unfamiliar look on his face. I felt my heart skip a beat, then pulse at the base of my throat. Fear was certainly a huge adrenaline buzz, and not in a good way.

"Maggie, I really don't like where we've gotten to in the past day or so."

"Y-you and me both, Frank."

"And I'm not happy about where we go from here, either."

"I'll go anywhere you want. Let's just get out of here, okay?"

I put one foot in front of the other and walked a single step in his direction, hoping to get us out of this nerve-wracking inertia that kept me landlocked in my own apartment. Once we were outside, I'd have some sort of shot at getting away from Frank. Standing here like this meant he had the edge over me.

Just then I heard a scrabbling, clicking sound behind Frank. It wasn't all that loud, and at first Frank looked as if he hadn't even heard it. But I lived here and I knew the sound of Seth putting his copy of my apartment key in that front lock.

And Vlad knew it, too. He'd been sound asleep on the recliner across the room not long after we'd come in, having discovered that we did not, in fact, carry foodstuffs with us. His disappointment had lasted a short while before he'd climbed back onto the recliner and went to sleep. I'd forgotten he was even in the same room with Frank until now. Until Seth had decided to show up.

It was Vlad who alerted Frank to the presence of someone on the other side of the door. When Vlad hopped upright on the recliner, ears perked up and eyes on the door, Frank whipped around and stood facing the door. I debated the pros and cons of speaking up, of warning Seth about the probable danger that awaited him inside his mother's apartment, but for the next few seconds I held my tongue. For me that was close to an eternity of saying nothing.

The next minute or two now seems like a blur of insanity. Seth finally got the key in the lock and forced it to turn. The copy I'd given him when he started staying with me again wasn't made properly and had to be massaged into the lock in order to work.

And then, the door was open and there was Seth, hands on the doorknob and lock, the door now open. He half stepped inside the apartment and froze. Frank was no longer facing me—he'd turned to see Seth coming in the door—so I stood in my spot in the hallway and frantically began waving my arms and shaking my head in a sort of "Don't!" gesture that I hoped he would pick up on.

Then my feet were in motion and I was dashing down the hallway into the living room and shouting at the same time.

"Get him! *Get Frank!*" I yelled, coming up behind Frank myself just as Seth began to understand what I was asking him to do. Frank, who had heard me shout this to Seth, was turning around to face me, and I quickly halted, coming up short.

Seth, on the other hand, rushed at Frank from behind now, throwing his arms around Frank's midsection and head-butting him in the back. He'd hit him fast enough to knock the wind out of Frank, and the two of them flew forward and down, with Frank hitting the coffee table, Seth on top of him. A double grunt escaped from both of them, and Vlad sailed off the recliner, yipping at the top of his little doggy lungs.

I ran down the hallway and into the living room, then panicked and grabbed the first weighty object I could find—the Smith Corona Clipper typewriter I kept on display on one of my bookshelves to my left. As I yelled, "Seth, move outta the way!"—raising the typewriter over my head—Vlad leapt onto the man-pile, barking his fool head off. Seth loosened his grip around Frank's waist just enough to move to one side, and I brought the typewriter down on Frank's head with both hands.

The adrenaline burst made me nearly faint, and I let go of the typewriter. Vlad had lost his balance as the two men tussled, and he fell off the coffee table just before the typewriter bounced and followed him to the floor on top of him. I heard a horrible doggy whimper, then heard Seth yell, "He's out cold! Call the cops!"

But my phone was buried in my stupid purse, wherever that was. I instinctively dropped to my knees and grabbed Vlad instead. "You call the cops, Seth! And then the vet!"

I remember sobbing and cradling Vlad, who felt lifeless in my arms, rocking us both back and forth on the floor. Somewhere far away I thought I heard Seth talking to the authorities on his phone.

Beyond that, I remember nothing.

CHAPTER 32

H E'LL BE FINE," I ASSURED ANNIE the next day as she sat on my couch with Vlad on her lap. She was softly crooning to him and gently stroking his back, taking care to avoid the area around his head and neck, as the vet had instructed us. I'd bought some puppy pee pads for the time being, so we wouldn't have to subject Vlad to the strain of the leash or the stairs from the second floor just to get him outside to do his business. The pads confused him a little, but not for long. With the weather turning much colder, my main concern now was that he might get used to the idea and balk at going outside once we'd been given the all-clear on his little doggy concussion.

With the right food—and some yummy human treats and meats—he had quickly forgiven me for bonking him on the head. I explained that it had been an unfortunate accident, and I apologized for letting the big bad Frank man into our lives in the first place. I was glad dogs were generally so quick to let bygones be bygones.

As for Frank? Well, both he and Alice were currently in the slammer awaiting trial, as the TV movies used to say. Alice had been taking trifluoperazine for anxiety and depression, and she'd been setting aside doses to use on Allen for quite a while. The Sport-Aide spiking had been Frank's idea, and he'd pulled it off before that ill-fated game while the field and dugout prep were usually little more than organized chaos. He made sure Allen got the right bottle.

Seth and I were both going to have to testify, but the glacial speed with which the justice system moved meant that wasn't going to happen till at least sometime next spring. In the meantime, we'd heard from our lawyer that Alice and Frank had ratted each other out, to coin more movie phrases. There was enough blame to go around for both of them.

ABOUT A WEEK LATER, SETH WAS FORAGING in my refrigerator for lunch on Saturday afternoon, now that Vlad's bottomless tummy was full enough to keep him from vaulting off the couch at the sound of the fridge door opening. I was once again behind on my freelance work, Annie was back at college, and although Seth had technically gone back to his apartment, he seemed to find reasons to show up at my door just in time for meals. I wasn't complaining. After all, I no longer had a boyfriend to pamper or cook for. I was surprisingly okay with that.

The Raging Avocados, whose post-season had finally wrapped up somewhere near Thanksgiving amid frigid temperatures, had pulled off an impressive third place upset in the whole league, even without Allen's speed or Frank's eagle eye and focused glove work. It was a record year for my favorite team, and we had all celebrated in a manner befitting the finest Little Leaguers everywhere: not with Sport-Aide, but with ice cream cones at Scotty's Scoops on the far edge of town.

Twenty-seven flavors... and not one of them was avocado.

THE END

Just a few of the real Raging Avocados softball team
Pittsburgh, Pa.

If you enjoyed Maggie's latest adventure, or even if you
simply had a chuckle at poor Vlad's expense,
please consider reviewing *The Tell-Tale Heart Attack*
on places such as Amazon.com and Goodreads.
Indie authors rely on positive reader reviews!

Thank you!

ACKNOWLEDGMENTS

ALWAYS HAVE FOLKS TO THANK when I put out another book. This one's no different. And I love them all.

Heartfelt thanks go to my high school classmate Jonathan Becker for answering a few questions about insurance policies (and regaling me with fascinating stories). What a fun and enlightening phone call that was! Also, Crystal Collins answered a few crucial questions about Vlad the Inhaler's post-concussion treatment. Vlad deserved only the best, and Crystal is the best.

Thank you to the real Raging Avocados for being awesome. Avocados are hip now, so you guys were ahead of the curve.

And my usual thanks to all the members of Crit Club, that online, worldwide (but purposely small) critique group that has been the impetus for most of my books finding their way into the world. Hard to believe we're inching toward twenty years together.

Much love to the St. Davids Roomies and also to Deep Creek Four. Sometimes I wonder how I was blessed by so many good, enduring friendships over the years. Thanks to you all.

ABOUT THE AUTHOR

IN THE EARLY 1980S, Linda pursued a writing degree from Carnegie Mellon University in Pittsburgh, Pa. She pursued it but it kept getting away.

She has since worked behind the scenes in publishing as a proofreader, typesetter, and copyeditor. She's worked with publishers, big and small, and with individual authors, big and small. (The big ones really ought to get a little more exercise.) She's also an 8th grade composition coach for WriteAtHome.com.

Linda is currently on the board of the St. Davids Christian Writers' Association and also serves as author wrangler for Beaver County BookFest in Pennsylvania. She enjoys comedy, computer gadgets, office supplies, reading, movies, adventure games, crocheting, "Weird Al" Yankovic music, and her office guinea pigs, who keep her company while she's working.

Her favorite writing challenge since 2004 has been the yearly contest known as National Novel Writing Month: writing 50,000 words of a single new fiction project during the month of November. She loves the pressure of a ridiculous, forced deadline. *The Tell-Tale Heart Attack* started out as a NaNoWriMo novel in 2015.

Linda currently lives in western Pennsylvania with her husband, Wayne Parker. They share six children between them, all of them now grown and living their own humorous stories.

Visit Linda online:
www.lindaau.com

Follow Linda on Twitter:
@LindaMAu

Stalk Linda on Facebook:
www.facebook.com/AuthorLindaMAu

Look at Linda's stuff on Instagram:
www.instagram.com/austruck1